Dedicated to the memory of Tom Shumate

Cover designed by Denny Klatt, illustrated by Dale McNiven

Printed in Victoria, BC, Canada

Note for Librarians: a cataloguing record for this book that includes Dewey Decimal Classification and US Library of Congress numbers is available from the Library and Archives of Canada. The complete cataloguing record can be obtained from their online database at:
www.collectionscanada.ca/amicus/index-e.html
ISBN 1-4120-4062-0

TRAFFORD

This book was published *on-demand* in cooperation with Trafford Publishing. On-demand publishing is a unique process and service of making a book available for retail sale to the public taking advantage of on-demand manufacturing and Internet marketing. On-demand publishing includes promotions, retail sales, manufacturing, order fulfilment, accounting and collecting royalties on behalf of the author.

Offices in Canada, USA, UK, Ireland, and Spain
book sales for North America and international:
Trafford Publishing, 6E–2333 Government St.
Victoria, BC V8T 4P4 CANADA
phone 250 383 6864   toll-free 1 888 232 4444
fax 250 383 6804   email to orders@trafford.com
book sales in Europe:
Trafford Publishing (UK) Ltd., Enterprise House, Wistaston Road Business Centre
Crewe, Cheshire CW2 7RP UNITED KINGDOM
phone 01270 251 396   local rate 0845 230 9601
facsimile 01270 254 983   orders.uk@trafford.com
order online at:
www.trafford.com/robots/04-1869.html

10   9   8   7   6   5   4   3   2

PROLOGUE

Blind people say that all objects have a sheet of air around them, and that when their senses become highly attuned, they can feel this thin cushion of atmosphere in time to avoid bumping into virtually any obstruction. In early 2001, the BBC aired a program, which showed blind cyclists "clucking" as they pedalled along a city street. They were able to distinguish not alone when objects were in their paths, but the size and shape of those objects as well, simply by the sound their clucks made in their own ears--"blind person sonar," so to speak. The show created quite a sensation, and of course, the odd prankster. One such character gave himself away by standing in front of a car, complete with assembled tabloid media, dark glasses and white cane, and declaring after sufficient clicking, clucking and cocking of his head that the automobile in question was a 1987 Volkswagen Polo--painted blue.

The killer standing in the garage had no such skills. He could tell neither from a cushion of air, nor from the sound of his own ragged breathing in his ears, that three tins of paint lay directly in the path of his Adidas running shoes. In the darkness that terrified him, but which was necessary to the task at hand, he clattered into the half empty five-litre containers of gloss paints. They made what seemed to him a deafening racket as they clumped and skidded on the concrete floor.

"Shit!" he raged, but didn't know for sure whether he'd cursed aloud, or that the thought was so clear in his mind it only seemed he had. Now his movements became jerky and unsteady; he moved his feet slowly, pushing them out, testing each inch in front of him before he allowed his body to follow. In a few moments, which seemed to last aeons, he reached the corner nearest the entrance, and waited for the prey which had brought him here in the first place.

He relaxed then. He could wait as long as it took. He knew the result would be worth every minute, every second.

Some time later, a two-year old Chrysler Neon pulled into the drive. "Now brake, nice and easy....." Bridget Sykes said to herself. "Hand brake on. Make sure the car's in neutral." Bridget had received the brown envelope telling her of her impending driving test just that Monday. She had already failed the test once, to her utter mortification, and was absolutely determined it wouldn't happen again. Her best friend, Patti, had seen a show about a Welsh woman who had failed her driving test 14 times, but who had refused to give up. The breakthrough came when one instructor advised her to talk her way through her test, to help improve her concentration. Sure enough, on test 15, she announced every move she made, as she made it, and at the completion of the test, nearly hyperventilated when she was told by the young examiner that she had indeed passed and could go inside to pick up her full licence. As for Bridget, she was quite willing to try anything--talking, sign language, smoke signals (she laughed to herself at this thought)--but she bloody well would not undergo the humiliation of 14 failures, nor anything like it, of that she was adamant.

"What are you laughing at, Mammy?" Bridget turned her attention to the source of the enquiry. Eight-year-old Danny was still bound by the secure restraint of his seat belt. An only child, he was the true centre of his adoring mother's universe. He was the complete package, wavy light brown hair, big blue eyes, a dimple in his left cheek that only needed the barest of smiles to coax it into the open, and an insatiable curiosity which led to countless questions from morning to night. To Bridget's delight, this curiosity was coupled with the patience to sit and listen to his mother's answers and explanations for as long as she cared to expound on any given subject. Bridget was sure Danny was a genius; Danny was sure all the cards in the shop which declared, "World's Best Mother" were manufactured solely to give him a wide variety from which to choose birthday, Mother's Day and Christmas cards.

"Oh, I'm just being silly, Danny. Mammy's mouth sometimes slips into gear easier than this car does." She laughed again at her own play on words. She mused that she really was in a good mood tonight, and she hoped it wouldn't be long before Brian got home. He'd been working so desperately hard. She thought, with equal mixtures of sympathy and warm affection, that he could do with the odd laugh himself, and tonight, for no apparent reason, she felt she might be able to brighten his life that little bit. If Danny was the centre of her universe, Brian was the sun which kept her world bright and warm.

"No wonder I'm in such a good mood," Bridget thought to herself as she stepped from the car. She held open the child-locked back door of the Neon, and watched as Danny extricated himself from his seat belt. Taking his hand, she led him into the garage, which was attached to their three bedroom home. The garage was always far too full of ladders, garden furniture and barbecue when the weather was bad, as well as assorted bicycles, sporting goods and DIY equipment, to even consider pulling the car in; they'd have to pick their way through this maze of organised chaos to get to the friendly, warm kitchen, where freshly baked chocolate chip cookies (all right, Bridget admitted to herself, the in-store bakery sign claimed they were freshly baked) and a glass of milk awaited Danny before bed. It had started to rain, and the trip through the garage was preferable to the path they'd have had to take to reach the front door of the house, which would have taken them around the rose bushes that lined the drive, then across an already mucky stretch of yard, a goodly portion of which, no doubt, would have come with them on the bottom of Danny's trainers.

As they stepped into the darkness of the garage, Bridget reached for the light switch. A blinding flash appeared, and for a single, confused moment, Bridget thought that the bulb in the ceiling had blown out, even though she was quite certain her hand hadn't reached the switch when the flash exploded before her eyes. Then an even more incredible thing happened; she saw as clear as day her own grandmother standing in front of her, albeit with a very concerned look on her face. She wanted so much to say, "What's wrong MoMo?" The name with which Bridget had christened her granny when she was 14 months old, because she couldn't get her mouth around Nana, or Grandma, was MoMo--the name stuck for life. Then, even before she slumped to the floor, blood welling from the wound at the back of her head, even before Danny started screaming in the most awful, pitiful terror, Bridget remembered. MoMo had been dead for six years.

ONE

Brian Sykes was tired. He was tired and annoyed and generally fed up. He knew why he was tired. He'd spent so many nights lately, tossing and turning, trying to figure out how to hit his ever increasing sales targets, that he started most days bleary eyed and wanting nothing so much as to hop straight back into the bed, next to Bridget. After 12 years of marriage, this thought still brought a brief smile to Brian's lips. But instead of getting back into bed, after his obligatory shower and two cups of strong black coffee, each day Brian dutifully took the keys to his Nissan company car off the hook on the wall, directly opposite the kitchen door, and headed into the city. As he drove, he mentally reviewed his list of prospective customers--his gold mine was how this list was referred to by Carl O'Dowd, Brian's sales manager. Each rep in the company was required to constantly keep this list updated, and to produce it at the Monday morning sales meeting and pep talk. Falsifying names on the list was grounds for instant dismissal, with no second chances. In addition, any name on the list for more than six weeks was struck off by Carl, who said if the deal hadn't been closed in that length of time, the name shouldn't have been on the list in the first place.

"Gold mine my backside," Brian muttered to himself as he struggled with the 7 p.m. traffic. "More like a salt mine lately!" he said as if the other tens of thousands of people battling their way home from the city like refugees returning home after a war could hear him. Like so many others who had found Dublin house prices virtually unattainable since the property boom of the 90's, Brian and Bridget had chosen a house in a very pleasant satellite town, which under normal traffic conditions would have a round trip journey time of something less than two hours. Unfortunately, as each month passed without Bertie Ahern's government delivering the promised road improvements, "normal traffic" was little more than an increasingly distant memory. Now the "nice little spin down the road," as the over-friendly estate agent had said, was more like daily penance, an ordeal to be endured before being allowed to enjoy the comforts and amenities that the seaside village of Dun Guaire offered. If Brian left for work early enough in the morning, he could reach his offices in Sandyford in just over an hour. But Carl O'Dowd's insistence that all reps be in the office right up to 5:30 meant that the drive home took place in the very worst that Dublin traffic had to offer. It was almost invariably the wrong side of 7:30 p.m. before Brian got home, and nearer to 8:00 on Friday evenings, when the weekend Dublin exodus added countless more thousands to the roads.

At 36, Brian had been in the sales game for 14 years. He'd started out selling supplies to hairdressing salons. After three years of conditioners and perm chemicals, he'd moved into a completely different field, selling industrial cleaning machines to factories, hotels, restaurants and schools. He'd enjoyed that job, and the money had allowed himself and Bridget to move out of their rented flat, into their current home. But the boss had been a complete ass. Ernest Truman was a fat slob who ate a lot of garlic and had once been a policeman in Brighton. Why he'd left the force had never been divulged. Brian had taken great pleasure in imagining many spiteful reasons and sharing them with his colleagues of the time. E.T. (the inevitable nickname with which Trueman was saddled) was also a bully, preferring mental intimidation to the physical variety. He even went so far as to call in the weakest member of the sales team, Frank Collins, to tell him that he smelled bad! Frank was 62 at the time and very near retirement. He told Brian later on that he hadn't known whether to smash E.T.'s face or cry. Brian dearly wished at the time that Frank had done the former, but suspected he'd succumbed to the latter. Frank did not have a happy lot after this episode. He stuck with the job--a wife who liked spending commission cheques before they were written and a daughter in Trinity College meant he had few options--retired at 65, and died of a heart attack less than a year later. Brian himself left just before E.T. did, and often wondered if he would have gone had he known his lout of a boss was about to vacate the office to become owner/manager of a B&B on the coast.

But leave he had done, and for four years now had been selling office equipment throughout the greater Dublin area. Three times he'd put his name forward for promotion. In each case, the job had gone to other candidates. Brian admitted to himself that the correct decision had been made each time, but it still hurt. He was a well thought of salesman, and had won numersous sales competitions. In his second year with the company, he'd qualified for the sales incentive trip to Barbados. He and Bridget had spent perhaps the best week of their lives marvelling at the Bajun sunsets, snorkelling in crystal clear waters and meeting some of the nicest people in the world. They had stayed at Coconut Creek, a small, spotlessly clean if unspectacular resort on the quieter west coast of Barbados. Their bartender had introduced himself as Evergreen George, who professed a great desire to live in Ireland one day. This came as no small shock to Bridget, given the 12 consecutive days of rain and temperatures near freezing they had left behind them at Dublin Airport. Why anyone would want to leave this beautiful...
"What the hell.....?!?" Brian realized he'd been daydreaming for most of his journey. The sight of an ambulance pulling away from his house with sirens wailing and lights flashing wrenched him back to reality and had virtually the same impact on him physically as would a sharp blow to his stomach.

Brian nearly chased after the ambulance. He was certain that it had pulled away from his house and not the neighbours', but as he tore his gaze away from the back of the rapidly disappearing ambulance-- oh, dear Lord, why was it travelling so fast?--Brian noticed the squad car parked opposite his drive. He pulled up nose to nose with the garda car, grabbed his door handle and went to jump from his car, not realising that he had neither switched off his engine, nor put the car into neutral. The Nissan jerked forward and straight into the nose of the blue Ford squad car, smashing the police car's left headlight as it did so. Brian nearly jerked the parking break clean off its mounting, he pulled so hard. He finally got out of the car and met the officer coming down the driveway towards him. Before a word was said, Brian noticed that Bridget's friend, Patti, was talking with a second garda at the entrance to the garage. Visibly distraught, Patti was gesticulating wildly toward the house. While Brian couldn't make out what she was saying, it was very clear to him that Patti was on the verge of hysteria. Panic now gripped him completely. As he tried to move faster toward the policeman, his muscles actually bunched into knots in his shoulders, neck and arms. Though he was less than 25 feet from the man, Brian felt incredibly, inexplicably angry that the distance was so great.

It was the policeman who spoke first. "Are you Brian Sykes?" queried Richie Brauders, at the same time looking with dismay towards his damaged squad car. "Never mind your bloody car," Brian said when he saw the direction of Brauders' gaze. "What the hell is going on here?" Brian asked, fear and anger mingling.

"Mr. Sykes?" came the gentle enquiry again, and this time Brian just nodded, afraid to vocalise anything lest his voice betray the numbing.fear that was growing inside him as each second passed. "Mr. Sykes, I'm afraid there's been a bit of an accident--umm, incident I guess. Your friend, Mrs. Lyons, rang us to say that she'd found your wife injured in your garage."

"Oh, God, was that her in the ambulance then? Is she going to be all right?" Brian still couldn't get a grip on this. If Bridget had tripped over something and hurt herself, why would the gardai need to be involved? He tried to remember if he'd been told once that the gardai had to be called out any time an ambulance is called. He just wasn't sure, and he wished the young policeman would speak an awful lot faster and tell him what had happened to his wife. Brauders response gave Brian none of the comfort he'd so desperately hoped for when he asked about Bridget. Instead, all that was offered was, "Your wife has been taken to St. Vincent's Hospital. She was unconscious when Mrs. Lyons found her. If you like, I can take you there myself."

"What? Umm, yeah, I guess…okay. I'll see if Patti will look after Danny for me for a couple of hours," Brian said. This was all just way too much, too fast. Brian looked around and saw Patti, eyes red, tembling uncontrollably, coming towards him, and instantly doubted that Patti could even look after herself at the moment, much less an eight year old. With an incredible effort, Brian forced his brain to work in a logical manner. Patti's daughter, Joanna, had done babysitting for them before; he'd ask Patti to get Joanna to come over for a while.

"Sorry, sir?" Brauders enquiring voice, for no reason that he could have identified at that moment, sent a chill straight down Brian's backbone, "Danny……..?"

Patti reached Brian a second after the policeman's voice. "Brian," she couldn't keep her voice from breaking, "what on earth could have happened? Bridget didn't answer the door when I called over. I was just going to ask if she wanted to go shopping with me tomorrow. I found her. Lying…..on the floor….the door to the garage was open…but Brian, where's Danny? I thought he might be with you. He's not in the house! I don't know where he is, and Bridget looked so--oh, God, she's hurt, there was blood--but where's Danny…?" Patti was rapidly becoming incoherent.

Fifteen minutes of phone calls, hammering on neighbours' doors, radio checks between Brauders and the station, and Brian and Patti running down opposite ends of the street calling, then screaming, and finally crying Danny's name, confirmed it.

Danny was gone.

TWO

St. Vincent's Hospital was unnaturally quiet, even for a Wednesday evening in April. Brian hated hospitals. He'd hated them for as long as he could remember. He found the smell of the disinfectant a pungent presence that lingered like a bad mood. Each ward, each room, each bed told a sad story, and sad stories aren't much fun, apart from black and white films like "Casablanca," at least in Brian's mind. As that thought came to Brian, he quickly said a silent prayer that Bridget's wouldn't be another story with a tragic ending.

But tonight there were only a fraction of the usual numbers of accident victims, burst appendix cases, children running sudden, frighteningly high fevers, and the inevitable heavy drinkers whose faces collided with light poles, being admitted to Vincent's. Brian passed a middle- aged couple on his way down the corridor. They were American tourists, and Brian heard the attending physician explaining briefly that the man would have to be admitted with a suspected deep vein thrombosis, possibly brought on by the long haul flight from Chicago. One of Brian's colleagues at work, Kevin Whyte, had suffered similar bad luck upon returning from a fishing trip to Canada. He'd been hospitalised, also in St. Vincents, for five days, while they thinned his blood, gave him injections of heparin to dissolve the blood clot behind his knee, and finally placed him on warfarin tablets for life, as Kevin was deemed a high risk for recurring clots. "Another sad story," Brian said aloud, but only to himself. He couldn't escape the feeling that there were sad stories, horrible stories, waiting in the grey darkness of his immediate future. "God, I hate hospitals," he said.

He'd already been told which of the rooms Bridget was in, and he'd already forgotten who had given him that information. In his darkest, most desperate nightmares, Brian couldn't have envisaged the scenario that now confronted him like a terrifying maze that led only to one dead end after another. His mind was a maelstrom of conflicting fears and emotions; at that moment he didn't know whether Bridget was conscious, or, he thought with a shudder and another of the countless waves of nausea that had washed over him since he saw the ambulance pull away from his house, whether Bridget was even going to survive her injuries. The next instant he thought that, if Bridget wasn't conscious, he at least wouldn't have to tell her that Danny was missing, and almost certainly in the most unimagineable danger. As that thought came to him, he was practically torn asunder with guilt for being, as he saw it, that incredibly selfish, to prefer his wife in a coma than to have to face her with his horrible news. He still didn't know if he would even tell Bridget that Danny was gone. He would ask the doctor in charge, and act according to his advice. Again, more guilt at the thought of putting even a molecule of responsibility for the decisions that had to be made in someone else's hands--tears of frustration, anger and fear now blurred Brian's view of the corridor. He wanted to stop, to collect his thoughts, yet knew he couldn't. In the storm that was the centre of Brian's soul, he felt that trying to put all the thoughts and feelings screaming inside him into some kind of reasonable order would be enough to drive him truly, and perhaps irretrievably, insane.

 He walked through the swinging doors that led into the Intensive Care Unit, to the second door on the left. He absolutely could not bring himself, at that moment, to look through the glass doors, even though he knew that Bridget was but a few feet away. Brian needed reassurance of any kind, from virtually any source, before he could face whatever awaited him on the other side of that glass door, and he looked for a nurse or doctor or anyone else with a long green or white jacket on, to whom he could go for a comforting word. He never heard the soft footsteps approach him from behind, and very

nearly jumped out of his skin when a gentle hand touched him
lightly on the shoulder.

"Can I help you, sir?" Brian turned with a start and looked into the
eyes of Dr. James Hickson. "Are you Mr. Sykes?" Brian figured the
doctor to be in his mid-40's, with thinning brown hair, kind-looking
blue eyes, and a slender frame. At just a shade under six feet tall, Dr.
Hickson was two inches shorter than Brian. He looked tired to Brian,
but alert all the same, and above all had a peaceful, calming
demeanour which, at that moment, was the tonic which Brian
craved.

"Yes, Doctor. Is my wife going to be all right? What happened to
her? Is she conscious? Did she lose much blood? Has she said
anything? Is she asking for me, or Dan............" Brian suddenly
realised that he'd asked all these questions without drawing a single
breath, or waiting for the answers. He was curiously soothed by the
fact that the man in front of him had tried neither to interrupt his
tirade of queries, nor did he seem unsettled by them. The doctor
simply stood there, patiently, and let Brian carry on, probably
sensing that one of the reasons Brian didn't stop for answers was
because he was terrified of what those answers might be.

"We've performed a CAT scan on your wife, Mr. Sykes. At the
moment, I can tell you that she has what appears to be a hairline
fracture of the skull. We're going to keep her here for a few days,
under observation, but I'd be very hopeful that she'll make a
complete recovery." Brian nodded, and the doctor continued.
"Blood loss was actually minimal, and thankfully, there appears to
be no internal bleeding, which would have been a concern. Your
wife is sleeping at the moment, but she did have periods of lucidity.
You can go in and sit with her if you like; I honestly can't say when
she's likely to waken." All this was said with very little emotion on
the doctor's part, but the reassurance in his voice and eyes was
something Brian was sure he wasn't just imagining. He felt
incredibly grateful to the doctor, as much at that moment for the
respite from dread and panic that had clung to Brian since this
waking nightmare had begun some four hours ago, as for the care

the doctor had imparted to Bridget. Dr. Hickson had given Brian hope, and comfort--good feelings.

They didn't last long.

"Your wife did say one thing, by the way, before she went to sleep." The doctor continued, without realising that in so doing, he was virtually ripping away the blanket of comfort which Brian had so gratefully wrapped himself in just moments before. "She said, 'Not Danny.'"

THREE

Detective Michael McCann carefully picked his way around the inside of the Sykes' garage one more time. The uniformed gardai who had been at the scene when McCann arrived had long since gone back to their stations. Even Patti, who had come back to answer more questions and enquire after Bridget and Danny, had finally gone home with Joanna and Ted, Patti's husband. The detective didn't mind being left on his own at the crime scene. He found it neither unsettling nor ghoulish to be in the place where, it was now accepted by anyone familiar with the night's events, a savage assault and probable kidnapping had taken place only a few hours before. On the contrary, McCann felt, quite rightly, that he did his best work when left to his own thoughts, without interruption. To him, a crime scene was a lifesize jigsaw puzzle. His ability to fit those pieces together with uncanny accuracy was what had propelled him through the ranks of the gardai, to the position of plain-clothes detective, before he had reached the age of 30.

From very soon after his arrival, McCann had sensed an extra-sinister situation existed, and within an hour, he was certain of that fact. He had noticed in his preliminary examinations of the property that no footsteps were evident around the Sykes house; none in the flower beds, none under the windows to the side and back of the house, not even in the garden leading to the front door, and this in spite of the persistent rain. Following on from this, McCann carefully checked the doors and windows for even the slightest hint of a forced entry. Finding no signs of anyone remotely attempting to gain access to the house, he nevertheless instructed that fingerprinting of the doorknobs and window frames be performed immediately.

Next came the garage itself. McCann was reminded of the garden shed at his home in Ballybrack. It was cluttered and unorganised. Three bicycles were leaning against one wall. Hanging on brackets above the bikes was an extension ladder; the gas fired barbecue occupying a good portion of the centre of the garage floor had probably been rushed in from a sudden shower of rain. McCann loved to barbecue for his own friends and family whenever the weather permitted. He thought for the moment that, once again, Ireland seemed destined for a wet, cool summer. Except for a week at the beginning of April, the last fortnight had been what the meteorologists at Met Eireann liked to refer to as unsettled, with promises of more to come right into May. Apart from one absolutely spectacular summer, in 1995, Michael McCann couldn't honestly remember a decent stretch of weather in the May to August period for many years. He allowed himself a small sigh. There wouldn't be many barbecues this summer, he figured. And with that, he thought, looking again at the Sykes' barbecue, that the family who lived in this house probably wouldn't be thinking too much about barbecues and weather for some time to come. He resumed his examinations.

The garage had the usual up-and-over door, but in addition, there was a separate, standard door that allowed entry to the garage from the driveway. Once inside the garage, there was access to the house, but McCann noticed there were no light switches near the entrance from the drive. There was only one switch, and that was near to the door that led into the kitchen from the garage. As Bridget had been found in the garage, McCann had no way of knowing whether the door from the drive had been locked or not. Patti had been adamant that the garage light was not on when she had found her friend, so McCann assumed that Bridget had not quite reached the light switch before her attacker had struck. McCann also mused that, being April, the evenings were getting longer, and that normally there would have been enough daylight for Bridget not to have even needed to switch on an overhead light. But the persistent rain of that day had come from heavy, black clouds that made the April evening look annoyingly like a November night. "Unlucky?" he wondered to himself.

The door to the kitchen was not locked, and the detective had to believe that the assailant could have easily gained entry to the house had he so desired. McCann's mind began to consider different scenarios. Perhaps Bridget had been in the house and heard a noise in the garage. Maybe when she went to investigate, she had startled a petty burglar, who panicked and lashed out before making his escape. McCann immediately discounted this theory. Bridget still had her coat on when found. No lights were on in the house, and the boy, Danny, was missing. McCann knew that Bridget had never reached the house that evening. He could then deduce that the police were not looking for a nervous burglar, because a burglar would have had no hesitation going into the house, after reaching the safety of the garage interior. No, this was a premeditated ambush, of that McCann was certain. And with that certainty came another. Bridget was not the target of the attack. Danny was. McCann sensed, then knew, that if Bridget had been the sole intended victim, the attacker wouldn't have risked taking the boy. Had the "perp" intended only to harm Bridget, he would have "hit and run." Given the light hadn't been switched on, there was no way Danny could even have gotten a good look at the attacker, and of course, there was no way an eight year old could have prevented an easy get away.

McCann summarised his early conclusions on a notepad. These were his personal notes; only he would ever refer to them. No one at the station, or in any courtroom would ever have access to them. Each assumption led rapidly to another, and soon the detective found his hand was rushing to keep up with his thoughts.

1.   *Attacker did not try to gain entry to the house.*
2.   *No sign of anything being taken-burglary very unlikely motive.*
3.   *Danny most probable target.*
   A. *Attacker must have known child lived in this house*
   B. *Attacker waited for opportunity, most likely in darkness*

> C. *Attacker, therefore, may have known something of family movements*
> D. *May have known something of house*
> E. *May be local, or at least familiar with immediate area*
>
> 4.   *If A through E are all positive, Danny's abductor is quite possibly known to the family--or even a member of the family. Or a neighbour.*
> 5.   *Danny is probably............*

McCann looked at his watch. It had now been more than six hours since Bridget Sykes had been found unconscious on the garage floor. Roadblocks had been put in place. Every garda in the country now knew there was an eight year old child missing under black-as-night circumstances, but, as of five minutes earlier, when he had last radioed in, there was no sign of Danny. The detective knew from lectures taken early on in his training that, in the disturbing majority of cases, if a kidnap victim, particularly a young child, hasn't been found within three hours of the kidnap taking place, he most likely would not be coming back alive. The exceptions were "tug of love" kidnaps, where one parent estranged from the other occasionally kidnaps their own child and flees the jurisdiction. Clearly, this didn't apply in Danny's case. McCann looked at his list of conclusions again, down to the unfinished sentence at the bottom. He couldn't bring himself to write the word "dead," though he knew it to be very likely true.

FOUR

Brian and Bridget looked at each other, again, still not knowing what to say. Brian, in particular, felt so many different kinds of horrible that he couldn't believe one person could feel so bad in so many ways at the same time. Dr. Hickson had called to check on Bridget; Brian had "buzzed" the nurse immediately after Bridget woke with a start and was clearly fully conscious. The doctor had asked her a few simple questions, checked her eyes, the lump at the base of her skull, and pronounced himself satisfied that Bridget was out of immediate danger, but that she was to remain at Vincent's under observation for a day or two. She had been moved out of ICU into a private ward, on Dr. Hickson's instructions. That was the solitary comfort in both their lives at that point in time.

Brian was desperately worried about his wife, in spite of the doctor's reassurances. He was as concerned about her ability to recover emotionally from the night's experiences, as physically. He was also inexplicably uneasy sitting by her hospital bed. He felt, deep down, that he ought to be out, doing something, anything, everything, to get their child back. He wondered for the barest instant what was happening to Danny at that moment. Immediately, he forced the thought from his mind, only to have it seep back into his brain. It was like trying to hold back a dark, cold, damp mist. The anger he had felt earlier had not dissipated, only evolved into fury at his own impotence regarding the well being of those he loved more than life. He wanted to issue demands-- for a phone with a direct link to the garda station, for constant updates on the progress in the search for Danny, for a private consultant for Bridget, for

...............for....................comfort. For peace of mind, which he knew would never again in his life be completely his.

"Bridget.....?" She jumped, his voice was that unexpected. She, too, had been lost in her own thoughts, and his voice, though she knew he was sitting right next to her, startled her as much as if he'd snuck up from behind her and shouted in her ear. It was Brian who had told her, more than 90 minutes previously, in a choked voice, and with a nurse standing close by, that Danny was missing. Tears had immediately begun to stream from Bridget's eyes; she only wondered later that night, in the quiet darkness, why she hadn't been more stunned by the news. She suspected it was because the events in the garage had been somehow imprinted in her brain, even though she was unconscious. Still, she cried--sobbed--for her missing child, and the nurse immediately perceived that Bridget could not withstand any further distress just then. She signalled quickly to Brian, who understood at once that he should save any further details, not that he had many, until Bridget felt strong enough to ask for them herself. But that had been more than an hour ago, and Bridget couldn't even remember whether they'd spoken since. But now he had.

"Yes, Brian?" she answered. She wondered for a millisecond if he'd thought of something that would bring her baby back to her. Maybe he'd suddenly realised where Danny might be, though, of course, she knew he hadn't. But there was that faintest glimmer of hope in her two-word response, and Brian was immediately annoyed and ashamed that he had given her any kind of false hope just by speaking her name. "Would you like a glass of 7-Up?" was all he managed to offer, and now it was Bridget's turn to be annoyed, because she remembered they had spoken, and not that long ago.

"You asked me that five minutes ago," she said sharply, "and I still don't want any."

"Do you think you could eat something, then?" Brian asked, wondering whether he'd also asked that five minutes ago.

"If I want something, Brian, I'll ask you, or the nurse." There was an edge to Bridget's voice now, and Brian, while eager not to aggravate an already impossibly tense situation, felt slightly piqued himself at Bridget's aggressive responses. He opened his mouth, closed it, clenched his jaws against the sudden urge to ask her again about the 7-Up, and drew a deep breath instead. For their entire marriage, Brian and Bridget had shared countless laughs, at each other's expense, over things as simple as ice. Brian always asked Bridget if she wanted ice in her drink. Bridget wouldn't take ice in her drink in a million years, and of course, Brian knew that. But he always asked. Her responses varied from an icy cool, "No, but thank you so much for asking," to a far less subtle, "Feck off, ya big eejit!" And then they would laugh. Occasionally, Bridget would threaten Brian with all manner of physical atrocities if he ever asked her again, and then they'd laugh some more.

"Water then?" He couldn't resist. He was as upset, confused and worried as she, and he was suddenly more than a little annoyed at her waspish retorts, so he twisted the screw just that bit too far, and waited for the response. He wasn't wrong.

"Brian! Are you actually trying to irritate me?" Her voice was raised now; he knew he'd crossed the line, but at that very instant, he just didn't care, so he pushed again. "How could I be irritating you by asking if you want a glass of water? I can't believe you're getting upset over someone trying to be nice," he said, extra quietly, because he knew that would drive her temper even further up the scale than if he matched her raised decibel levels. Again, he was right, but this time, he didn't anticipate her furious reaction.

"Do I want something?" She practically hissed the question at him. "Right then, if you want to get me something, then get up off your backside, get out of my sight, and go find my son!" Three times in one short sentence she had crucified him. To Brian, getting off his backside suggested he wasn't doing anything useful. It only served to underscore his own, as yet unspoken, feelings that he ought to be doing something more to help end this unthinkable nightmare. 'Get out of my sight' was equally hurtful, but the topper was the

suggestion that Danny was "her" son; that somehow, with those
words, she had stripped him even of the right to be Danny's father,
as though he didn't deserve that honour. The pain he felt at her
words was real, physical and wrenching.   For almost 10 seconds,
Brian struggled in silence with the ferociousness of Bridget's attack.
He got up, put on his jacket, and, without a word, turned for the
door. His anger and hurt, on top of what was already happening to
him (and that was how he thought of it at that precise instant,
happening to him, rather than to the two of them) rendered him
speechless. His face literally turned white with temper, then, before
he even reached the door, tears threatening the backs of his eyes yet
again, he had turned red with sheer frustration, and even
embarrassment, that his wife could think so ill of him. Then, as his
hand touched the door handle, he went cold inside. A part of him
died, as certainly as the nameless teenage car crash vicitim who was
still lying on the trolley in A & E had died five minutes previously.

"Brian." Bridget was still impossibly upset, but knew she had
gone way, way too far with her attack. "I'm sorry. I know you can't
help what…….." Her voice trailed off as she realised she had started
her sentence horribly wrong.

"Don't worry about it," Brian said, as calmly as if she'd only spilled
a glass of milk. But it wasn't right, Bridget thought. Something
wasn't right, beyond everything else that was wrong that night, now
something else was being added, and Bridget felt a new panic rise in
her chest. She looked at the man she had loved for 14 years, and
whom she had shared every day of her life with for the past 12, and
she relaxed ever so slightly. She was sure they would endure,
whatever happened to the rest of their lives, so she said the thing
that she believed was right, and that had always been the right thing
to say to make things better. Right because it was true. Right
because it mattered, in any circumstance.

"I love you, Brian." She meant it.

"I love you, too," he said. He should have walked back to the bed
and smashed his fist into her face, because the effect that action
would have had would have been far less painful and devastating

than that caused by his four-word response. Bridget actually gasped.
Brian couldn't meet her astonished stare, and didn't actually feel the
need to right then. Again, he felt nettled, because he knew virtually
without looking that he had upset her again, though he had no idea
how badly. He had said the right thing, in his own mind. The
problem was, Bridget was horrified by the absolute, undoubted
certainty that Brian's words were as without meaning and feeling as
a politician's lying promise. It wasn't even that he hadn't meant the
words; it was that he hadn't felt them. And knowing that fact, as
certainly as she knew her son was not safe home in his bed, she
couldn't forgive him for throwing out those words as easily as he
might throw out the garbage. The words were cold as death, and
they had hurt Bridget more than any curse or insult he would ever
deliver.

   It was the beginning of the end of their marriage.

FIVE

Michael McCann took another sip of his steaming cup of coffee, looked over the rim at the man who had given it to him, and waited patiently for Brian's next question.

The two men were sitting in the kitchen of Brian and Bridget's home, at either side of a rectangular pine table. The matching pine chairs had colourful seat cushions; the kitchen itself was decorated in creams and brighter yellows. The window over the sink looked out onto a small back garden, in which an impossibly deserted swing set seemed to testify to the fact that someone was missing from the picture presented by this middle class "family" home at No. 11, St. Michael's Terrace. Then Garda Brauders walked past the window, head down, searching for clues in the brighter sunlight of the day after Danny Sykes had disappeared. He would "work" the garden, back and forth, and, McCann was quite sure, would find nothing.

His gaze came back to Brian, who alternately looked hopelessly at McCann, and occasionally questioningly out at Brauders, who was now looking under the evergreen hedge that separated their garden from the Doyles' next door. Brian didn't really like Brauders being out there; it wasn't as though he'd find Danny hiding under the little cherry blossom tree that had been planted in the sunniest corner of their garden. But he forgot about the uniformed garda for the time being, and asked the same question of McCann that he'd already asked twice.

"Have you found anything, anything at all, or heard anything, that might help?" McCann was used to these questions. The same queries came up, in one form or another, in nearly every

investigation in which he'd ever taken part. There was always the
"What leads have you got?" followed sooner rather than later by
"Isn't there something more you can do?" Then, invariably, the
accusation came, sometimes veiled, sometimes far more direct, that
the gardai weren't doing their jobs properly, or that they were afraid
of the criminals they sought, and, surely, that if it was "one of their
own" that was missing, there'd be an awful lot more done. McCann
always kept his composure in the face of these allegations, regardless
of how personal or bitter the delivery, because he understood the
stress these people were facing. And at the very back of his mind, in
a whisper that he mostly didn't allow himself to hear clearly, came
the disturbing notion that maybe, if it was one of his neices, or the
son of one of his colleagues, that bit more would be done. For the
moment, he dismissed the thought as irrelevant.

   "To be honest, Mr. Sykes....." McCann was cut off by an impatient
wave of Brian's hand. "Please, Detective McCann, call me Brian. Mr.
Sykes is my father's name," Brian said, forcing a smile to show that
he was attempting, albeit awkwardly, a bit of humour.

   "Okay, Brian," McCann returned easily, "I was hoping you might
actually be able to help us come up with some leads." He saw the
frown form, and knew some of what was racing through Brian's
mind as he considered what had been said. McCann was sure that
Brian was asking himself *exactly* what McCann meant by 'helping.'
The phrase, "helping gardai with their enquiries" was widely
accepted in any circle Brian had frequented to mean that the police
had the guilty party in custody, and were working their way
towards a confession. Brian and Frank Collins once heard that a man
who'd been arrested with a suitcase full of cocaine was "helping
gardai with their enquiries," and, knowing Ernest Trueman as they
did, figured the police were beating the hell out of the suspect in a
dark basement room at Dublin Castle.

   McCann didn't tell Brian that he had been removed from any list of
potential suspects hours previously. He simply didn't need that
information, as it would only upset Brian hugely to know that he'd
even been considered. But the sad fact was that McCann and his

team had phoned Brian's office to confirm that he hadn't left the office until 5:30 the previous evening. Carl O'Dowd had politely informed Mary Simmons, McCann's colleague of three years, that Brian definitely had been at his desk up to the prescribed hour. Given the traffic delays that Brian couldn't possibly have avoided, there was no way he could have been home in time to attack Bridget, secret Danny off to God knows where, and then drive up and hit Richie Brauders' car. Unfortunately, that was the very first scenario McCann had felt it necessary to rule out, and he actually felt a small measure of relief when he was able to do so.

Likewise, four other members of the force had been assigned to check, as quickly and discreetly as possible, other members of the family, as well as friends and neighbours. McCann had not shaken the belief that the person responsible for this attack was known to the Sykes family. In fact, he was more certain than ever, but he wanted to be very careful about the manner in which he shared this information with Brian. It wouldn't be easy for any man to hear that someone he knew, and possibly trusted completely, and maybe who was even a member of his own family, had attacked his wife and taken his child. Yet McCann had been turning the events of the previous night over in his head for more than 16 hours now, and he knew that, if there was any dim hope of finding Danny alive, it lay with Brian, or Bridget, providing some insight as to who this monster might be.

Tommy Morris had done a check on Patti and Joe Lyons, and even their daughter Joanna. Joe and Patti had been at home, together, from about 5:45, when Joe had gotten home from his job as janitor at St. Joseph's, the Dun Guaire primary school, right up to the time Patti had found Bridget lying unconscious in the garage. Joanna had been studying at a friend's house on the opposite side of the street, and knew nothing of the events of the previous night, except that she really, really hated French class.

Patti had decided she was now virtually certain the door that led from the drive into the Sykes' garage was open when she arrived to see Bridget. Other than that, she had not remembered seeing anything unusual, nor thinking of anyone capable of, or with a reason, to do any harm to Brian, Bridget or Danny. After speaking with Patti, Morris held similar discussions with Conor and Adam, Brian's two brothers, neither of whom had been anywhere near Dun Guaire when Bridget had been attacked. Both men had arrived at Brian's house late the previous night, and had spent several hours checking every garden shed in the estate, then down past St. Joseph's to the local cemetery, then to the DART station, all the while calling Danny's name and listening in vain for the reply that never came.

Colin Forde spoke with Brian's parents. Brian's mother and father lived on Vernon Avenue in Clontarf, just north of the River Liffey. Geraldine Sykes was 72, wore a hearing aid, and weighed just over seven stone. Liam, Brian's father, was 75, and had undergone hip replacement surgery in 1999; he regaled Forde with every detail of that operation over three cups of tea, while Geraldine looked at the detective with sympathy etched all over her wrinkled face. Then she turned her hearing aid off before sitting down with the two men.

Bridget's parents, on the other hand, had travelled to Dublin from the small village of Kilcormac, County Offally, immediately upon hearing of Bridget's injuries. David and Roisin Fitzgerald were both in their late-50's. Bridget had been their first child. Danny was their first grandchild. Detective Patrick O'Shea met them at Vincent's, and asked David and Roisin if he could have a quiet word with them after they'd seen Bridget. The Fitzgeralds readily agreed, but wanted as much time as possible with Bridget first. O'Shea waited on a mock leather armchair in the TV room located halfway down the corridor. Judge Judy was on, telling a used car salesman who was bald on top but had a greasy ponytail, that he was a very poor liar, and that therefore he should maybe consider a career outside the automobile industry. Judgement for the plaintiff, who was suing the salesman for not honouring the promised three-month warranty on the Ford Taurus he'd sold, was in the amount of $1,276, and the whole case lasted just 3 minutes and 20 seconds. O'Shea guessed that Judge Judy must have had a bad experience with a used car salesman at some stage in her life. It was simply pay back time.

After just under two hours of waiting, during which time O'Shea
also watched "Countdown" and a bit of Rikki Lake, the Fitzgeralds
arrived into the room to speak with the detective. David told O'Shea
that he was a mechanic at a Toyota dealership in Tullamore. Roisin
worked part time in a small bakery. Both had been at work the day
before, and neither could give any inkling as to who might want to
hurt their daughter. O'Shea gently enquired whether Bridget had
mentioned any extra stress or marriage troubles to Roisin, even in
passing. But Roisin and David both waved away the notion as one
would an irritating insect. They were both clearly eager to help, but
had absolutely nothing to offer that would assist in the case.

Likewise, Detective Fran Kennedy was having no success with the
neighbours. All had been shocked; Bridget was clearly well liked,
and the tension caused by the abduction of Danny was palpable. It
was somewhat difficult to believe that no one had seen anything at
all out of the ordinary. But this seemed to be the case. Not one
stranger had been noticed by anyone in the small housing estate, nor
in either of the two streets that ran parallel to St. Michael's Terrace.
When he relayed this information to McCann via mobile phone, it
only served to strengthen McCann's belief that whoever had
committed this crime was no stranger. He was someone who "fitted
in," or at least appeared to.

McCann was about to relay to Brian the conversation he'd just had
with Detective Kennedy, when he noticed that Richie Brauders was
now crouching down very near the cherry blossom tree, and looking
intently at the ground just to the right of that tree. McCann stopped
in mid-sentence. Brauders, without even looking around, seemed to
know that he had McCann's attention, and he raised his right hand to
beckon the detective to come out.

"Excuse me a second, Brian, please," McCann said, and started out
the back door. He could have saved his breath, because Brian was
up out of his chair and had followed the detective out to the back
garden. He had no intention of sitting quietly and waiting for news
if there was any way of avoiding doing just that--sitting, and waiting.

"What you got, Richie?" McCann asked the garda.

"Earth here's been turned, but with all the rain lately, it's hard to say how recently," Brauders said, pointing at the ground that was mushier, in a roughly rectangular pattern, than the surrounding area.

McCann looked and saw exactly what Brauders was getting at, and for an instant, he had a flash of alarm that maybe he'd completely misjudged the situation, and that the gruesome truth of what had happened less than a day earlier was right in front of him in the shape of Brian Sykes.

Brian saw the look on McCann's face. Brian was intuitive by nature, and years in the selling game had taught him to be extra receptive to signals given out, be they negative or positive, by the people he came in contact with. The look on McCann's face was not giving out positive vibes.

"Tell me you don't think that's a grave," Brian said to McCann. He could understand, even appreciate, that the policemen were doing their job to the best of their ability, but it still angered him that McCann could have the slightest doubt about his innocence.

For his part, McCann was actually embarrassed to have had his thoughts that easily interpreted, though he did his best not to show this. Instead, he responded quietly, "Why don't you tell us what that is, Brian. I mean, did you start a flower bed there, or were you going to plant some vegetables, or what?"

"No," came Brian's reply, and for once, McCann could not read the tone in Brian's voice at all. The next few words did not fill him with confidence in his perceptive abilities either. "Actually, Detective, it is a grave." Brian kept his face like stone. He actually wanted to impart, at the very least, some discomfort to the two men who were standing in his garden and wondering if he was capable of the unspeakable acts that had occurred in his home just a few hours before.

McCann didn't respond at all, just looked at Brian and waited for him to continue. The pause lasted nearly 10 seconds, and McCann wondered if Brian was going to elaborate, or if he was going to make them dig up the ground to find out what lay beneath the surface. Then, finally, Brian carried on.

"Our family pet died in February. His name was Bandit, and he was a springer spaniel. We'd had him since Danny was a year old. He caught the pavro virus, because I'd forgotten to get him his injections last September. He died within three days of first getting sick. We were all devastated, so we had a little funeral for him. I don't know if the council allows you to bury pets in your garden. I didn't ask, and I honestly don't give a damn."

"Danny must have been heart broken," McCann offered, and while he knew he'd have to get someone to dig up the grave--hopefully when Brian was out of sight--he had no doubt that Brian was telling the truth.

"It was the only time in his life that Danny was really angry with me," Brian answered.

"Why would he be angry with you?" McCann asked. "It's not like you ran the dog over."

"No, but I told Danny the truth about me forgetting Bandit's injections. He never stopped asking how Bandit could have died. The dog was only seven, and springer spaniels usually live to 15 or 16 years. Danny probably assumed the dog would be with us forever. I finally told him that it was my fault, and he knew I was telling him the truth." Brian's eyes weren't focusing on McCann now. He was picturing the evening in the sitting room, and the look of pure fury on Danny's little face, when he learned the truth about Bandit's death.

"He got over it, though?" It was a question, not a statement. McCann was genuinely interested.

"Yes, but he never wanted another dog from that day to this. Bridget and I offered to get him one, but he didn't want to know. And there was my little punishment as well." McCann thought Brian was grinning ever so slightly, but then saw the tears welling up at the back of the man's eyes. "I told Danny that, since it was my fault, he could give me a good hard slap on the face, or a box in the belly. He took me at my word. He said, 'Right then, a box in the belly,' and he swung his little fist as hard as he could. Naturally, I pretended to be winded, nearly keeled over, but he didn't laugh. He was so mad. I was afraid he'd never................" Brian's voice started to break, and the tears were flowing freely now "...............ever forgive me. But he did. On my birthday, March 4th, he gave me a card, and drew me a picture of himself playing football, and he thanked me for teaching him how to sell a dummy to a defender.............and, and..." Brian was sobbing now, "...he told me he loved me! We never mentioned Bandit again. Jesus Christ, man, you've got to bring him back to me!"

McCann knew instinctively that this was the time he might get the information he needed from Brian. He knew Brian's mind was in turmoil, that thoughts were whirling around like a tornado in his skull. But he figured that, exactly when Brian wasn't thinking like a rational, normal person, he might grab the one idea out of the heart of that tornado, as it whizzed past the front of his brain. Because what had happened to this family wasn't a normal, rational thing, and thinking this through logically wasn't going to solve the puzzle of what happened to Bridget and Danny. So he gambled.

Brian, let's go to the garage. I want to take you back to where this all started and see if we can't come up with something. Go with me on this, Brian.

"But you've looked for clues," Brian protested weakly. He wasn't eager to revisit the scene, but hated to admit that to McCann.

"That's right, Brian, we have," McCann came back, "but I need you to look at things that we couldn't possibly see, like what little thing might be out of place, or if you notice anything at all that might be missing, or that might be there that shouldn't be. Trust me, please."

Though Brian's emotions were stretched to snapping point, he agreed and went back into the house, through the kitchen, and out into the garage.

"Brian, the person who did this knew a lot about your family, I'm sure." McCann knew he was going out on a limb giving Brian this information, but he knew with every passing instant, Danny's life was in greater danger. If it wasn't already too late, he was willing to risk breaking standard protocol to jar something loose in Brian. "He or she also had more than a passing knowledge of your house, or at least this part of it," McCann went on. "Look around. Feel what isn't right about this garage. Don't think, just sense what this place has to tell you."

Brian saw the tins of paint that had been kicked over; he pointed to them and said, "Those wouldn't have been left like that. They were stacked one on top of the other, just inside the door. Even if Bridget or Danny had kicked them over, they would have put them back. I get kind of cranky about things like that." He was getting upset again, knowing that he was in the spot where his wife, and the child they both lived their lives for, had been savagely assaulted.

"Stay with me, Brian," McCann said softly. "Keep looking. What else is there?"

Brian looked at the bicycles. He noticed that the tyres had gone flat since last summer, and would have to be pumped up again before they could be taken out. But they hadn't been moved. The barbeque was also exactly as it should be, and his tools were hanging on the garage wall, under the extension ladder, which was hung on brackets. There was a box of magazines and newspapers, destined for the recycling bin at Tesco, but they didn't....

"What did you say?" asked Brian.

"Nothing. I didn't say anything just now," McCann answered.

"Not just now, but a minute ago....." Brian's mind was trying to seize something whirling in the tornado, but he couldn't get a grip on it. Something was out of place--not out of place, but something just--dammit, why couldn't he think?!?

"I said stay with me." McCann could see the strain on Brian's face, and knew he was struggling desperately to grasp a detail that was just beyond his reach. It was like trying to see through a dense fog, knowing something was out there, but not being able to put a form to it.

"No, before that. You said that the person knew our family well." Brian was turning frantically, looking this way and that, almost spinning around now. "You said they knew the house, or at least this part of it, didn't you?"

"What is it, Brian? What do you see? What do you sense?" McCann could see Brian's face was now bright red with the strain of trying to remember. No, not remember, but to make sense of something, but if everything was in place, then everything made sense. Maybe he was asking too much, but he felt Brian was close. "Say whatever is in your mind, Brian, it doesn't have to make sense, just say it," McCann urged.

"The paint cans shouldn't be there. I yelled at Danny once for leaving things....." This sentence trailed off. "They should have been put back. I was going to paint the next dry weekend. I would have got the paint, then the ladder and brushes out."

"Paint. The paint........no!"

"The brushes. Damn it all to hell! The bucket...."

"The ladder."

"The ladder........."

He turned to McCann, with a dazed look. His breath was coming in short bursts, and his face was shiny with perspiration. His heart was pounding so loudly in his ears that, had it been McCann who spoke next, it was doubtful whether Brian would have heard him.

"I have to go, I have to go get Danny," Brian was actually turning towards the entrance to the garage, and for a crazy instant, McCann thought he was going to be left behind.

"What about the ladder, Brian?" McCann asked, but Brian didn't really hear. Instead, Brian just looked frantically around, at nothing and no one, and suddenly released what was screaming in his brain like that howling wind.

"Oh, dear God above!" Brian shouted. "I know who it is! I know who has Danny!"

SIX

The slate grey Alfa Romeo 166 was capable of 140-plus miles per hour. McCann couldn't get it up to within 100 miles per hour of that maximum, because they were travelling through a series of housing estates--as the crow flies, less than half a mile from the Sykes' home. Brian sat next to McCann, who had told Richie Brauders to radio for backup to be sent to No. 41, Fr. Cullen Terrace, an end of terrace, run down, 63-year-old house that was the current rented accommodation of Geoffrey Staines. It would take approximately 15 minutes for the five additional gardai to arrive. Brian and McCann would be there in four.

Brian explained to McCann, in short sentences, as he stared straight ahead and willed the narrow, short streets, with cars parked on either side, to open into a wide avenue that would take them more quickly to their destination, that for the past 16 months, Geoffrey Staines had been cleaning their windows. Coming up to the Christmas before last, Bridget had decided that she wanted her windows cleaned properly for the holidays. She had found Staines' hand written message on the Tesco notice board, offering his services and giving an address and mobile phone number. Brian, who had a number of excuses for not cleaning the windows himself, given the fact that he never got home in the winter until well after dark on weekdays, pointed out that the weather was unreliable at the weekends, and refused to admit what Bridget knew for certain--that he was mortally terrified of getting up onto anything higher than a step ladder--quite happily consented to Bridget spending the £20 Staines quoted for cleaning all the windows, upstairs and down. He would have done them inside and out, for £35, but Bridget decided she'd do the inside herself, and use the saved £15 to get her hair done at Suzie's Scissors in town.

Staines had arrived when he said he would, with his own extension ladder strapped precariously onto the roof rack of his 1988 Nissan Micra. When he had finished the first time, and Bridget had paid him, she noticed him struggling to secure the ladder back onto the roof of his car. Bridget told him that, if he ever did the job for them again, he was welcome to use their ladder, to save him the bother of bringing his own. Staines immediately offered to do the job at a discounted price if Bridget would agree to get him back on, say, a monthly basis. Bridget and Brian discussed it briefly over dinner that night, and between them, agreed that every six weeks would suffice. Brian had phoned Staines the first Saturday after Christmas, and told him he could start whenever he wanted in January, and every six weeks thereafter, at £18 per time. Staines accepted, and briefly enquired whether it would be all right to use Brian's ladder, as Bridget had suggested. Brian, secretly delighted that it would be someone else, anyone other than himself, scaling that aluminium death trap, said it was absolutely no problem.

Every six weeks, from that time to the present, Staines had called to clean the windows. His work was fine, though Brian noticed it almost always seemed to rain within a day or two of the windows being cleaned. He also noticed that Staines always put the ladder back in the garage, exactly as he'd found it, when he finished his work. Brian had a bit of a "thing" about tools, utensils, even the hoover, being put back into their allotted spaces after use, so he was pleased that Staines followed this practice. He mightn't have been as pleased to see Staines smiling in through the upstairs window at Danny, who was in his bedroom, colouring a picture of his dog Bandit running through a garden of red and yellow flowers. It was only Staines' third visit to the house.

For McCann's part, he didn't know whether Brian's hunch was right or wrong, though he was leaning to the belief that the man sitting beside him had "clicked" on something. It was more than just having the penny drop. It fit, thought McCann, with his own beliefs that the person they sought knew the Sykes family and house. It would also explain why no one in the neighbourhood had noticed anything out of place. Staines would have been regularly seen in the estate, as would his car. In McCann's experience, some people, by virtue of the fact that they are such a regular part of a given scene, become virtually invisible. Post men, milk men, supermarket delivery vans, even garbage collectors, with their big, smelly trucks that invariably held up traffic, were as accepted in people's minds as were grass and trees, and therefore, unless behaving erratically, came and went unnoticed by the vast majority of people. "Would this also apply to a window cleaner who had been coming and going for nearly a year and a half?" McCann wondered to himself.

Yes, it probably would, he decided. Even if someone had seen Staines going into the Sykes' garage, they would have thought nothing of it. His car would have attracted no interest whatever. The dark clouds and rain would have added to his cloak of anonymity. As it happened, no one in the neighbourhood had actually seen Staines that night, but had they done so, no mental alarms would have been triggered.

Still, he was determined that Brian not go charging in like the cavalry, spouting unfounded accusations that could get both of them in serious trouble. He would have left Brian behind, given almost any other scenario, but he knew to do so would have been fruitless. Brian would have simply taken his own car, and arrived at Staines' house within seconds of the detective anyway. So McCann determined that he might have more luck holding Brian under some kind of control if he kept him close by. A sideways glance at Brian gave McCann no great confidence in his ability to keep this man under any kind of control at all, should they find that Staines was indeed the criminal they sought. Brian was pretty powerfully built for a man who wore a shirt and tie to work every day. And McCann had often experienced the strength of people, men and women, who were either terrified or furious. Still, he had to try to maintain some semblance of order to the situation they were rushing into, so he spoke quietly to Brian, unsure of whether his words were registering or not.

"Brian, you have got to let me handle this, ok?" No response. "We know nothing yet; we're only checking this Staines fellow out; we'll see if he knows any......."

Brian cut him dead with a look. "We don't know anything?" he snarled. "I know my son has been missing for almost a day now! I know you told me that whoever took him was someone we know, and that this person knew the house, and I know you should just drive the goddamn car faster and get us there!"

McCann said nothing for a full five seconds, then responded, "What I know, Brian, is that you've come up with a possible suspect, and fair play to you. It's more than we've been able to do," he said placatingly. The dark glare from Brian told McCann in no uncertain terms not to patronise his passenger any further, so he continued in a firmer tone, "but if you want to screw up any evidence that may or may not be at this man's house, as well as any chance of convicting him if you rush in like a bull elephant, then you just keep it up, because you're going about it in the right way. We haven't got a search warrant, and we can't even go into his house, unless by some miracle he invites us in. If you get in his face straight away, he's not going to be too eager to have you in for a cup of tea, is he? Now if you're not happy with that, then I can stop the car right here and let you out. Is that what you want?" McCann briefly thought this last idea might just be an excellent suggestion. They were still about a quarter mile from Staines' house. If he put Brian out of the car, he'd either have to go the rest of the way on foot, or go back to his own house to get his car, either of which would give McCann and his colleagues time to, at the very least, make an initial assessment of whatever situation they might find at No. 41, Fr. Cullen Terrace. As quickly as the idea came to him, he dismissed it. He would need nothing less than a crow bar and stick of dynamite to remove Brian Sykes from his car, and he didn't want to waste time fighting with a man who was clearly right on the very edge.

For his part, Brian was again torn asunder by a range of emotions. Anticipation that he might be on his way to finding his son gave him an enormous surge of hope. The next millisecond, blind rage seared through his soul, because he could now put a face on the monster that he was sure was responsible for his waking nightmare. Then, just as abruptly, the rage was gone, only to be replaced by a tidal wave of guilt. Why hadn't he noticed anything about Staines' behaviour? Why hadn't he worked out earlier who had taken Danny (there was simply no doubt in his mind)? He even wondered why he couldn't get over his own fear of ladders and do the windows himself. Then a picture of Danny reaching out to him flashed through his head, and the joy that vision gave him was almost something he could touch. The joy turned to terror that this image would never be a reality, only what might have been if he'd acted sooner. Not for the last time that day, a wave of nausea made his stomach cramp, and rose to his chest and throat. He only barely held it at bay.

When they arrived at No. 41, Fr. Cullen Terrace, McCann instantly took in the scene that confronted them. Firstly, McCann noted that No. 40 was deserted, because the windows were broken out and boarded up, and the tiny front garden appeared not to have been tended in a considerable length of time. On the other side of No. 41 was a "green strip," as the council liked to call it. They used this term for just about any piece of ground that was too small for them to cram another council house onto, and called it "green" to show how environmentally aware they all were. The strip was only about eight metres wide, blanketed by weeds, and bordered by a low wall covered with graffiti. The lack of neighbours on either side did not sit well with McCann. "No one to hear anything through the thin walls," he thought to himself, though he didn't share this with Brian. There was no driveway at No. 41, just the frame of a gate, the main bulk of which was rusted because it hadn't seen paint in more than fifteen years. Staines' Micra was parked in the street, directly in front of the house. McCann drove down as far as No. 35, ignoring Brian's furious protest that he had gone too far, and pulled into the curb.

"I'm telling you now, Brian, don't make me lock you in the car, which I probably should do anyway," McCann warned. "You follow me, identify Staines to me, and let me ask the questions," he continued, emphasising the word 'me' each time.

They got out of the car and started the short distance up the street. Brian was level with McCann until they got to the rusty gate, then suddenly bolted to the front door. He raised his fist, and only when it was an inch from the first, crunching knock, did he have any doubts about what he was doing. It's incredible how many thoughts can go through a man's mind in the time it takes his fist to travel an inch. He wondered if he had gotten it totally, completely wrong. This was surreal. The sun was actually shining. People were going about their business; everything was normal. It wasn't possible that he could be standing at the front door of the man who had kidnapped his only child. And worse. Was it?

So the first knock was tentative. By the time his fist struck the rotting timber doorframe a second time, the doubts were already gone, and he pounded so hard, it seemed entirely possible that the tired wood with the few flakes of white gloss paint still left in place might just splinter and give way.

"Damn it, Brian, don't make me arrest you!" McCann hissed, trying unsuccessfully to grab Brian's right arm as it launched another assault on the door.

"Danny, are you in there?" Brian yelled, not caring in the slightest who might hear, or whether he would eventually be shown to be making a complete fool of himself. "It's Daddy! Just shout if you can hear me!" The word 'daddy' caused a lump to form in Brian's throat, and he was about to attack the door for a third time, when he felt McCann lock both arms around his waist from behind. The detective literally picked Brian up off the ground, spun him round so the two of them were now facing back towards the street, and half dropped, half shoved him away.

"Back off!" McCann raised his voice far more than he would have liked, but he had to regain control. Far from having the desired effect, it appeared that Brian not only hadn't heard McCann, but it was as if he couldn't even see the detective standing in front of him. McCann braced himself for what now appeared was going to become a physical confrontation. He still had his back to the house, so he didn't see the face appear in the small rectangular pane of glass in the middle of the front door. Brian did, though, and he immediately stopped his advance and looked intently over McCann's shoulder. When McCann noticed this, he too spun around.

The door opened slowly, and Geoffrey Staines stood in front of the two men. At 5 foot 10 inches, and with a scrawny build, Staines didn't present a particularly menacing figure. His dark brown hair was receding around the temples; what was left was wispy, scraggly, and clearly hadn't been washed in some considerable period of time. He wore jeans that had pizza sauce stains in several places on the left leg; some form of liquid had been spilled on the right. It was as if he'd had his takeaway meal without the use of a plate or even a glass. Both sleeves had been torn off his grey sweatshirt, right up to the shoulders; the front bore the slogan, "Screw you if you can't take a joke!"

Staines' brown eyes surveyed the scene in front of him--but only just. His pupils were dilated to the point where only the barest bit of brown encircled the black centres. Red lines made crazy designs in what were meant to be the whites of his eyes, and very dark circles underneath completed the package. "If eyes are the windows to the soul," McCann thought, "then this man's soul is not getting a lot of daylight."

Brian was speechless. All the fury had gone out of him, and not through fear, or a sudden change of heart that maybe he had been wrong. It was simply a situation for which he wasn't one bit prepared. He literally had nothing to say, and he just stared blankly at Staines.

Staines returned Brian's look, and as the mist temporarily cleared from his eyes and brain, recognition dawned. "Brian Sykes, isn't it?"

he said. His words were slurred, and whiskey was as thick as stale vapour on his breath.

"Mr. Staines?" McCann asked, noticing Brian's seeming paralysis, and being silently grateful for it at the same time.

"Who are you?" Staines asked, but his voice betrayed the fact that his mind was already drifting elsewhere. Though the question was directed at the detective, his eyes had lost focus, and were now scanning the street, then the sky, and then somewhere between the two. McCann suspected that Staines had indulged in far more than just whiskey in the not too distant past. Naturally, McCann had seen the symptoms of drug use before. Depressingly, they were more frequent now with every passing day, not just on the streets of Bray and Dublin, but in once quiet communities, like Dun Guaire, Greystones, and, he was assured by his colleagues in the Narcotics Unit, in virtually every town, village and parish in the country. And within 30 seconds of meeting Geoffrey Staines, he knew that the window cleaner had far more than just a passing familiarity with hard drugs. The eyes suggested heroin. Subsequent investigation would prove this to be accurate, along with the alcohol, and, when funds permitted, cocaine. Hard core users frequently ingested cocaine to fuel an instant high, then used heroin to come back down.

"I'm Detective McCann, and you already know Mr. Sykes," McCann replied, keeping his voice as casual as was possible under the circumstances. He was on edge himself, and this was in no small way due to his conviction that Brian could snap out of his current state of suspended animation at any second.

"Oh, uh, yeah, I know Mr. Sykes, and the missus," Staines barely got the words out over his ever-thickening tongue. Then, even though he was standing relatively upright, Staines' eyes started to roll back in his head, and it appeared that he would pass out right in front of the two men. He fought against the darkness, but his mind was all over the place. It was like he was just waking up from a dream, and couldn't distiguish between that which he had dreamt, and that to which he was awakening.

"Windows," Staines managed to get out, but he couldn't put any
substance onto the thought. "Has this got something to do with
windows?"

Brian was lost. This couldn't be right. He'd had visions during the
drive over of breaking into Staines house, and of the villain making a
run for it, panic stricken. He would have chased him down and
beaten him into mushy lumps until, afraid for his life, Staines would
have told him where Danny was. Staines wasn't frightened. He was
drunk and drugged, but he didn't have the look of a man who was
capable, or guilty, of a savage attack and kidnapping. Hell, it was all
he could do at the moment to stay on his feet.

"We're wasting our time here," Brian said to McCann, with a
defeated tone.

"Are we?" McCann asked quietly. He'd seen Jeckyll and Hyde
characters before, and after all, hadn't Dr. Jeckyll used drugs to
achieve the effect? He turned back to Geoffrey Staines, whose eyes
were now as frosted over as beer mugs coming out of a deep freeze.

"We're investigating the disappearance of Danny Sykes, Mr.
Staines," McCann said, unsure of whether his words had penetrated.
"You wouldn't have been in the Sykes's neighbourhood yesterday
evening, by any chance, or seen anyone or anything suspicious,
anywhere in this general area, would you?" Again no response.
"We were wondering if you might have even seen Danny with a
friend, or getting into a car, or talking with a str...."

"Danny?" Staines had picked this one word out of the hum that
made up the rest of McCann's questions. He was weaving now, from
side to side. Twice he actually bumped off the doorframe. "You
here looking for Danny?"

Brian had been ready to leave moments before. Now he wasn't
even breathing. Staines knew something, and the adrenalin building
in Brian sent his heart rate to double the norm. But still, he said
nothing, just waited.

Staines had lost the battle of distinguishing between reality and
dreamland. He nodded once, looked at Brian, and said, "Umm,

windows, right, yeah, sure." He still wasn't sure what this had to do with windows, but his brain was only registering odd words in half sentences. " Next week be all right?" Staines actually giggled. "And Danny's around here someplace. Prob'ly time for him to go home, right? You'd better come in and get him."

SEVEN

Danny was in the third room they checked.

Upon entering the house, Staines slumped onto the tattered, filthy brown sofa, sitting like a lump of muck under the window that looked out onto the green patch at the side of No. 41. There were three rooms that led from the sitting room. To one side, there was a small bathroom. Straight ahead was the kitchen, and off to the right was the single bedroom.

McCann saw that Staines was going nowhere. He'd felt entitled to enter the house, even without a search warrant, because Staines had invited them in. This eliminated the need for the warrant. Brian and McCann took a brief look into the kitchen, which held nothing more than a rickety table, two unmatched chairs, a small fridge, gas stove and hob, old fashioned ceramic sink, and a floor covered with linoleum that looked straight out of the 60's. It even had a floral pattern, but the lino was now wearing paper thin from 40 years of traffic.

Coming out of the kitchen, McCann saw Richie Brauders arrive in his own squad car, followed within a few seconds by an unmarked Nissan Maxima containing four plain- clothes detectives. McCann took the three steps from the kitchen entrance to the front door, and waved quickly out at his colleagues to come into the house. He then turned and saw Brian walking directly into the bedroom to his right. The detective quickly followed, but he needn't have bothered. Brian stood just one step inside the bedroom door, rooted to the floor, incapable of movement, speech, or for the moment, action.

McCann entered the bedroom and stood at Brian's side. What he saw stayed with him for the rest of his life. It haunted him at times, depressed him often, and, more than once in the years that followed, led him to consider leaving the force, thinking that by doing so he could distance himself from the evil which that moment had brought into such horrifically sharp focus.

Danny lay on the stained sheets of the single bed, eyes half open, but unseeing. Dry tear tracks were still visible on his cheeks. His wavy hair was matted and stuck to his skull. Dark, purple-red bruises contrasted horribly with the otherwise whiteness of Danny's throat. His lips were cold blue. Brian couldn't understand how he hadn't known that Danny had contracted chicken pox; it was, bizarrely, the first thing he later remembered that had struck him. What he didn't realize was that the 20 or so marks on Danny's naked torso weren't from chicken pox. They were cigarette burns.

Brian took a faltering step nearer the bed, and saw that Danny had been left only in his little Dunnes Stores briefs. They were meant to be white. Bridget insisted that Danny put on a clean pair every day, even at weekends. Now, Brian saw the red staining the back of those briefs, and his knees buckled. Once again, bile rose in his throat; again, he fought back the nausea and reached for his tiny, battered, broken child.

"Don't touch him, Brian!" It was McCann. From the time they had walked into the bedroom, less than 15 seconds had passed. Now McCann knew that he must take charge. No. 41 was a crime scene, and evidence had to be preserved. "Brian, just step out of the room. We've got to seal this house off, and I've got to get the forensics people down here." He also needed the coroner, but didn't say so. He turned away from Brian for just a moment, and looked back into the sitting room. "O'Shea, take him into custody, now!" he barked, pointing at the semi-conscious Staines.

"Custody?" Staines looked out from under his droopy eyelids. "Oh, man," he slurred, "have I fucked up or something?"

"Jesus, the lights are on, but no one's home," Fran Kennedy said to O'Shea, before moving to the side of the sofa and beckoning Geoffrey Staines to stand up.

Then Brian turned away from McCann, and with absolutely no emotion on his face, walked out of the bedroom and back into the living room. "He's in shock," thought McCann. Brian, though his face was impassive, was walking directly toward Staines. Fran Kennedy saw this, and moved to stand between Brian and his target, though he didn't think from Brian's facial expression that he was going to actually cause any trouble. He put a hand out. Kennedy was all of six-foot-three, and weighed in at more than 16 stone, very little of it in body fat. His physical presence alone generally dissuaded anyone with thoughts of violence.

"Mr. Sykes, we'll take care of this. Do you want to wait outside?" The detective's voice was sympathetic, but he didn't move out of the way of Brian's advance. Brian slowed, but didn't stop. Still, his face betrayed nothing. He didn't even seem to see the large detective standing before him, until Brian's chest came into contact with Kennedy's burly hand, which remained outstretched.

In one continuous motion, Brian used his left hand to sweep aside Kennedy's outstretched arm, followed by a crunching right fist to the side of the policeman's stunned face. The blow knocked Kennedy backwards, his left jaw broken. He staggered, and fell half across Staines, who looked on as though he were a spectator at a prize fight. Even when Brian, his face now unmasked and covered with blind rage, reached for Staines' throat, the drugged man appeared not to realize that his life was in real and immediate danger. Brian's face was white, except for matching red dots the size of five cent coins that blazed on top of each cheek bone.

McCann again grabbed Brian from behind, much as he had done on the porch earlier. Patrick O'Shea moved in quickly as well, and, with the element of surprise gone, Brian couldn't overcome the attentions of the two policemen. They moved in a kind of rugby scrum towards the front door. Richie Brauders opened the door, and in one tangled mass of arms and legs, the three men stumbled out

into the front yard. O'Shea and McCann pulled quickly away from
Brian, who almost instantly started to rush back in the direction of
the door he'd just exited. He pulled up, though, when he saw the
entry blocked by the considerable frames of Brauders and O'Shea.

"Brian, please, for Christ's sake!" McCann shouted. "We've got a
job to do, and you're just making things.......look, man, you can't
help your son this way!"

McCann wondered, late that same night, when he tried to close his
eyes to sleep and instead saw the lifeless eyes and broken body of
Danny Sykes, why he chose those words. It was obvious that no one,
ever, would help Danny again. His words, though, had stopped
Brian Sykes more forcefully than would have any type of physical
restraint.

"You'd protect him, that filthy bastard, from me?" Brian asked, half
pleading, half accusing. Neither policeman answered, nor did they
look Brian directly in the eye.

The reality of what he had seen in Geoffrey Staines' bedroom
slammed into Brian's brain like a freight train. He staggered
backwards, his world spinning wildly out of control. What would he
tell Bridget, his own parents, his brothers? At that moment, he had
no answers, only a torment that burned like the fires of hell. Brian
turned to his left, and vomited into the scraggy, uncut grass.

EIGHT

Bridget's heart was broken. Brian's had turned to stone. Three days had passed since the horrific discovery in Geoffrey Staines' house.

And three nights.

Sleep was not possible, not even with the strong sedative that Dr. Hickson had prescribed for Bridget, or the half bottle of Powers Gold Label that Brian felt compelled to drink before going up the stairs to the bedroom each night. Their tortured brains could be neither quietened nor stilled by drugs or alcohol. Bridget had come home on Friday, the day after Danny had been found at No. 41, Fr. Cullen Terrace. Her injuries were sufficiently healed that she could have come home a day earlier, but once word of what had happened to Danny reached the hospital, nurses kept a constant vigil at Bridget's bedside, mourning with her while at the same time watching for any sign that she might lose control.

Brian himself had told Bridget that Danny was never coming home. When he stood in the hospital doorway, flanked by Patrick O'Shea, she knew from his face that her worst fears had become reality. She couldn't recall the words he'd used to tell her that her son was dead. She saw his white face, and red eyes filled to overflowing with tears,

noticed the torn pocket on his shirt from the scuffle with the two
detectives, and wondered if all that was happening was just a
nightmare that, God willing, she would wake from at any moment.

Bridget ached. Her heart seemed to have swelled in her chest, but
that only allowed the pain she felt there to be enlarged, almost all-
consuming. Tears were never more than a few seconds away from
the back of her eyes, and they poured forth till she wondered herself
where all the salty liquid came from. Likewise, she felt true pain
below her stomach, as though her womb had been ripped open
without anesthetic, and something removed. That "something" she
knew to be Danny, and though he'd been born more than eight years
earlier, he was surely as much a part of her as were her heart, her
lungs and all the other things she required inside herself to live.

Bridget remembered the night Danny was born. He had arrived at
the end of a 14-hour long labour, which had only been truly painful
for the last 90 minutes or so. Brian had been there throughout the
day, and was present at the birth. Bridget cursed him like a sailor at
the height of her labour pains. She threatened him with a do-it-
yourself-at-home vasectomy performed with a rusty scissors coated
in sea salt if he ever came near her side of the bed again in his
lifetime. They laughed about it later. Not for a few months, but after
that, Brian often looked under Bridget's pillow before getting into
bed, muttering something along the lines of "Hmm, no scissors here.
Could be a good night tonight!"

Danny arrived just after 11.30 on a Tuesday night. He had cried for
only a few seconds, and Bridget secretly thought that he was already
so clever, he'd only cried so they wouldn't worry that he was
breathing all right. Of course, she knew this not to be true, but she
liked to pretend that it was, even if only to herself. After the first
minute or so, Bridget, then Brian, was allowed to hold Danny before
he was whisked away to be cleaned, weighed, and have his
identification bracelet attached. When he was returned to the
recovery room, his eyes were wide open, and he genuinely appeared

to be trying to take in his surroundings. He was a very contented baby, and, being the first, and only child, well and truly spoiled. The love he received hadn't ruined him, however. He was a genuinely good and happy boy, whom Bridget was sure would have grown into a wonderful man, with a lovely wife and gorgeous children of his own.

The memory melted away. Bridget felt that she had actually been smiling with the vision she had just recalled. But as it dissolved, it turned bitter in her mouth. Then, as the reality that Danny was going to be placed under ground, in a small white coffin, came screaming back to her, Bridget fell apart. The screaming she heard came from her own throat, and from deep, deep within her.

Brian heard the screams from downstairs. They had only a slightly greater effect on him than if they'd come from the late night TV mystery movie he was watching at the time. He hadn't cried since he left the side of Bridget's hospital bed. He didn't cry when he contacted his mother, or his brother. He didn't cry when he leaned into the coffin at Tarpey's funeral home and kissed his son's stone cold forehead. He recoiled slightly from the touch. A part of him still expected Danny's skin to be warm to the touch. Apart from that, he was impassive and unfeeling. It was as though his mind was protecting him from the trauma he'd experienced. He was conscious of everything that was going on around him, including Bridget's ghastly pain. But even to that, he was numb. He felt only emptiness each time a person came to him, put their arms around him, and told him how incredibly sorry they were. Their tears were real; many of these neighbours, friends and family were utterly heartbroken at the loss of Danny, even more so for the way he had been taken from them. But Brian felt that he himself was as dead inside as.......as.......as

......Danny.

This was late Sunday night, two weeks since Easter Sunday, a day when Danny had found his Cadbury's Miniature Heroes Easter egg at the foot of his bed when he woke up. He'd walked into his parent's bedroom, holding the chocolate egg aloft with a delighted smile and proclaimed, "Thank you, Mr. Easter Bunny," looking directly at Bridget as he said it.

It had been a lovely day, not because of the changeable weather, which had delivered the promised mixture of sunshine and showers, but because they had spent the day together. Father Brady had given the midday Mass; he'd kept it relatively short for an Easter Mass, which pleased Brian, and Danny, immensely. Bridget then presented her "two favourite men in the world" with an excellent dinner of roast ham, mashed potatoes and gravy, sweet corn and garden peas, accompanied by hot bread rolls, milk for Danny and red wine for herself and Brian. After dinner, Danny tucked into his chocolate egg; Bridget got her box of After Eights and placed it on the sofa between herself and Brian. She watched "Easter Parade" with Judy Garland, while Brian scanned the *Sunday Independent*. "Perfect," Bridget remembered thinking at the time.

But in a few hours time, Father Brady would be saying Danny's funeral Mass. The coroner had finished the inquest into Danny's death on Saturday. "Death by asphyxiation," was the official verdict. He would testify at Geoffrey Staines' trial as to how that asphyxiation was probably caused.

So Saturday evening and all day Sunday, Brian and Bridget had spent at Tarpey's, while a constant stream of visitors came and went. There wasn't a single man, woman or child who entered the funeral home that didn't break down in tears once they saw Danny, lying serenely in his coffin, dressed in his First Holy Communion suit, tiny hands crossed and clasping his rosary beads, hair done to perfection, skin without a visible blemish. The tear tracks had been washed away. The suit covered the cigarette burns, and the kindly, elderly Tarpeys had done the rest of the makeover.

Bridget went to the coffin only occasionally. She knew it would make her hysterical to look at her baby boy lying in a box. So she sat with her parents and let them try to comfort her, and, in fact, she was comforted when her mother put her arms around her and told her that she loved her. Brian went to the coffin just twice, once Saturday evening before leaving the funeral home, and then again Sunday, in the last moment before they closed the lid of Danny's coffin, just before the removal to St. Joseph's Church. Brian knew he would never see his son's face again, waiting for him as he pulled up the drive after work, or peeking into the bedroom on a Saturday morning, far too early, asking whether Daddy was going to give him a game of football. So just those two times, he kissed Danny's forehead, then leaned close to Danny's ear and whispered, so quietly that no one, besides Danny, could hear, "Sorry, son."

The late night movie ended, and Brian mechanically switched off the television, turned out the lights, and checked the locks on the doors before climbing the stairs to the bedroom. It had been several hours since the Fitzgeralds, Patti and Ted had left them with hugs and assurances that they would see them at the church the following day. As he reached the landing at the top of the stairs, he avoided glancing to his right. Danny's bedroom door was closed, and locked. "Who are we trying to keep out?" Brian asked aloud, but there was no one present to answer.

He entered the main bedroom and saw Bridget's accusing stare aimed at him like a weapon. "What?" he asked, though he knew perfectly well that, because he hadn't rushed up the stairs when he heard her screaming, more than half an hour earlier, he was going to pay a heavy price.

Bridget turned her dark brown eyes on Brian, and scowled for another several seconds. Her pain was now mixed with anger. They were a potent and dangerous combination. "Didn't you hear me, Brian?" she asked, but knowing full well he had ignored her cries.

He had been attentive on Friday, when he'd brought her home from St. Vincent's, and had stayed by her side for the most part during their time at Tarpeys, but he had become, over the three days, increasingly distant. He wasn't coping well, she knew, but what she couldn't understand was the lack of any noticeable type of emotion. Outwardly, Brian wasn't displaying anger or grief, not even self pity. Likewise, there was no discernible compassion, concern or sympathy directed towards herself. She needed pity. She needed to grieve, but not on her own. She needed him to worry about how her head still hurt, and whether she needed one of the painkillers she'd been given to bring home. She wanted him beside her, holding her hand, sharing her pain. She expected this from him, and felt she was entitled to the care he now appeared to be willfully withholding from her. He wasn't being loving. He wasn't even being caring. He was turning cold, not just to herself, but, Bridget noticed, to anyone who approached him. Still, she thought it strange and frustrating that he wasn't...anything. Brian had lost, or locked away, the ability to show any kind of human feeling, and while this would later come to frighten Bridget, for the moment, she was just getting fed up, seeing it as one more thing she just didn't need to deal with at that particular time.

"Answer me, Brian, please," Bridget said, her voice now just beginning to break. "Weren't you even worried enough to check if I was all right? Was the movie that good, or were you in the kitchen getting ice for your drink?" She'd damn well get a response from him, shake down the hard, thick wall he was erecting between himself and every person with whom he happened to be sharing a room.

"I don't want to fight, Bridget," Brian said, utterly dispassionately. "Are you okay?" he asked, and it was blatantly obvious that he didn't care to hear her answer.
"Oh, yeah, I'm brilliant," Bridget practically sneered the answer. "Like you give a damn."

"All right, now I'm asking you," Brian said, but without raising his voice a decibel, "Let's not do this right now." He spoke the words in a virtual monotone, with no indication that he was asking her anything more important than to pass the sugar.

"Brian, what's wrong with you?" Bridget shouted this question. His answer was to give her an "I can't believe you just asked me that" look, followed by a snort, but he wouldn't rise to her question with anything more. She found this completely maddening. By God, it wasn't good enough! It wasn't fair; he was hurting her, and she didn't deserve another ounce of pain to go with the tonnes of anguish that were already crushing her heart.

"You're drunk," she accused him with a disdainful tone.

"I'm not."

"Did you stop off for a drink on your way home from work last Wednesday? Is that maybe why you were a bit late getting home?"

She knew she had never insinuated anything as cruel in her life, not to anyone she had ever known. She wouldn't have made such a suggestion to someone she disliked immensely, and she was shocked that she could have said these words to Brian. But she set her chin, refusing to withdraw the remark, though she knew it to be utterly without foundation. She had lashed out, and it was too late to take back the words. They found their mark. Colour drained immediately from Brian's face; he was white with shock.

"You're saying I'm to blame? That I should have been home earlier, and that if I had been, then Danny would still……"

"No, Brian." Bridget felt she had to try to defuse the nuclear warhead she had just activated. "I didn't mean that. I just meant that--if only….."

"You think it's my fault," and now Brian's voice was raised, not shouting, but loud enough to cause Bridget to shrink back. She desperately regretted what she'd said, until Brian launched his own attack. "Well, maybe if you'd been home, cooking my dinner, instead of swanning around in the shops, you wouldn't have anything to be screaming the house down about! Maybe if you weren't so concerned about your precious carpet getting dirty, you'd have used the front door instead of taking Danny into a dark garage! Maybe if you'd locked the garage door before you left to practice for *another* driving test, that maniac wouldn't have been able to get inside in the first place!"

Bridget stared, horrified. This couldn't be happening. Her husband couldn't, wouldn't ever be able to say these things. Yet he continued.

"And why didn't you fight back? Staines is a weed; you probably outweigh him! Why didn't you stop him?"

"Brian, stop it! You bastard!" Bridget screamed. He had blasted her with every terrible, scathing thing he could think of, knowing that not one word of what he had accused her of was true. The fact that he secretly blamed himself, without even being able to justify that guilt in his own mind, made Bridget's implied charges as painful as if she'd stuck a red hot poker through his skull and into his brain, branding him as a failed father and human being for eternity. Like most animals when wounded, he had lashed back blindly, and without thought or concern as to the damage he himself could cause.

Brian's anger ebbed as quickly as it had risen. The ice inside him won the battle with the fire Bridget's words had sparked off. The living fury was replaced with lifeless stone, and his eyes now looked blankly at Bridget. Her eyes, though, were flooded with tears, which in turn flowed down her bright red face, and mingled with the mucus that dripped from her nose. Her husband would never be forgiven for this attack. In their twelve years of marriage, he had never struck her, and would never have considered doing so. She knew that a physical beating would have been far easier to recover from than what he had just done to her. From that precise moment, to the day she died more than forty years later, Bridget would carry those horrible words in her heart. She even knew he hadn't meant them, but that wasn't enough. The fact that he'd been able to say those things to her, even under the circumstances they were facing, was not something Bridget could let go.

Like Brian, she'd believed that maybe she could have done something different on that Wednesday, and that, in so doing, could have saved their son. Neither could accept that the evil which had ripped their lives apart by an unspeakable act, was not something they could have avoided.

"Get out of this house, and don't ever come back," Bridget hissed. "Stay away from the funeral tomorrow. I don't ever want to see you again." She had stopped crying, and believed the words she was speaking.

"No," Brian answered, in the same dull tone he had used earlier. "If you don't want to see me again, then maybe *you* should stay away from the funeral tomorrow." He went back onto the landing, took two blankets from the hot press, and went back downstairs to the sofa, where he spent the night.

Danny's funeral attracted more than 2,000 people to St. Joseph's. Many hundreds were forced to stand outside. RTE sent a news van there, but the cameras kept a discreet distance, and neither Brian nor Bridget even noticed they were there. Father Brady talked of the taking of innocence, and how it was natural to ask why God would call someone like Danny, but how it was all going to make sense when his family were reunited in heaven, where Danny had surely gone. Conor, Danny's godfather, read the 23rd Psalm, and Patti's daughter, Joanna, sang "Amazing Grace." Twenty-five of Danny's classmates formed a guard of honour when the coffin was wheeled out of the church to the back of the funeral car.

Brian and Bridget sat side by side in the church, and walked together, behind the hearse, to the cemetery. They both looked on as Danny's coffin was placed in its grave, Bridget weeping uncontrollably, while Brian's eyes couldn't be seen behind a pair of dark glasses. No one noticed that, from the time they arrived at the church, then throughout the rest of the entire funeral, not once did Brian and Bridget touch.

That night, Brian slept again on the sofa. Tuesday, he packed what he could into three suitcases, and by early in the afternoon of the day after they'd buried their son, Brian and Bridget were no longer living together. He had moved out. The marriage was over. There would be no going back.

NINE

Wicklow Town, like the rest of the country, was in that peculiar limbo that occurs just before the start of the Christmas rush of buying presents, partying, and general over-indulgences. Mid-November was dull, dark and wet, and since Daylight Savings Time had ended, and the clocks had been set back an hour three weeks previously, the days had taken on that horrible characteristic of still being dark when most people went to work, and already dark again when they were returning home. Restaurants were quiet, and shopkeepers took on a nervous disposition, wondering when, if ever, the spending sprees would start in earnest.

The large, grey, imposing court house, which stands on the corner of Wicklow's Main Street and Kilmantan Hill, seemed impervious to the upcoming holidays. Perhaps that's because, in this particular building, there is never a seasonal lull. Business is always brisk. Between the district court proceedings, which deals with everything from shoplifting to joyriding to drug dealing; family law courts covering judicial separations, child maintenance payments and applications for barring orders, and days like today, when the Circuit Criminal Court would begin hearing the case of the Director of Public Prosecutions vs. Geoffrey Theodore Staines, this old structure had neither the time nor the inclination to pause and take note of the impending festive season of peace and good will to all men.

Perhaps, given everything its walls had seen and heard over the decades, the soul of the building itself was cynical to the notion that there could ever be good will to all men.

Staines' first court appearance after his arrest was at a special sitting of Bray District Court, just two days after Danny Sykes' body was found in Staines' bedroom. On that April Saturday, Staines had been charged with Danny's murder, and the gardai had made an application that he be remanded in custody. The police argued that the crime was of such a heinous nature, there was a danger Staines would flee the jurisdiction if released on bail. They further argued that, given the close proximity of Staines' residence to the family of the deceased, at least one of whom would be called on as a State witness, there was a real danger that the defendant may try to interfere with that witness. The third point raised was the danger of committing further offenses while out on bail, and finally, the State solicitor felt that, given the outpouring of grief and anger in the community, as well as the wide-spread press coverage, Staines could be in real danger of retaliatory attacks if allowed to return to the community pending trial.

Judge Dominic Pritchard asked Staines how he wished to plea to the charge of murder. Staines, flanked by a garda and appearing very blasé about all that was happening around him, said, "I don't know. I suppose not guilty--or something."

Judge Pritchard looked despairingly at the accused, then accepted the gardai's application on the basis of three of the four grounds named. He didn't feel Staines was likely to flee the jurisdiction ("The fool couldn't find his way out the front door without a roadmap," the judge thought to himself), but he did accept the other points, and remanded Staines in custody until the full trial. He also instructed that the State appoint Staines free legal aid. Given that Staines could express no preference himself, Judge Pritchard appointed Mr. Gavin Shaw, SC, to represent the accused.

Seven months had elapsed; a file had been passed to the Director of Public Prosecutions, and, according to the press, this was as close to an "open and shut" murder trial as had ever taken place in the history of the State. The *Examiner* listed the main points they felt would be central to the trial on that morning's front page, in an article under the headline "Bloody Staines All Washed Up." No other suspects had ever been arrested or questioned by the gardai. Sources "close to the investigation" had revealed that all the forensic evidence recovered at the scene tied Staines directly to the crime. Those same sources stated that the defendant would be shown to have been heavily under the influence of a "cocktail" of drugs at the time the crime was committed. Staines lived alone and had not even thought to suggest someone else might have been in his house, or otherwise involved, in the taking of Danny. The *Examiner* could also exclusively reveal that Staines had regularly been seen, by neighbours of the deceased, peering in through the Sykes' windows!

Judge Cyril Evans, presiding, upon hearing of, then reading for himself, the *Examiner* article, immediately placed a gagging order, preventing any further publication or broadcast of facts or information relevant to the trial. He threatened the newspaper with contempt of court charges, and, before commencing the trial, instructed any member of the jury who may have read the offending article to disregard its contents entirely. If they could not, then they could ask to be dismissed from the jury. Mona Warren very nearly took the judge up on his offer. She didn't really want to be on the jury at all, but she was afraid to say that she had been overly affected by the newspaper story, in case the judge would ask her detailed questions. The fact was, she only ever read *The Star*.

Brian and Bridget arrived at the court house separately, but within five minutes of each other. Bridget wore a navy blue pant suit, and a black wool coat to hold back the November chill. She wore no jewellry at all, and her makeup was confined to the barest touch of lip gloss. Brian was dressed in a camel coloured sport jacket, dark brown slacks, cream coloured shirt and matching tie. He appeared to be unaffected by the cold weather, and his face was impassive as he walked up the court house steps, towards Bridget. She wondered whether he wanted to speak to her, given that he had not made a single contact since July 17th, the day they'd sold their house. They had agreed on the sale; Bridget couldn't bear to live with the reminders that every nook, cranny and corner of the house threw in her face every minute of every day. Brian had never returned since the day after the funeral. His brother, Adam, had called to the house for the rest of Brian's things, which Bridget had helped pack.

Adam told Bridget how sorry he was, and that maybe Brian would come to his senses once all this was behind them. Bridget nodded and tried to smile, but she knew that what had happened would never be behind herself and Brian. It would be there, in front of them and between them, for the rest of their lives. It was also Adam who later delivered the news that Brian wanted nothing from the sale of the house; once the mortgage and legal bills were paid, she could keep whatever was left for herself. Given that house prices had literally doubled in the six years since they had bought their home, Bridget was left with nearly €115,000. Her parents cashed in an endowment policy, and gave Bridget another €50,000; this allowed her to buy, free and clear, a nice one-bedroom apartment in Loughlinstown.

She decided, against the advice of Patti, not to pursue Brian for any further payments or support. Bridget had neither the energy, malice, nor the motivation to even contemplate such action. She had other demons to face. Depression threatened to swamp her like a tidal wave. Remorse, anger and guilt were unwanted, daily callers to her tormented mind. Regularly, the old saying that "time heals all wounds," was questioned by Bridget. In her case, time was a plague to be suffered, and a horribly empty vessel to be filled. And all Bridget had to fill it with were thoughts of Danny, which were unbearably poignant, or equally painful thoughts of Brian. Their twelve years of truly happy marriage had paled to nothing because of one screaming match the night before Danny's funeral.

Bridget had since lost far too much weight. Brian's sneering "...you probably outweigh him!" hissed in her head like a venomous serpent each time she tried to face food, and she now weighed barely seven stone, compared with the nine stone, ten pounds she had been at Easter. She regularly felt weak and dizzy, and couldn't remember

the last time she'd been able to muster enthusiasm for any task or
event. A part time job at Marathon Videos in Shankill helped fill
some hours, but mostly her energy went into finding ways to avoid
thinking about Danny and Brian.

Now Brian was within a few feet of her, and Bridget found herself
becoming a bit nervous, wondering what he'd say, and equally, how
she would respond.

"Right, what can we expect today?" Brian asked, and Bridget was
horribly confused until she realised the question was not meant for
her, but for Sean McGillicuddy, Senior Counsel for the State. He was
standing just behind Bridget, and to her left. Open-mouthed, Bridget
stared at Brian; it couldn't be that he hadn't seen her there. He now
passed within two feet of her, and walked directly up to the man
who would be trying to convince a judge and jury to send their son's
killer to prison for the rest of his life. Had Brian forgotten that
Danny was indeed "their son?" Was Bridget to be ignored, shut out,
as she had been from Brian's world for seven months?

"Like hell," she thought.

"Brian, I'd like to ask some questions, too, if you don't mind,"
Bridget said firmly. "Well, even if you do mind, actually," she
added, flushing slightly at her own clumsy display of aggressive
petulance.

Again, Brian looked, sounded and acted as cold as the November
air. "Why would I mind?" he asked, with utter indifference. Bridget
knew there was no answer that she could articulate that would
sound any way reasonable, so she looked at McGillicuddy and asked
him how long the trial would take, and whether or not she would be
called on to testify. The solicitor, a pudgy man in his early 50's, with
a shocking head of brown curly hair, wire-rimmed bifocals perched
on his large nose, and watery, dull blue eyes, nodded slowly, with a
grave look on his face.

"We may call on you, Mrs. Sykes, but if we decide that's necessary,
we'll give you as much advance notice as possible. Your husband
will be called, possibly as early as tomorrow. Our opening statement
will be relatively brief; I can't imagine what the defense counsel will

offer in terms of his remarks, but we should be through the entire
proceedings within the next four or five days. That's a very, very
short time for a murder trial, but this one's quite — umm--direct.
There's also always the possibility that the accused may change his
plea to guilty; given the preponderance of evidence against him, I
must confess to being somewhat surprised that he hasn't already
done so."

Bridget found, to her horror, that McGillicuddy's voice was
practically putting her to sleep! He was talking to her about a child
killer, but he might as well have been giving the weather forecast.
There was no intensity, no passion, for what this man was about to
undertake. He seemed to be taking success for granted, but didn't
appear that he would be particularly overjoyed if that success were
achieved. Bridget felt something was terribly, terribly wrong. If
Brian felt the same, he certainly wasn't showing it.

"Why would he plead guilty, Mr. McGillicuddy?" Bridget
enquired. "Surely, he has nothing to lose by chancing his arm."

"Please, call me Sean," the solicitor said, trying, and failing
miserably, to create some kind of rapport with Bridget and Brian.
When he got no response, he continued, "If he pleads guilty, the
judge may consider a less severe sentence, because it would spare
your husband and you the pain of sitting through the whole trial,
and the anxiety of having to testify. It would also save the State a
considerable amount of time and money," he concluded.

"Spare me nothing," Brian replied, with perhaps more emotion
than Bridget now thought him capable. "I'd rather walk over fire
than see that...that...than to see that man serve one less day in prison
than he deserves."

"I understand," McGillicuddy replied. "Now if you'll both excuse
me, I want to have a quick word with my adversary."

With that, the man representing Brian and Bridget's best chance to
begin putting Danny's memory to rest, turned and waddled over to
Gavin Shaw. Brian and Bridget both looked on, and though not
speaking, sharing the same thoughts. Shaw and McGillicuddy were
supposedly about to be locked in legal conflict; several lives would

be seriously and permanently affected as a result of their efforts over the next number of days. Yet they stood together, speaking quietly, as though they were members of the same rugby club, or sharing an old school style reunion. At one point, Shaw actually appeared to chuckle at something McGillicuddy said to him. Why was it, both Sykes wondered, that these two men could engage in friendly conversation, and probably meet for a drink in Jack White's later that evening, when they were supposed to be, legally at least, mortal enemies?

Bridget stared in the direction of the two men, slowly shaking her head, partly in despair, mostly in disbelief. "What's going on here, Brian? I have a very bad feeling about this."

She turned her head to look at Brian. He had already walked away.

TEN

"Have you reached a verdict upon which you are all agreed?" Cyril Evans asked the foreman of the jury.

The trial had passed that quickly, like the blink of an eye. Barely three days had passed since Judge Evans' opening instructions to the seven men and five women of the jury. In the meantime, they had heard evidence from the coroner, who confirmed that little Danny Sykes had died from lack of oxygen. The marks on his neck and the underlying damage to the ligaments and muscles in his throat and windpipe were conclusive proof that he had been strangled. As no rope burns or other ligature marks could be identified, it appeared that his assailant had strangled Danny with his bare hands. Given everything else he had gone through in the time before his murder, it would have been a blessed release.

He had died sometime between midnight of the night he went missing, and six a.m. the following morning, just a few hours after he had been taken. In that short span, he had suffered through what must have seemed an eternity of evil acts. Not alone were there some twenty-three cigarette burns on his body, but he had been sexually abused as well. DNA evidence tied Staines directly to that hideous perversion. Three of the women jurors-- including Mona Warren-- and two of the men, had wept openly upon hearing the details of what the eight-year-old boy had endured. The coroner also revealed that Danny's lungs contained water, but not enough to have been the cause of death. He did surmise, however, that at some stage before he died, Danny's head would have been held under water, probably in the kitchen sink. Spots of Danny's blood had been found on the kitchen draining board.

Throughout the coroner's testimony, Bridget sat clenching her mother's sleeve, choking back sobs, unable to bear the thoughts of what her baby must have been thinking as horror upon unspeakable horror had been inflicted upon him. Brian sat quietly; the stone in his chest turned, crushing another small bit of humanity within him, as each new detail was laid bare.

Dr. Tony Pearce gave evidence that, after his arrest, Staines' blood had been tested. The samples showed that Staines had indeed ingested a large amount of cocaine prior to his arrest, and his blood alcohol level was alarmingly high. There was also heroin in the defendant's system. Under cross examination, Dr. Pearce admitted to Gavin Shaw that he couldn't say with any assurance when Staines would have taken the drugs and alcohol. Shaw seemed quite anxious to push this point, almost too anxious, to Brian's way of thinking. He thought that it surely didn't matter whether Staines was high on drugs before, during or after Danny's murder. .

Michael McCann was called to give evidence of the events leading up to the arrest of Geoffrey Staines. He kept his version of events as simple and direct as possible, from his arrival at Staines' house, to the invitation from Staines to come in, and finally the discovery of Danny's body in the bedroom, after which Staines had been taken into immediate custody. He did not mention Brian's assault on Fran Kennedy.

Gavin Shaw wanted to know under what circumstances did McCann decide to travel to his client's home. "We had received information that led us to believe Mr. Staines may be able to help us with our enquiries," McCann said, beginning to feel uncomfortable.

"Information of what sort?" Shaw pressed.

The detective was loathe to say that he had travelled to Fr. Cullen Terrace on the hunch of a desperate man who noticed his ladder was in the right place in his garage. He tried to sidestep the question. "Staines had been seen in the neighbourhood," McCann said weakly.

"Correct me if I'm wrong, Detective McCann," Shaw said, with the air of a boxer who had spotted a weakness in his opponent and was moving in quickly, "but wasn't Geoffrey Staines a window cleaner for the Sykes? Wouldn't it be quite normal for him to have been seen in the neighborhood? Doesn't he, in fact, live in that general area? Why would his appearance have been unusual enough to trigger a rush to his home?"

Before McCann could answer, Sean McGillicuddy struggled to his feet and said, "Whatever information the detective was acting upon appears to have been quite reliable, your Honour, so is this line of questioning particularly relevant?"

"I wouldn't have thought so," Judge Evans replied, before turning to Shaw. "Can you come to some point, please, Mr. Shaw."

"My point is made up of a few strands, your Honour. Please may I continue for a short time longer?"

"I'll allow you to make some rope out of your 'strands', just see to it that you don't hang yourself with it," Evans replied.

Without even thanking the judge, Shaw turned back to McCann. "Did you have a search warrant with you when you went to the house?"

"No," McCann replied, "but we were invited into the house by the defendant, so we didn't..."

"Who is *we*?" Shaw interrupted.

McCann knew there was no point in trying to circumvent the issue, so he met it head on. "Myself and Mr. Sykes. He came to the house with me, and we arrived before Garda Brauders and Detectives Kennedy, O'Shea, Morris and Forde."

"Would it be normal practice to take a civilian along with you when conducting an investigation?" Shaw asked with sickeningly obvious innocence.

"No, but the circumstances were highly unusual, and I felt the best way to maintain control over the situation was to let Mr. Sykes accompany me to Mr. Staines' house," McCann said, waiting for the inevitable question about what those circumstances could possibly have been. Shaw had other plans; he changed direction without warning.

"When my client came to the door, did he seem to you to be fully coherent?" Shaw was probing with real purpose now.

"I detected the smell of alcohol on his breath; he appeared intoxicated," McCann answered.

"Out of it? Legless? On another planet?" Shaw wanted something, and McCann couldn't work out exactly what.

"I'm not a doctor, and wouldn't be in a position to make that judgement."

"Would he have been capable of making rational decisions?" Shaw asked insistently.

"Your Honour, the detective has already stated that he's not medically qualified to make such a determination," McGillicuddy protested.

"And yet the prosecution felt qualified enough to assert in their opening remarks that the defendant had embarked on a 'drink and drug-fuelled fantasy that concluded in an orgy of kidnap, depravity, torture and murder.'" (Again, Shaw had been able to recall McGillicuddy's remarks without reference to notes or court transcripts.)

"All right, then, let me ask you this," Shaw said before the judge even had a chance to rule on McGillicuddy's objection. " If you had seen my client getting in his car and preparing to drive off, would you have let him do so?"

"No, I wouldn't," McCann answered truthfully. "He was in no fit state to drive."

"Did he struggle when arrested?" Shaw asked, seeming to change direction again.

"No, he wasn't in a really fit state to do that either."

"But you determined that he was mentally fit enough to invite you into his house, without a search warrant, which you knew by law he was entitled to ask for?" Shaw had everyone's full attention now, including the judge and jury.

"Once we were invited in by the defendant, we did not require that search warrant," McCann insisted.

"Hmm, so let me get this absolutely straight in my own mind," Shaw was about to tie all his 'strands' together. "You arrived at Mr. Staines' home, with a distraught civilian, and no garda backup. From the court records, it is known that you hadn't even applied for a search warrant before you went to the house. You pound the door down, until my client, clearly the worse for wear, answers. You *claim*, though you have no garda corroboration, that my client invited you into his home, which, by the way, he states he has no recollection of doing. You also state that Mr. Staines did not struggle, yet there is a hospital record of Detective Kennedy being treated, after being called to the Staines' residence, for a broken jaw. Do you deny that he sustained this injury in the course of protecting my client against an attack by Mr. Sykes?" McCann shook his head weakly; Shaw's information was very good. McCann had hoped Brian's understandable outburst could have been kept out of the court records.

Shaw now moved quickly to drive his point home to fullest advantage. "Your Honour, surely my client's rights have been horribly infringed here. If he was under the influence of drugs and drink, and operating in a fantasy world, as the prosecution claims, then he was not capable of making a rational decision regarding inviting the detective into his house, if indeed he made such an invitation," Shaw was in full flow now.

"You surely are not calling the detective a liar, Mr. Shaw?" Judge Evans enquired, and the look on his face told Shaw to be very careful indeed when giving his answer.

"No, your Honour, but I am saying that my client does not remember inviting the detective in, which would actually substantiate the prosecution's own claims regarding Mr. Staines' mental state, and that what happened on that day was, therefore, one way or another, an illegal search. Any evidence uncovered in that search should be deemed inadmissable to this court. I also submit that by taking the unfortunate victim's father to the house, the authorities placed my client's well being in jeopardy, as is clearly evidenced by a detective sustaining a broken jaw trying to prevent just such an attack. I think the only fair and proper course now is to declare a mistrial and dismiss the charges against my client. Given the huge amount of negative pre-trail publicity, it is not possible that Mr. Staines would ever receive a fair trial, in this or any other jurisdiction, and his rights have been that badly violated, he should be released immediately."

Shaw knew that the odds of him getting this case dismissed were roughly akin to winning the lottery. His actual aim was to create some sense of confusion amongst both the judge and jury, a feeling that all was not as it should be. In so doing, it was just possible that Staines might receive a slightly lesser sentence. That would be victory enough, and as much as could be hoped for. Any victory was important to a solicitor, and Shaw was no different to any of his colleagues in that respect. He saw every trial as a kind of competition, and he liked to win. But not at any cost. Shaw wondered what the jury must think of him, defending what seemed indefensible. He also wondered what they would think if they knew that, deep down, he hated even being in the same room as his so-called client. He had seen the coroner's photographs of Danny Sykes, and he knew beyond reasonable doubt that Staines had committed the murder for which he was being tried. Shaw had children of his own, and it wouldn't cost him a minute of sleep if Geoffrey Staines never saw a day of freedom again.

"The problem with your suggestion, Mr. Shaw," said Judge Evans, "is that a murder has apparently been committed, and we need some questions answered. Now, while I'm willing to take what you've said into consideration, can you offer the court anything by way of evidence in support of your client's not guilty plea, or that will in any way contradict the evidence presented thus far by the prosecution?"

"The defence will not be calling any witnesses, your Honour, and my client has decided to exercise his right not to testify in his own behalf," Shaw replied. Try as he might, the defense team had been unable to find a single witness to testify to Staines' 'good character.' The man was a loner. His parents had separated when Staines was just six. His father had emigrated to England shortly afterwards, and all contact with him had ceased at that time. His mother was now living with a sheep farmer in County Wexford. She had told her son almost the instant he'd turned eighteen that she wouldn't support him any longer. As far as she was concerned, she'd fulfilled her responsibilities and was now intent on making what was left of her own life as comfortable as circumstances would permit. When contacted by Shaw's office, she had stated frankly that she would be no use in assisting her son's defense, though she did enquire as to whether she'd get witness expenses if she travelled up to Wicklow.

There were no brothers, sisters, aunts, uncles or grandparents. Staines was well and truly on his own. He functioned as a window cleaner long enough to get some cash together. When he had enough, Staines would buy some whiskey at Tesco, then go to the seafront in Bray to score heroin and, funds permitting, cocaine. When the drugs ran out, he would use his dole money, which he collected in addition to his window cleaning income, to buy some food and pay his rent, and then the cycle would start all over again. He was a functioning addict--just about.

A quick consulation between McGillicuddy, McCann and Brian led to the decision not to put Brian on the stand. Likewise, Shaw had no objection to Brian being removed from the witness list; he had no desire to be seen to be persecuting the father of a murdered child. He'd already made his point regarding Brian's attack on Fran Kennedy. To belabour it could be counter productive. Kennedy had already said that he would not be pressing charges against Brian, and the jury would almost certainly sympathise with any man who had walked into a house and found his son dead. Who wouldn't momentarily snap?

So after final submissions by McGillicuddy, who basically read through some four pages of notes, and who might as well have been reading from the phone book for all the effort he put into it, and Shaw, who reiterated that his client was the victim of a culture of drink and drugs, whose own rights had been horribly violated to the point of being placed in the way of physical danger, and who deserved help and treatment for problems that would never be sorted out behind bars, Judge Evans gave the jury their final instructions and sent them away to deliberate. They hadn't taken long, just four hours to reach a unanimous verdict.

Now Thomas Dwyer, the foreman of the jury, was standing and facing Judge Evans. "Yes, your Honour. We, the jury, find the defendant, Geoffrey Staines, guilty."

There was no uproar in the court, although a handful of journalists rushed from the room to phone in the story of Staines' conviction to their respective newspapers and radio stations. Several people, including a number of the jury, turned to see the reaction of the parents. Bridget sat with her mother, Roisin, and cried quietly. She felt no happiness at the conviction, but perhaps the tiniest bit of relief that her earlier misgivings regarding McGillicuddy were apparently unfounded. Brian sat on the bench directly behind Bridget, with his brothers. He actually wanted to feel good about what had happened, but the stone that had taken the place of his heart was again silent and still. He was, truth be told, relieved and at the same time somewhat...unsettled...that he hadn't testified. Even with the guilty verdict, he felt he could have done something more. What that something was, he hadn't an inkling.

Judge Cyril Evans remanded Geoffrey Staines in custody until Monday, December 19th, at which time he would be passing sentence. What neither Brian nor Bridget realised was that Judge Evans would also soon be taking what little comfort Geoffrey Staines' conviction had offered them, and replacing it with a new nightmare, something they couldn't have imagined or foreseen. Gavin Shaw had done his job very well indeed.

ELEVEN

Three weeks had passed since Geoffrey Staines had been found guilty in the death of young Danny Sykes. During that time, very brief Victim Impact Reports had been prepared for Judge Evans, at his request. This really only concerned Brian and Bridget, and the report concluded the obvious; the parents had been severely traumatised, and were unlikely to emotionally recover from their ordeal for some time, if ever. The report also noted that the marriage had suffered dramatically, due in large part to the severity of the stress they had faced. The psychologist responsible for compiling the report did not speculate on the likelihood of reconciliation.

Staines had also been examined, and that report dealt with somewhat more complex issues. Dr. Bernard Doolin conducted three interviews with the convicted killer. His report stated that Staines' was indeed capable of distinguishing right from wrong, and that his intelligence, while slightly below the norm, would certainly not be deemed a serious impediment to normal social interaction. He added, however, that it was impossible to gauge what effect the large amount of drugs in Staines' system would have in distorting his perception of reality. Further, he noted that, while the subject was aware that he had been convicted of a horrific crime, he seemed neither particularly concerned as to the consequences, nor overly remorseful.

Dr. Doolin noted that, at most, Staines seemed "a bit uncomfortable" discussing Danny Sykes. Persistent questioning about the boy simply led to Staines becoming unresponsive. Final conclusions from the doctor were sparse. He detected no obvious

sociopathic behaviour, nor did he deem that Staines would one day
be fit to be returned safely into the community at large. Effectively,
he fudged the issues, not because of incompetence or laziness, but
simply because in the time allotted, Bernard Doolin couldn't
penetrate through the rather dense persona of the man before him.

Judge Evans read the reports with equal mixtures of interest and
concern. The Sykes/Staines case had disturbed him more than most
that had come before him in his time on the bench. None of the nine
murder cases over which he had presided had involved a child.
Well, that may have been technically true, but in four of the cases,
either victim or perpetrator had been in their teens. While the law
allowed them to be tried as adults, to Evans way of thinking, they
were still children. However, none of the victims had been as young
as Danny Sykes.

This wasn't the only unsettling feature of the trial, in Evans' mind.
He had been disappointed in the prosecution of the case by
McGillicuddy, who had seemed to feel that he could stroll through
the proceedings. It hadn't been the first time that McGillicuddy had
tried a case in the judge's court. The plain truth was, Judge Evans
found him lazy, pompous, and sloppy in his preparation. The
prosecutor's failure to tackle Shaw's motion for dismissal head on
was alarming. "Aw, hell," Evans admitted to himself, "I just don't
like the boring son of a bitch."

He wasn't crazy about Shaw either. He found him a bit too
ambitious, and somewhat pushy. It bordered on arrogance. But he
admired his work rate, and the apparent enthusiasm he brought to
each case he tried. Primarily a defense attorney, Shaw was often
presented with apparently hopeless situations, but he approached
each case with an obvious desire to do his best for his client. He had
created a lot of smoke with his cross examination of Detective
McCann, but hadn't actually crossed the line by accusing the
authorities of impropriety.

Judge Evans liked the way that Shaw generally worked through
both his questions and his summations without referring to any
notes or documents. He always kept his facts straight; this showed

Evans that considerable effort was being put into the case before it came to trial. He had seen enough hot shot barristers try to "wing it" on the day, only to "crash and burn" because they ran up against someone who had worked through the weekend in the law library instead of on the golf course.

These things and more were still running roughshod through the judge's mind as he prepared to pass sentence on Geoffrey Staines. He noted the assembled media, many of whom had already prepared their stories stating that Judge Cyril Evans had sentenced the killer to life imprisonment. No one doubted it was going to happen; they just wanted some meat to put on the bones of their articles and sound bites.

Sitting below the judge, and to his left, were Geoffrey Staines and Gavin Shaw. Staines was in handcuffs, but looked otherwise as though he might be about to take in a movie at the Bray Cineplex. Judge Evans tried not to stare, but he did note the dilated pupils of the convicted man's eyes, and supposed with a degree of despair that Staines had already discovered the ease with which he could get heroin in Mountjoy Prison.

To the judge's right sat Sean McGillicuddy, along with an assistant whose name the judge could not recall. Judge Evans also noticed Brian and Bridget Sykes in the public area, and he was truly sad to see that they weren't sitting together. "They've lost so much," he thought. "Can't they see that, for every reason imagineable, this is the time they should be together? Or are they going to lose each other as well?"

Bridget, for her part, was there to hear the judge pass a life sentence on the man who stole from her the most precious thing in her life, her own reason for living, her little blonde-headed boy. She could now feel anger when she looked upon Staines. She saw the handcuffs, and she hoped that, whoever had placed them on him had put the cuffs on too tight. She had heard in "cops and robbers" films that handcuffs could be quite painful, though she didn't actually know anyone who'd ever been placed in them. Looking at the killer before her, she prayed the cuffs hurt like hell.

Some fifteen feet away sat Brian. He, too, wanted to hear the judge say the words that would put Staines away forever. Brian knew that a life sentence seldom meant life, but was hopeful, after questioning McGillicuddy, that the judge would give a recommendation that Staines serve a minimum of 25 years. There was even the possibility, McGillicuddy had hinted, that the judge could sentence Staines to consecutive terms for drugs offenses. It was more normal, however, that any such sentence would run concurrently, and therefore not add any real time to the more severe sentence.

Brian knew that he would get no satisfaction from whatever sentence Judge Evans handed down. He had heard that child killers were sometimes subjected to severe treatment at the hands--and fists, and boots, and the odd homemade weapon--of other inmates, who looked on criminals convicted of offenses involving children as scum not worthy of sharing their cells. This thought gave Brian no joy, either, but he felt at the same time that it would be, perhaps, some measure of justice.

Out of the corner of his eye, Brian caught sight of Bridget. He wondered how she was coping, but admitted to himself that, whatever the answer to that question, he was not inclined to go past wondering about it. It was as if the ability to care, to sympathise, to want to ease Bridget's pain (or anyone else's), was contained like some body of cool water within him. Under normal conditions, he could have doled out comfort as and when it was needed, and still have enough left over for his own needs. The water would have lasted his and Bridget's lifetime, being constantly replenished by the love and experiences that he, Bridget and Danny would have shared. What had happened to Danny had acted like a fireball, or a nuclear explosion. The water had been vaporised in an instant; all that had been left behind was poisonous dust and rock that would never sustain any kind of meaningful life again. But dust and rock cannot help their sterile inability to support or generate life, nor can they regret it. They are simply there, unfeeling.

"...and so, Mr. Staines, it would appear that you have no regret for what you have done, nor any desire to express such remorse to those you have wronged."

Brian absolutely could not believe that he hadn't noticed Evans begin his comments before passing sentence. He had no idea how long the judge had been talking, nor of a single word that he had said to that point.

"This is not in your favour. The taking of any life is unspeakable. To compound this with the unprovoked attack, torture, and killing of an innocent child goes beyond the comprehension of any right thinking human being. To feel no regret for this act, to my mind, makes you something of a monster. There is nothing that can be said in your defense to mitigate in any way what you have done."

Sean McGillicuddy was looking smug. Gavin Shaw sat impassively listening to the judge. Geoffrey Staines was looking at some cracks in the wall behind Judge Evans, thinking that they formed the pattern of a small bird with a broken wing.

"Having said all that, there are aspects of this case, beyond the crime itself, that disturb me." Judge Evans looked directly at McGillicuddy as he said this, and had to admit to himself that he was not unhappy to see the prosecutor's self-satisfied smile replaced with a furrowed and worried brow.

"First, there's the question of the search of the house. It would be wrong to say that I am one hundred per cent satisfied over the failure to secure, or even seek, a search warrant before travelling to Mr. Staines' residence. Given the obvious and understandable belief held by Detective McCann that time was of the essence, and his assertion that he was invited into the house, this alone would not be enough to sway any decision regarding sentencing."

"But there's more. It is clear to me, and in fact was a feature of the prosecution's case, that the defendant was very much under the influence of intoxicating substances. The question in my mind is whether or not he would have committed this crime had he not been experiencing some drug-induced psychotic episode. That he did kill

Danny Sykes is certain. This has been proven beyond any reasonable doubt. That the public must be protected, and a custodial sentence imposed, is likewise without doubt."

Brian found that he had been holding his breath since the time Judge Evans had started to turn from what appeared to be a direct course towards a life sentence for Staines. The knuckles of his hands were white from gripping the bench in front of him. Bridget was sure she wasn't hearing properly. She also began to feel faint.

"If a drunken driver kills a pedestrian, or another motorist, they have killed that person as surely as if they'd used a gun," Evans continued. "But is it murder? The law says that it is not, because the act of that killing is unintentional, but the law still allows the courts to sentence such an offender to a term up to and including life in prison, for manslaughter. In this case, however, the act was intentional, but I am not convinced Mr. Staines was fully aware of what he was doing, particularly given his actions when confronted by the police and the father of his victim. He did not flee. He didn't try to hinder the detective's investigation. He made no attempt whatever to cover up his crime in any way. He actually invited a member of the gardai into his home to…" Evans consulted McCann's notes of Staines' arrest "….'come in and get him,' referring directly to the victim. This is not rational behaviour, and cannot, under any circumstances, be attributed to someone who knew what they were doing. Is Mr. Staines insane? No. Does he know right from wrong? In spite of his unwillingness to express regret for his crime, the reports I've received indicate he is capable of making this distinction."

Judge Evans noticed that Brian was moving forward towards Sean McGillicuddy. He glanced toward the uniformed garda sitting behind Staines and saw that he, too, had noticed Brian's movements and was prepared to act, if necessary, so Evans continued.

"It is the duty of this court to remove itself from the emotive nature of the crime, and to pass a sentence that is fair and just. Given the fact that he has never before come to the attention of the authorities, and the serious doubts I have regarding his state of mind during the carrying out of this crime, I hereby sentence Geoffrey Staines to a term of imprisonment of 14 years, to include time already served. For possession of narcotics, a term of 3 years is imposed, to run concurrently."

The judge noticed that Brian was whispering frantically into McGillicuddy's ear. Each time the pudgy prosecutor shook his head, Brian appeared to become more insistent. Then there was a sudden cry from the other side of the courtroom, as Bridget fainted. She slumped unconscious to her right, collapsing against Michael McCann, who had taken time off from work to be in court for the sentencing. Noise welled up from every corner of the court; reporters were tearing from the room, switching on their mobile phones as they went.

Brian continued to accost McGillicuddy, who was becoming visibly flustered.

"Do it!" Brian demanded, and there was no one in the court who didn't turn when they heard the sound of his voice.

At that, McGillicuddy got to his feet. "Your honour, I know this is a highly unusual request, but Mr. Sykes would very much like to address the court."

"I will not tolerate any outburst in my court, Mr. Sykes. I would like to extend to you--and your wife-- my deepest sympathy on the loss of your son. But it would serve no purpose to allow you to make a statement at this time," Evans said, trying to mix compassion in with stern words.

Bridget was coming around. As she did, she started to cry. She tried to stifle her sobs, but they grew louder.

"Please, judge," Brian said softly. "I need to...." the words trailed off.

Evans wasn't particularly pleased with himself just then. He had dispensed justice to the best of his ability, at the same time wondering whether he had dug too deeply into things that, at the end of the day, didn't really matter. He asked himself whether he should have just taken the obvious course and sentenced Staines to life. No one, including the defense, would have faulted him for doing so. He couldn't help but feel sympathy for the man standing before him. He relented and decided silently that unless Brian got totally out of hand, he would let him have his say, uninterrupted.

"What do you want to say, Mr. Sykes?"

"I want to say that today would have been Danny's ninth birthday."

Bridget gasped. She hadn't believed that Brian would remember, and now her crying quietened, as she listened to what came next.

"You've sentenced this--I think the word you used yourself was 'monster'--to 14 years, Judge Evans. The dogs in the street know that means my son's killer could be out in about seven years. If that's the case, then he will have served less time in prison than my son spent in this world." Brian spoke slowly, quietly, with unnatural intensity. Not another sound came from the room.

"Justice doesn't really come into it, does it? Danny was a good person. He smiled all the time. He wasn't cheeky to his mother or me. He didn't cry when his front teeth fell out. He even liked school. For seven months, he's been lying in a cold, dark place; Danny didn't like the dark, judge. It scared him a bit, you know? Whereas Mr. Staines here has been receiving three meals a day, in a warm, brightly-lit place, watching some television, taking the odd bit of exercise, and let's not forget the little trips to the doctor's, so we can find out what makes a man like him torture, sexually abuse and then kill a beautiful child. Is it true that they get a special menu in prison on Christmas Day? Never mind."

"Justice? Real justice would have been dispensed hundreds of years ago, before courts even existed. You know what I'm talking about, but I guess we shouldn't mention that here."

"Seven years, maybe eight, certainly he'll be out in less than ten. And that's because you think he wasn't in his right mind when he killed my boy? Let me ask you, Judge Evans, though I don't expect you'll answer, would the crime have been any greater if he'd been in full control of all his faculties?" Brian's voice began to rise now. "Or to put it another way, you've actually just sat there and told us that because this sick, depraved pervert was out of his mind on drugs, he doesn't deserve to be treated as harshly as if he'd been stone cold sober--*as sober as a judge*--when he pushed cigarettes onto my son's naked chest and back, or when he pushed his head under water in a sink....."

"Mr. Sykes, this is truly pointless," Judge Evans interrupted. It was getting out of hand, and it was time to put an end to it. He was now sorry he'd broken with standard protocol and permitted the man to speak in the first place. "Again, you have the court's sympathy, but..."

"All right, I'll finish." Brian suddenly seemed deflated. "I just want to say one thing to Mr. Staines." He turned toward the table where Staines sat, and looked directly into the eyes of the killer. Staines appeared untroubled. No one would have noticed the tiny shiver that ran up his spine, as he looked back at Brian and heard a voice that was as cold as steel. Staines simply raised an eyebrow, and gave Brian a questioning look, as though nothing he could say would have any affect on him.

Brian stared without blinking. His words were spoken clearly, and he didn't raise his voice now. What he had to say could be done in three words.

"Don't come out."

TWELVE

Ger Simmons was the postman who delivered the brown envelope, with the official harp insignia, to Bridget Sykes, care of the Fitzgerald Residence, Kilcormac, County Offaly. He was a happy, colourful man in his mid-thirties, who knew everyone in Kilcormac on a first name basis. He also knew, from reading postcards sent to friends and relations in the town, where most of the population of Kilcormac spent their holidays each year. Not one of the villagers minded when he commented on their trips to the Canaries, or Cyprus, or even Florida, except Peggy McCarthy, who thought him a nosy little man who had nothing better to do than read the mail that he was meant to be delivering. Nothing escaped his sharp eye and quick wit. He had known for a fact, for example, within two hours of her arrival, that Bridget had moved back from Dublin, and in with her parents. That had happened more than five years previously, and some two years after the death of her poor son.

The years since Danny's murder had not been kind to Bridget. She was drawn and always looked tired or on the verge of tears. Now 41 years of age, Bridget appeared at least a dozen years older. "Not that she was seen out much," Simmons thought. She spent most days indoors and out of sight. Occasionally, she'd be spotted making a quick trip to the Super Valu store, her mother always close by her side. She wore frumpy clothes, but it looked to Ger like she'd lost an awful lot of weight since the time she'd gone off to the city and married that Dublin fella. He also noticed that she never really spoke to anyone, either; she would acknowledge a greeting from a well-meaning neighbour, family friend or shop assistant, but she certainly wouldn't initiate a conversation under any circumstances, and her replies, while polite, were always short enough to discourage further attempts at friendly chit chat.

No one in Kilcormac knew what had become of Brian. It was a subject never broached, and Roisin and David would not be receptive to any queries along those lines. In The Knights Bridge Tavern, speculation, fuelled by pints of Guinness, often ranged from divorce proceedings being imminent, to ongoing efforts at reconciliation, to one suggestion that Brian had left the country with another woman. Any blame being attached to the situation was generally levied on Brian. Bridget had been well liked from her school days in Kilcormac, and sympathy was heartfelt, sincere and abundant when news of Danny's kidnap and killing hit the town like a mortar bomb. The natural instinct of the townspeople was to close ranks around one of their own. Therefore, virtually all of the gossip sessions that took place in the pub ended with the assumption that, whatever was wrong with Brian and Bridget's marriage, it had to be Brian's fault.

Bridget hadn't moved back in with her parents out of economic necessity, or a desire to escape Brian, or even to "start a new life." She simply could think of no reason, not a single one, to stay in Loughlinstown. There was Patti, but she lived in Dun Guaire, and didn't drive; Bridget had never taken the scheduled driving test and still didn't have a full license. Since she didn't feel it right to be a "named driver" on Brian's insurance policy, she had sold the little Chrysler Neon that Brian had left behind when he moved out. So seeing Patti was not as simple as it might have been. Other friends had drifted away and ceased contact once she and Brian had separated. Some found it desperately uncomfortable being around Bridget after the tragedy with Danny; the marriage splitting only compounded their unease. In the end, it simply became more trouble than it was worth for most of her former acquaintances to make regular contact. Many went out of their way to avoid it altogether. It was understandable, in a way, but seeing people she had known as friends avoiding eye contact, or making quick, feeble excuses to evade any conversation, made Bridget wonder what would make her stay in or near Dublin.

Contrary to popular belief, she had no desire to be close to Danny's grave. She hated going to the cemetery. There was no comfort to be found among the dead. She didn't want to remember Danny in his coffin, or what had put him there. Her memories of Danny were made of cuddles and tickles, good night kisses and giggles, not funerals and graveyards. She'd be happy to never see his headstone again.

So she had stayed in her apartment in Loughlinstown for twenty-two months. When she made the decision to put it on the market, a young school teacher had snapped it up within three days of the first advertisement appearing in the estate agent's window. The sale had allowed Bridget to pay her parents back the €50,000 they had given her, though David and Roisin were adamant they wouldn't accept the additional €5,000 that Bridget had wanted to give them in interest. They also asked Bridget, without hesitation, if she'd like to move back into the family home, and Bridget, for her part, gratefully accepted.

She saw her name on the brown envelope lying on the hall floor. She didn't think much of it, except that the harp signifying some form of government business always made her just a bit nervous. "Probably some tax demand," Bridget said to herself as she opened the envelope. Within a few seconds, she knew this was far from the case.

Padraig Keane delivered the post most days to Brian's rented flat in Cabinteely. Unlike his Kilcormac counterpart, Keane knew little or nothing of the people to whom he was carrying letters, bills and junk mail. And what Brian received in the post would have given few clues as to what his life was like, had Keane been bothered enough to be curious. There were no holiday postcards, no birthday cards or parcels, no periodical magazines to indicate a hobby, only the usual assortment of E.S.B. bills, monthly bank statements, phone bill, and a very occasional letter from one of his brothers, who had moved to New York.

Brian still worked at Office Solutions (Ireland) Ltd., and was now
in his twelfth year of selling digital copiers, colour printers and
software packages. At 43, Brian should have long since either moved
into management, or left to start a new career elsewhere. He had no
desire to do either.

His job was not really demanding any more, oddly enough. Many
of his customers knew Brian's personal history; the few that didn't
had grown used to dealing with him over the years, and gave him
their business without much negotiation. He never once won the
company's monthly sales award in the seven years after Danny died,
but he did consistently achieve his targets, or at least get close
enough to them to keep management off his back.

When Carl O'Dowd had been made Sales Director, Brian hadn't
even applied for the vacant Sales Manager's position. He didn't
want any extra responsibility, and he didn't need any more money
than he was already making because his needs were very sparse. He
paid his rent, phone and electricity bills, and bought his food, period.
The company looked after his car expenses as part of his package.
There were no holidays, no nights out or weekends away, no
presents to buy and no one to buy them for.

Brian was functioning on automatic pilot. He was efficient if
unenthusiastic in his work, courteous though not friendly to his
customers and work colleagues. He attended the compulsory sales
team meetings, and his time keeping was practically robotic. Where
attendance at staff functions, like Christmas parties and company
picnics, was not mandatory, the one rule of thumb that could be
counted on was that Brian would not be there. He gave no excuses
for absenting himself.

On one occasion, the company accountant had been foolish enough
to ask him why he'd missed a farewell do for a departing executive.
Brian immediately enquired, turning dead eyes on his offending
interrogator, whether he should bring in a note from his mother.
There was no one he called a friend. Kevin Whyte, now managing
the telesales division, often tried to strike up a conversation with
Brian, and while never directly rebuffed, rarely got more than a few

words in return. For a short time, a typist named Caroline Sheppard
made numerous, and pointless, efforts designed to spark some
romantic interest from the relatively well-paid man she knew threw
her enquiries to be separated from his wife. She gave up,
exasperated, when it became clear that Brian's attentions were — not
exactly elsewhere — more like....nowhere.

The night he'd turned forty, Brian had gotten drunk. It happened
to be a Friday night, and his brothers had wanted to take him out to
celebrate, but Brian had insisted on staying in, so Conor and Adam
had called round with Chinese takeaway and four bottles of wine.
Adam was driving and stopped after two glasses of red. Conor
wasn't as shy, and drank the rest of the red, and half a bottle of rosé.
That left a bottle and a half of rosé and a full bottle of chardonnay,
and Brian consumed every drop with a vengeance.

He seemed to take no pleasure from his intoxication. Adam put it
down to a combination of letting off steam, and the desire to forget
the fact that he'd just reached his fortieth birthday. To forget that he
would spend the rest of the night, after Conor and Adam left, on his
own. To forget the otherwise empty flat and empty bed.

And to forget other things.

While Conor and Adam weren't especially close to their older
brother, they were nevertheless worried about his well being.
Nothing concrete could be pinpointed to justify their concerns. On
the outside, Brian appeared physically healthy; the depression over
Danny's murder was understandable, and neither was qualified
enough to know how long it should or would last. In addition, both
were married, with families of their own, and the accompanying
mortgages, car payments, school expenses and the standard day to
day fare of "normal" life.

Conor would soon move to Taunton, Massachusetts, a bustling
New England town 30 miles outside of Boston. He'd been offered a
position there, working for a company specialising in the
construction of fire engines.

The day after his fortieth, Brian had gone to the off license at
Cornelscourt Shopping Centre, and had bought two more bottles of

the Australian white, one bottle of a Chilean merlot, and another bottle of the rosé. By Monday morning, they were all gone.

After that, a pattern had slowly developed, whereby Brian would abstain, more or less, during the week, then on Friday he'd stop at Cornelscourt or Stillorgan and buy as many as five bottles of wine to drink over the weekend. Where Saturday mornings had once been used as a time to wash the car, pay bills or do the shopping, it quickly became a penance to be served until whatever appointed hour arrived that Brian had deemed in his own mind would be late enough in the day to open his first bottle.

Within six months, he'd need to make another trip to the wine merchant before the weekend was out. Three months more, and Brian had convinced himself that it was okay to have a little bit on Thursday evenings, without waiting for the weekend to arrive. Before the year was out, he had decided that it was also acceptable to drink late into Sunday night.

He started to put on weight, and his face took on a haggard look, including regularly red eyes, with dark circles underneath. Getting to work by 8:55 Monday morning became more difficult, in spite of the relatively short journey from Cabinteely to the Sandyford Industrial Estate. The drink didn't fill the emptiness that was Brian's existence. It simply made it more hazy, neither good nor bad, just different.

Then, as suddenly as it had started, the drinking stopped. It wasn't that Brian couldn't afford it, or that his work had suffered dramatically. He just couldn't be bothered, even to get drunk. His life moved along, month by month, with no laughter, no love, nothing. Brian simply expected to carry on, get old enough to retire, and then, eventually, to die. Of that prospect, he had neither fear nor expectations. It would just happen, and then he would be no more. "The end," he often thought to himself. Speeding up that ending never really entered his head. In young people's parlance, he "couldn't be arsed" to go to the bother of killing himself.

He took the brown envelope with the harp on it from his assigned letter box, fixed to the wall outside the main entrance to his apartment building. "Probably a new tax free allowance certificate," he thought to himself, tearing the letter open before he had reached the door to his flat. The first paragraph stopped him in his tracks, and in spite of the fact that he didn't feel cold, Brian began to shiver.

The governor of Mountjoy Prison, Cathal Dempsey, opened his brown envelope with the harp insignia, and scanned its contents quickly. The words neither surprised him, nor caused him any discomfort. He'd received many such letters, and acted upon all of them professionally and dispassionately. This one would be no different. It was from the Department of Justice, signed by the Minister's assistant, in his name. The letter stated in part "........and so I hereby order the release of Geoffrey Staines within 90 days of receipt of this letter. He will be subject to normal conditions of parole, and upon his release must report to his probation officer on a weekly basis pending further review."

The letter concluded with the request that, if the governor knew of any reason why this release should not take place, he should forward his concerns to the Minister's office without delay. Dempsey had always secretly thought that this last provision was a classic exercise in a politician covering his own backside. He quickly checked his computer's database, and noted that Staines had been in Mountjoy for seven years and three months. During that time, there had been nothing of note to report about the prisoner's term of incarceration. On four occasions, Staines had privileges revoked for drugs offenses, but he had never displayed violent or aggressive tendencies towards staff or other prisoners. The prison psychologist expressed no particular concerns about the likelihood of Staines reoffending; his report concluded that further evaluation would be desirable, but not enough to prevent his release from custody. The governor would be making no request to prevent Staines being set free.

"Dear Mr./Mrs. Sykes," began Brian and Bridget's letters respectively, "I am instructed by the Minister for Justice to inform you, as a matter of courtesy, of the impending release from custody of Geoffrey Staines."

"The Minister wishes to take all necessary steps to minimise any distress this action may cause. If you have issues which you would like the Minister to address, please feel free to contact these offices, and we will make every effort to allay your concerns."

"While ultimately the definitive date of Mr. Staines' release will be determined by the governor of Mountjoy Prison, please be advised that we expect this to take place within the next 90 days."

The letter was signed by Sheila McConville, for Noel Travers, Minister for Justice.

"Oh, dear God, no," Bridget gasped, dropping the letter to the floor, tears instantly springing to her eyes.

"Oh, is he really?" said Brian, as he entered his apartment and violently slammed the door shut behind him.

Two days later, Staines received the first of the anomymous letters. From that day till the day he was released, at least one card or letter was delivered to him every morning at Mountjoy. The first was a hand printed message on a plain sheet of A4 paper; the envelope sported a Dublin 18 postmark. The three-word message stirred something in Staines' memory, but he actually couldn't remember whether he'd heard the words in an old Humphrey Bogart film, or if it came from somewhere else. "Don't come out" just seemed familiar.

As the date of his release drew nearer, the messages became increasingly intense, without ever altering the content. "Don't come out" was always there. Once, the letters were pasted on the page, having been cut out of a newspaper. Another time, there were spots of what appeared to be blood dripped onto the paper around the three words. That one caused a bit of a shiver in Staines' spine, but not enough for him to report the contents to anyone else. The code of keeping his head down had served him well for more than seven years; he wasn't going to abandon it now.

Bizarrely, a greeting card meant as a get well message was sent. The outside of the card showed someone comically chained to a hospital bed, and the door next to that bed sported prison bars on the glass. The bright letters declared, "Bet you feel like you've been locked up for ages!" Where it had been printed on the inside of the card, "Hope you're out soon!" the message had been changed to read, "Hope you don't come out soon!"

For his part, Staines didn't really know what to make of it all. He got the point that someone didn't want him on the outside, but it wasn't as if he could just tell the guards that he preferred to stay where he was, even if he wanted to, which he most definitely did not. Not that he had any plans for after he got out of The Joy. He hadn't. He'd been introduced to the man who would act as his probation officer, or P.O. Accommodation, a FAS course that would help him become employable, and, if required, suitable counselling services would all be made available to him. In truth, he doubted if he'd take advantage of any of those things. But he knew for a fact that no "nutter" sending unsigned notes was going to stop him from getting back into the real world. He'd be out in June, the sun would be shining, the days would be long, and if Sullivan's Ale House was still on the promenade in Bray, Staines' first appointment would be with whoever was behind the bar, not some stuffed shirt asking him if he'd been a good boy for the past week.

In the final seven days before he was set free, the neat printing on the sinister messages was replaced by what looked like frantically scrawled letters. On one page, the pen had been pressed down so hard that it had gone right through the paper. And on his last day in prison, Staines received three separate notes, and on these, an additional word had been added to the normal command. Bemused and confused, Staines just couldn't get his head around the idea that someone had sent him more than six dozen notes, cards, and letters, and now the final three, in huge letters covering the entire page, each saying, "PLEASE!!! DON'T COME OUT!"

THIRTEEN

The Fit 'n Trim Health Studio in Ballybrack, according to its own promotional literature, boasted the most modern, technically advanced equipment for those wanting to get in shape for their summer holidays. Fliers advertising the centre had been placed on the windscreen of every car in the Office Solutions parking lot. Besides the 25-metre indoor heated swimming pool, there was also a sauna, Turkish steam room, jacuzzi, and plunge pool. The main workout room held eight treadmills, six rowing machines, and four each of step climbers, exercise bikes and cross training machines, as well as a wide selection of abdominal crunch, lateral pull, bench press, and quadricep/hamstring curl apparatus. Dumbells ranging in weight from 2.5 to 20 kilograms filled racks standing beside floor-to-ceiling mirrors.

'Before and After' pictures of men with pot bellies and white skin transformed into tanned, lean Adonnis types, and women who had turned cellulite, flabby arms and saggy bottoms into figures that would be the envy of any model, lined the walls of the entrance to the gym. Brian had always wondered why anyone with a grain of self respect and an ounce of dignity would ever pose for the "before" shots.

He had entered Fit 'n Trim on the Monday evening after receiving the letter from the Department of Justice, informing him of Staines' impending release. He had asked the receptionist about membership, and she had told him that he could opt for a six-month or annual subscription, or he could just pay for each visit individually until he decided which way he wanted to go. Brian immediately signed up for the six-month plan. He didn't want to pay for each visit, because he planned to be there very, very often.

And he wasn't at all sure he'd need it after six months.

The weekend after the correspondence arrived had been spent in varying states of confusion, helplessness, and an awakening anger that had been buried for so long, Brian had thought it was gone forever. But the official announcement that the man who'd killed his little boy would soon be walking the streets free, had acted like a spark touching down on a tangled mass of seemingly dry, dead wood. First, the tiny speck of fire settles onto a dry twig, seemingly harmless and incapable of generating anything of substance. Then, with no more encouragement than a puff of air, smoke starts to rise as the wood smolders. And the deader and drier the wood, the more violent and intense are the flames that spring forth, all-consuming, savage as a wild beast, and far more dangerous. Even a wild animal can be selective about its prey; fire cannot. Even if the will to do so was there in the soul of the inferno, it could not confine itself to specific targets.

Anything close enough will get burned.

Brian felt the fire build in the place that once his heart, then, for so many years, only heavy stone, had occupied. It caused him no pain. If anything, it gave him a small sense of pleasure that he could actually feel anything at all. It was like coming alive, being reborn. He did not recognise the danger of what was happening to him. Had he been able to do so, he would not have altered his path one iota. For more than seven years, he had been walking through darkness, like a vampire, more amongst the dead than the living. Now he saw purpose in each sunrise, and he welcomed the reason to live that had so unexpectedly been thrust upon him. He even occasionally allowed himself to picture Geoffrey Staines' face in his mind, something he would not have been remotely interested in doing before.

To the contrary, he would have done almost anything to avoid such a vision. Now, once the image was clear in his mind, he would open the vault of emotions that had been sealed like a tomb deep inside him. He felt the black, horrible hatred fill him, and admitted to himself that it felt good. He could live with these thoughts, he could live among them, and feel a sense of harmony with them. Certainly, it was preferable to the vacuum that had been his utter and total existence — if you could call it existing — up to this point.

Brian's routine was frighteningly intense. He would rise at 5.30 each morning, eat a light breakfast of fresh fruit and muesli, then arrive at the gym by 7 a.m. sharp. His early morning session consisted of stretching, then doing four miles on the treadmill. Sweat poured forth in torrents, but Brian ran in a heavy fleece, with T-shirt underneath, tracksuit bottoms, and two-pound weights strapped to each ankle. After nearly two months, he was able to cover the four miles in 21 minutes flat.

Immediately after finishing on the treadmill, Brian changed into his swim trunks and obligatory bathing cap, and swam 20 lengths of the pool, as hard as he could manage. A quick shower and change saw him arrive at the office by the appointed hour. Each weeknight, after work, Brian would arrive back at the gym no later than 6.30. He would invariably be the last to leave, and always trying to push out the 9.30 closing time. Evening sessions involved weight lifting, including five sets of 50 repetitions each on the bench press, single arm curls, quadricep curls, lat pulls and abdominal crunches. In the beginning, Brian's muscles cried out for relief from the torture he was inflicting upon them. Brian ignored his own body's pleadings, driving himself like a lunatic.

Like a lunatic with a timetable.

Bobby "The Brick" Burgess was another patron of the gym. He had earned his nickname by developing a physique that Brian and others thought only ever appeared in magazines. Muscles bulged from every conceivable part of The Brick's body. At six-foot-two, he appeared much taller; it seemed impossible that so much bulk could be attached to an otherwise "normal" frame. Dark brown eyes, and matching eyebrows, proved the lie of his spiky blonde hair. He had entered many body building championships in Ireland and the U.K., and had won his fair share. Brian heard other members say, only when Bobby was well out of earshot, that there was no way Burgess had developed muscles like that from clean living and lifting weights three nights a week. Brian knew, of course, that they were referring to the use of steroids.

Watching the ease with which Burgess would take a 20 kilogram dumbell in each hand, alternately curling them up towards his massive chest, then straight back down to his side, one after the other, over and over, made Brian more than a bit curious. He wouldn't mind having that kind of strength in his arms—it might just come in useful.

So one night, after Brian had been attending the gym for three weeks, he had decided to speak to Bobby when there were only the two of them left in the changing rooms.

"Excuse me," Brian said, "but have you got a minute?"

The Brick looked at Brian. "A minute for what?" he replied, indicating that he wasn't totally receptive to strange men approaching him in empty locker rooms. Not that he would have any difficulty repelling unwanted advances from any quarter. Burgess looked as though he could snap Brian, or men much larger than Brian, in two, without breaking a sweat.

Brian didn't really know how to broach the subject, so he barged awkwardly ahead, unsure whether he'd get what he was looking for, or a black eye and fat lip for his efforts. "I'm interested in getting some....ummm....product, that might help me with my weight lifting regime. I thought you might be able to help me, or let me know where I could get what I need."

Burgess looked warily at Brian. He knew precisely what the man was looking for, but he knew absolutely nothing else about the person asking him to supply the illegal steroids. "Who are you, anyway?" Burgess wanted to know. "Are you the law? What makes you think I could help you, and what the hell would you want them for, anyway?"

Brian had, at least, anticipated these questions. "I'm a salesman, nothing more than that," he said, holding his hands out to his sides and shrugging his shoulders. "And as to what I want them for, well, it's not like I'd be a threat to you in your next competition, is it? I'm 43, and I sit behind a desk for a living. The truth is, there's someone I want to.....impress."

Bobby was inclined to believe him. He'd seen Brian in the gym each of the last six times he'd gone himself, and it wasn't unusual, in his experience, for middle-aged men to make sudden, desperate attempts to lose a few pounds and put on some muscle. Health reasons, like heart attack scares or high cholesterol levels, were sometimes the incentive. More often, it was something to do with a woman. Still, he wasn't absolutely sure. "Why me?" he asked again.

"Because you strike me as the kind of man who'd be willing to help someone who's serious about his weight lifting, especially if there were mutual benefits." Brian had decided to go for broke. "I'm willing to pay a good price, and I guarantee there will be no questions asked and no comeback."

The last assurance had been added because Brian had done a bit of research into steroids on the internet. He'd heard, as had anyone with more than a passing interest in virtually any professional sport, that steroids had potentially harmful side effects. Dozens, if not hundreds of athletes lured by the glamour, fame and big-money rewards of sporting success had made the conscious decision to ignore the danger. It was suspected to the point of near certainty that the performance-enhancing substances had found their way into amateur sports as well. Ex-coaches, trainers and managers had come forward to admit their parts in expanding on the theory that sport, virtually any sport, was like warfare. If you didn't come to the battlefield with the best, most up-to-date weapons, then you got slaughtered. This had always referred to modern equipment, diet and training techniques. Now, steroids had turned sporting warfare into "chemical" warfare.

After just an hour looking through the various medical journals that were available on the internet, Brian knew that the dangers poised by steroids were caused by what doctors referred to as cardiovascular toxicity. The most commonly affected organs were the heart and lungs; the liver was another frequent casualty. In addition, there were questions over reduction in fertility, to the point of complete sterility, in users of the drugs that turned fat into muscle, as if by magic.

Brian also discovered that there were a wide variety of drugs legally available, without prescription, which body builders used. Creatine, a high protein diet supplement, was one of those more favoured by athletes trying to take the honest route to super-fitness. There were steroid websites, offering "legitimate and legal" anabolic steroids. Brian had neither the time nor inclination to chase the drugs over the world wide web.

"What do you want?" Burgess asked, then added, "Not that I'm saying I can get you anything at all."

"I've heard of Nandrolone, and HGR (human growth hormone). They can be taken in tablet form, right? I don't really want to inject. Can you get me a supply of those, enough to last, say, three or four months?" Brian was reaching for his wallet; he pulled out enough €50 notes to hold Bobby's attention for real. "A deposit," Brian smiled at Burgess as he handed over eight of the crisp bills.

Once the price was agreed, it was a simple matter of meeting back at the gym, and accompanying Burgess to the car park after their next workout. The Brick came up trumps, and Brian gave him the balance of the cash. He didn't know if or when he'd need more product, he told the now eager body builder, who counted the proceeds of what had been a highly profitable transaction. Brian told him that he kind of wanted to see how the first lot went before making any further purchases. "It might just be a short term thing," he said.

He also declined Bobby's offer to help him with his weight lifting exercises, and how to get the most definition out of his muscle groups. Brian didn't want or need any new friends. He didn't like Burgess; his feelings toward the man were totally ambivalent. He was a means to an end, a vehicle to be used like a hired taxi. Brian's priorities lay elsewhere. So Burgess told him when, and how many of the tablets he should take, and the two men effectively went their separate ways.

The regime became even more manic. As the ingested steroids went about their business of stimulating tissue generation, Brian found that he could push himself harder, and longer, than he'd ever dreamed possible. Even as a relatively fit teenager, playing rugby and Gaelic football virtually year round, Brian would never have stood the pace that he now considered part of his daily routine. Coupled with the demanding workouts he was putting himself through twice a day, seven days a week, the drugs began to transform Brian. His biceps now measured 18 inches. His chest expanded from 42 to 48 inches, and his stomach looked like a kitchen draining board. Slacks with a 34-inch waist were now two inches too large. The four-mile treadmill run became more of a warmup than a full session; by the time he'd completed the run, only the barest of perspiration dampened his brow.

For Brian, the highlight came when he moved to the bench press machine one Saturday in mid-May. When he'd started his first few workouts, Brian had struggled mightily to push up 80 kilos, just one time. After six weeks on the "magic tablets," he almost laughed to himself when he lay down on the bench and pushed 140 kilos over his head 20 consecutive times.

The resident fitness instructor was a young man in his early twenties. He'd observed Brian's determination and progress, and admired both qualities. But he grew concerned when he noticed the huge leaps in Brian's capabilities, and the extent to which the new member was driving himself. One evening, he approached Brian, introduced himself, and offered the gentle suggestion that pushing as hard as Brian clearly was, could have consequences in later life. "After all," he said with a friendly smile, "we all need a break now and then. Maybe you should go a little easier, or take the odd day off."

Brian looked directly into the eyes of his would-be advisor. "Consequences in later life?" he enquired coolly. "For all any of us know, young fella, this might just be later life."

Something in Brian's eyes, and the tone of his voice, insured there were no further suggestions forthcoming. "Now if you'll excuse me," Brian continued, "I want to get going."

"Got a date?" the young trainer enquired, eager to put distance between himself and his earlier comments.

"No, I just want to drop something off at the post office before I go home."

FOURTEEN

At the south end of Bray, a roundabout leads onto the N11 motorway, north towards Dublin, or south, in the direction of Wickow and Wexford, the "Sunny Southeast." Once on that fast-moving stretch of road, Brian drove exactly 2.4 miles straight south, to the turnoff for Roundwood. Passing through the peaceful little village of Kilmacanogue, known for not much more than a pub that, each Christmas, puts on the most beautiful display of outdoor lights in the area, Brian found himself on Rocky Valley Drive.

This winding tarmac road curls around and behind the Sugarloaf Mountain, which hundreds of years ago ceased to be Ireland's last active volcano. Following the directions he had written down less than an hour earlier, Brian continued along past the Roadstone quarry, which appeared on his left. After another six hundred yards, he turned left onto an even narrower, more treacherous road, which appeared to be not much more than a laneway. "After you get onto this road," the man on the phone had directed, "go exactly a half mile, then turn right through the green gates. There aren't any sheep out in that field today, so if I get there before you, I'll leave the gates open. Just drive right up to the cottage, and I'll meet you there at 2 o'clock. And you did say cash, right?"

As Albert Stevens had promised, the green gates were right where he'd said they'd be, but Brian had arrived twenty minutes early, intentionally. He stopped his new Nissan Primera Estate, which was now the fleet car of choice for Business Solutions, and stepped out into an early-June, Saturday sunshine that was as rare as it was welcome. All around him, birds were singing, and he could see large

numbers of sheep grazing in the fields that stretched nearly as far as
the eye could see. As he stood looking further down the road that
he'd travelled, Brian could see in the distance the sparkling waters of
Bray Harbour. Over his left shoulder, the Sugarloaf looked stunning,
awash with colour in the summer sun.

Beautiful without question, serene and peaceful certainly. None of
this impressed Brian in the slightest. But he was undoubtedly
pleased. He noted that, from the time he left the newsagent's shop
on the busy Bray Main Street, to the place he now stood, his car had
travelled less than nine miles. Yet he might as well have travelled to
the moon, for the difference between the two locations. Not another
person was in sight, nor would there likely be. The section of the
dual carriageway, less than a mile away, that ran through the Glen of
the Downs, had been completed in 2003. People now rarely strayed
off that busy thoroughfare in their mad rush to get to or from Dublin.
Had he shouted at the top of his lungs, in the middle of the day, the
only ones to be disturbed might be the sheep, and they'd have to
have been listening carefully.

The *Bray People* newspaper came out once a week. Brian had
purchased one in the hope of finding…just this. The small ad, which
Brian didn't know had been running for three consecutive weeks,
offered, "Charming, secluded, old world stone-built cottage, with
magnificent views, for sale or lease, by private treaty. Long and
short term rental considered." A quick phone call to the number in
the ad confirmed that the property was still available, but Albert
advised Brian to "move quickly if you want it, because there's been a
lot of interest."

Brian had known that what he was looking for could have been
found through enquiries at any of the various auctioneers and estate
agent offices that were dotted throughout the area. But estate agents,
or solicitors handling property for retired farmers, emigrants or
elderly clients, would have required contracts, paper trails, and
details Brian didn't necessarily want to share, so he was delighted to
see the 'private treaty' clause in the ad. Innocent enquiries about
whether cash in advance would be acceptable to the landlord yielded

similarly satisfactory results. The price could be haggled over and agreed once Brian saw the cottage, and a handshake would be the only contract the two men would ever enter into.

Having seen the surroundings, and before ever setting foot in the house itself, Brian knew he'd found the right spot. The little stone building was only barely visible from the gates, set back some 200 yards from an already isolated entrance, and sheltered behind a stand of old, majestic oak trees.

For what Brian needed it, the place was perfect.

Albert arrived at the appointed hour in an ancient Land Rover that looked like it was held together more by rust and mud than bolts and welded metal. As round as he was tall, the farmer greeted Brian with a wave and a smile. They shook hands, and for the next fifteen minutes, Brian had to pretend to be interested in all the magnificent qualities that Albert ramblingly attributed to the little house. In fairness, Mrs. Stevens had done her best to make the place presentable once Albert had decided to rent it out. An old bed had been put into the solitary bedroom, and she had stocked the kitchen presses with spare delph, knives, forks and two pots and pans. The open fireplace in the "sitting/dining room" had been cleaned out, and there was even a small supply of turf stored in a tiny room off the kitchen.

Albert assured Brian that the smell of damp, which couldn't be ignored, would disappear after a couple of fires had been lit, and the place "aired out" for a day or so. A cooker that worked on bottled gas was as clean as half a bottle of Cif cleanser could make it; there was no refrigerator.

Albert said that the electricity was in his name, and that, if it was agreeable to Brian, he'd keep it that way, and they could just settle up when each bill arrived. Brian readily concurred; "another contract that didn't have to be signed," he thought silently and gratefully.

"Well, that about covers it," Albert said, peering at Brian with thinly disguised hope. "She's a cracker, ain't she?" he said with as much enthusiasm as he could muster.

"Nice all right," Brian replied, "but I have one or two questions for you."

"Oh, damn, he's not happy about the smell, or else he's going to want that cracked toilet seat replaced before he moves in," thought Albert. But he said, "Sure, fire ahead, but I honestly think this place is as nice as you're going to find."

"First, you haven't even told me how much the rent would be, and the ad didn't mention it either," Brian said.

"Oh, yeah, that's right...right!" Albert stammered. "Well, how long were you thinking of staying?" he countered. "I mean, if you're only going to be here a little while, then the rent would have to be a bit higher than otherwise. The missus put a lot of work-- and expense-- into getting this place ready, and..."

"I'm thinking three or four months," Brian interrupted. "And that leads me to my next question. If the price is right, would it be okay to pay three months in advance, with an option on another three months after that?" Brian didn't want to appear too eager. He was now quite certain that the cottage had probably been up for rent for some time. The place was run down, to put it kindly; a dump, if he wanted to be cruel.

But it suited him.

"Do you mind if I ask what it is you do?" Albert asked, more to stall for time than out of interest, because he just couldn't work out in his own mind how much money he could extract from his potential tenant.

"Well, I'd rather not say exactly," Brian replied, giving a little disarming nod-and-a-wink smile at the same time. He wondered if Albert thought he was famous or maybe a mid-life crisis victim, looking for a secluded hideaway for himself and some younger lover. "Let's just say I'm working on a kind of project, and I need a lot of solitude to give it my best. And one thing's for sure. I really, really, don't want any interruptions when I'm working."

"Oh, you won't be seeing me, anyway," Albert rushed to reassure Brian. "My house is about two miles from here, back towards Glendalough. I bought three of these fields from the old man who used to live in this house," he said, indicating with a sweep of his big, beefy hand the area of land around and behind the cottage. "Poor man died, and I kind of inherited this house with the fields. I graze sheep here when the grass is good, but you wouldn't even see me out this way more than once in a blue moon. And you can see for yourself, you wouldn't get too many unexpected visitors out here."

Brian was convinced. He smiled again, took out his wallet, and offered €1,500 cash for the first three months. It was higher rent than the place was worth, and certainly more than Albert had expected to realise; now it was his turn not to appear too eager. He really wanted to reach out and grab the money before the fool in front of him changed his mind. But maybe, just maybe, Albert thought, he could do a bit better.

"Well, now there are other people who want to look at this place — highly desirable location and all," Albert was now enjoying himself. "But I suppose I could be convinced to disappoint them, if you were to up your offer to, say, €650 per month."

"Mr. Stevens," Brian deliberately used the formal address, "I'm going to put this money back in my wallet in ten seconds, and after I do, it won't be coming back out again. Not ever. Now do you want me to start counting backwards from ten? Is another prospect likely to show up, like, by the time I reach three or something? You now have five seconds left, by the way. Four. Three...."

"You drive a terrible hard bargain," Albert said, grabbing the money with both hands. "When were you thinking of moving in?"

"I'm not exactly sure," Brian answered, "but let's just say my three months starts on Monday, unless you want to haggle some more."

"Monday it is, then," Albert was taking no further chances that might cost him his unexpected windfall. "Would you like any help moving in your furniture? And do you want a receipt?"

"No, and no," Brian said, answering both questions in a tone that Albert couldn't quite read.

Whistling to himself, Albert pulled the Land Rover up to the door of his modest farm house. He walked into the kitchen, where his wife was peeling potatoes for that evening's stew. "How'd you get on?" she enquired.

"Oh, he was a tough one, but you're married to a helluva businessman," Albert lied. He pulled €1,000 from his trouser pocket. "Look at this. A grand, for three months rent, and I insisted he pay in advance, too. I mean, I don't want to have to be calling over there every month to collect the rent, do I?"

The other €500 was tucked away in the toolbox at the back of his jeep. He planned on several good nights in the pub, when his wife was off at the bingo. That idea seemed so good to him that he handed her the thousand and said, "Put most of that in the bank on Monday, but why don't you treat yourself to bingo in Laragh tonight? And maybe you'd give me €20 back, for a couple of pints at Oscar's, if you do decide to go." He knew she'd be grateful and suspect nothing of the extra cash. And she wouldn't go near his toolbox in a million years.

She looked at him and knew beyond any doubt that he was up to something. "He must have got more money than he's letting on," she thought. Still, she let it go. "What's this fella like?" she asked her husband, who was now rooting in the fridge for a can of draught Guinness.

"Bit strange, kind of eccentric, like," Albert replied, then knowingly added, "I'd say he's one of those writers, or maybe a painter or something. Says he's working on a big, secret project or something. Probably writing a new poem," he sniggered.

"A writer, really? Did you get his name?" She liked to read, and was mildly excited to think that a famous author might be renting their property.

"Of course I got his name! What kind of a fool do you think I am, anyway?"

"Don't get in a huff. I just thought I might recognise the name, that's all. So what is it then?"

Albert had been so excited about the easy money, he'd nearly forgotten. He took a long pull of stout from his glass, stalling while his mind raced to recall the name of the man to whom he'd just rented a piece of property. Then he had it, the name he was positive he'd been given over the phone.

"O'Brien," Albert said with certainty. "Danny O'Brien."

FIFTEEN

Tuesday, June 11th, was the day that Geoffrey Staines said good-bye to Mountjoy Prison. At 11 a.m. precisely, he walked out the front door, and then the main gate, swearing silently to himself that he'd never be back on the wrong side of prison bars again in his lifetime.

"Still," he mused, "it hadn't been all that bad."

He had made no mortal enemies — that he knew of — and through his work in the kitchen, peeling potatoes, scrubbing pots and pans that were too large to fit into the industrial dishwasher, and mopping floors over the seven years, he had actually walked out of Mountjoy with more money than he'd ever dreamed he could acquire. Even with the days he had missed, through illness, suspension of privileges (he couldn't believe they called working in the kitchen a privilege) for drug offenses, and the occasional sit-down strike, the €3.75 per day had added up to a truly tidy sum. Even taking away the money he'd spent in the tuck shop, buying cigarettes, snacks and toiletries, Geoffrey Staines was positively giddy when he'd been handed a cheque that morning for €5,581.25. He shuddered to think how many windows he would have had to clean to put that kind of brass together.

Even before reaching the Dart station for the trip to his new "home" in Bray, he was making plans on how to spend some of the money. Beer featured heavily in those plans. He toyed with the notion of a night of purchased passion with a Leeson Street lady. Heroin was also definitely on the agenda. He'd never kicked the habit, though he'd found access to the drug considerably more restricted in Mountjoy after new regulations had been introduced during his third year there.

If anyone asked him where the cash had come from, and he sincerely hoped they would, he was going to tell them that he'd been doing serious work for the government. "Staines. Geoffrey Staines. Licensed to thrill," he intended to say.

Cathal Dempsey, Governor of Mountjoy, had personally handed Staines his written instructions, and at the same time had given the standard, "We hope not to have you back visiting with us in the future," speech, an hour before Staines walked away from his home of the last seven years. Included in the list of do's and don'ts was an order that he must meet with William O'Neill, who would be acting as his probation officer, once every 30 days.

This actually pleased Staines, who had expected to have the P.O. breathing down his neck every week or so. He was quite sure he could keep his head straight enough to say "Yes sir, no sir, three bags full sir," one day a month, and he was equally pleased that the meetings would take place at a mutually agreed upon location in Bray, rather than in some stuffy office filled with stiff secretaries and starched shirts.

But Staines was far less content with what appeared further down the page, and which Dempsey had emphasised during their farewell encounter. Due to the nature of part of the attack on young Danny Sykes, Staines had been placed on the Sex Offenders Register. And even though he was being released early, the government had the right to stipulate that Staines report to a garda station, every week for two months, then fortnightly thereafter until further notice. As a bedsit on Quinsboro Road was to be his new home, the garda station in Bray was nominated as Staines' point of contact.

This was not good news, as far as Staines was concerned. But he knew better than to even question the dictates from Dempsey and whoever wrote the damn rules. So he took his cheque, and the black plastic bin liner containing all his worldly possessions, and walked as far as Connolly Station in Dublin City Centre. He actually wanted to savour his first day of freedom in seven and a half years; the sun was warm on his face, and he felt as carefree as his mind could ever recall.

That would explain why he never noticed the man in the dark glasses, walking a dozen paces behind him, from the time he left Mountjoy until he got on the Dart. When Staines jumped on the fourth green carriage, his shadow rapidly stepped into the fifth, just before the train pulled out of the station. Since it was now just midday, and there were no children still heading to school, or throngs of people trying to get to work, Staines had no difficulty getting a seat.

The man who had followed him could have had his choice of any number of seats himself, but chose instead to stand at the very front of the car, glancing every few seconds through the plexi-glass partitions into the compartment where Staines now reclined, putting his feet up on the vacant seat directly opposite.

As the Dart pulled into Bray Station, a voice came over the loudspeaker announcing that all passengers must disembark, as, due to essential line maintenance, this train would not be travelling onwards to Greystones.

Brian didn't even hear that message. He had evacuated the Dart the instant he saw Staines stand and head for the door. Knowing there was only one station exit available, Brian got there first, turned left, and waited for Staines to come out. Incredibly, Brian thought to himself, he felt neither nervous nor even angry. He had left his Nissan Primera a quarter of a mile from the gates of Mountjoy, the same as he had done every day for the past two weeks.

Having made a routine phone enquiry to the Mountjoy Prison information desk, posing as a freelance reporter, as to when he could expect Staines to be released, Brian had been pulled up short when the lady at the other end of the line had asked, naturally enough, for the caller's name.

"Murphy. Joseph Murphy," Brian had lied, praying that there was at least one Joseph Murphy working for at least one newspaper in Ireland.

"I'm afraid we can't give out that kind of information, Mr. Murphy," the lady had replied politely.

"Ah, sure, I know that, and I know you're just doing your job. But listen, be an angel, and just tell me what time of day the prisoners — any prisoners--are usually released," Brian coaxed. "You don't have to give me exact names, or even times, just a general idea. Please."

"Well, let's just say that we try to give them breakfast, but not lunch. Would that be enough information, Mr. Murphy?" she asked, knowing she probably shouldn't. But it had been a long time since anyone had called her an angel.

"Perfect. Thanks a million. You're a star," Brian answered.

From that day, the 3rd of June, until the day Staines was set free, Brian had been waiting. He would report to the office in Sandyford each morning, but as soon after nine o'clock as was possible without rising suspicion, he would head out the door, telling anyone who asked that he had appointments set up, and that he didn't want to be late. From there, he drove straight to his parking spot near Mountjoy, and then he watched, and waited, through the lunch hour.

Every day, he saw prisoners walk out the main gate. Often, there were people — family, friends, wives, lovers--waiting to meet and greet the men, or women, who had served their time. This time. Usually till the next time.   Each day, by two o'clock, when there had been no sign of Staines, Brian would return to his car and work at his "day job," including a return to the office every evening, even if only for a few minutes.

"Working hard, Brian?" Kevin Whyte enquired one evening.

"Knocking 'em dead," was Brian's answer.

Now that Staines had been released, the part of Brian that had begun to come alive turned cold, but not in the same dead way as before. It was a different kind of cold, more lethal from without than within. He recognized that the man who faced him in the mirror each morning bore little or no resemblance to the husband and father that once existed. He often stared at his own reflection, looking hard and long to see where the old Brian had gone, and occasionally, but not often, wondering whether he would ever come back.

Brian wasn't sure he wanted the old one back.

Certainly, the old Brian had never been as fantastically strong, as hard and steel-like as was the new version. What Brian's business suits and sports jackets hid from daily view was a physique now carved from stone. The steroids, and Brian's relentless workouts, had achieved a transformation that was incredible to behold. The veins in his arms stood out dramatically, as though the muscles beneath them had left no room for anything else, forcing the blood vessels to the surface, where they looked as if they might break through the tightly stretched skin. The stomach was ridged with the much sought after six-pack, and his thighs and calves might as well have been cut from granite. He looked as though he had the strength of ten men, and he could literally run for an hour at five-minute mile pace.

Mentally and emotionally, the changes were every bit as dramatic. Every sound was amplified, every colour magnified. Feelings...well, they were something not to be faced or thought about, not yet anyway. All he allowed himself to feel, for the moment, was that he was alive again, and anything more than that — and he knew there was much more — could be dealt with at a later stage. A plan had slowly formulated in his head. Thinking backwards, he was never able to pinpoint when it had started, nor how. He only knew the "why."

The part of him that had developed this plan was linked directly to the vision he now saw in the mirror. But where was the part that had written the daily notes for the last three months? Was that the old nine-to-five Brian, the solid citizen, good neighbour, reliable husband and — something twisted inside him at the next thought — loving father, trying to resurface from the dark depths? Trying to hold back the new, relentless, rock hard Brian? Trying to prevent something that was too horrible and destructive to contemplate from unfolding? Trying to save...himself...from only God truly knew what?

"If it is," thought Brian as he had turned away from the mirror, "then the old Brian can go straight to hell."

Now Staines was walking away from the train station and the seafront, toward the centre of Bray, a short distance up to Quinsboro Road. Further ahead, he could see the cinema; to his right, the offices of the Wicklow Citizen's Information Centre stood flanked on either side by a bicycle shop and a solicitor's office.

Behind him, Brian Sykes had closed the gap between them to a few feet.

Staines turned left onto the footpath that led up to the entrance of number 279, a three-storey building that once had been a magnificent private house, but which had since been turned into a collection of bedsits. O'Neill had organised for him to stay here. If Staines didn't like it, he could move out at any time, but this was to be his starting point, and if he did decide to move, the probation officer would want to know about it first.

Brian hesitated for the barest fraction of a moment, then continued up the road. He walked up as far as the Main Street, then doubled back to the train station, taking the Dart back into Dublin, where he collected his car. By four o'clock the same afternoon, he had sold a digital colour photocopier to Stillorgan Furniture Mart. They wanted to produce their own fliers advertising special offers, and Brian convinced them that it would be cheaper to buy and maintain the new Canon IRC3350 than to run to the printers every few weeks.

Geoffrey Staines would wait. The plan was taking on shape and form.

The old Brian had lost. And gone back to hell.

SIXTEEN

"Doctor McCarthy, you've got to help me. I can't get to sleep; I'm exhausted, and the tablets you prescribed last time just aren't working," Brian complained.

The fact was, Brian had never taken a sleeping tablet in his life, but that was, to Brian's mind, information the good doctor simply did not require. "Isn't there something better — stronger — that you could prescribe?"

"Look, Mr. Sykes, you only came in here for the first time a week ago. I gave you a 'script' that should last you a month, and I don't want to give you anything more until…"

"I brought them back," Brian interrupted, displaying the bottle of relatively mild sleeping pills, from which he'd removed seven (in case the doctor decided to check), flushing them down the toilet. "I don't want you to do anything you're not comfortable with, doctor, but you do know why I'm not sleeping, right? I did tell you."

"Yes, and I understand that you're upset over your son's killer being released." The doctor was genuine in his sympathy, and felt certain the man sitting before him was being truthful. Also, he clearly wasn't trying to hoard a supply by getting two prescriptions within a week of each other. The doctor had seen patients get hooked on everything from pain killers to sleeping pills to anti-depressants, and then go so far as to visit different doctors, and pharmacies, on the same day, to acquire a large supply of the medicine they felt they couldn't live without.

Obviously, Brian was making no such attempt, or else he wouldn't have brought in the unused portion of his earlier prescription.

"All right, Mr. Sykes, I'm going to prescribe you with something I'm quite sure will be effective. They're very strong, so please — please — don't exceed the stated dose."

"What are they?" Brian asked.

"Rohypnol," came the doctor's reply, unaware that it was precisely the response Brian had hoped for. "Just a single, one-milligram tablet before bed. Avoid alcohol, and under no circumstances drive or operate machinery after taking one," the doctor instructed.

"Thanks, doctor. You have no idea how much this helps."

There was no need for the doctor to give him another physical, as he had done the week before. Heart rate was 52 and strong, comparable to a professional marathon runner. Blood pressure was 105 over 65, well below the norm for a man in his early-40's. Without question, Brian was one of the fittest people Dr. McCarthy had ever examined, and that wasn't going to have changed in just seven days, so the visit was over within five minutes of Brian walking through the door.

Driving back into Cabinteely, Brian pulled into the perpetually busy car park of Cornelscourt Shopping Centre. The pharmacist in the small outlet opposite the huge Dunnes Stores that occupied the vast majority of the building paused only slightly when he saw the 'script' for the thirty tablets. Rohypnol had received a bad name in media circles as the "date rape drug." He keyed Brian's name into the pharmacy's computer and saw nothing to cause concern, but Brian had noticed the slight furrowing of the brow, and the accompanying, albeit brief, hesitation.

He wasn't worried. In the unlikely event that the chemist decided to phone Dr. McCarthy, his story would stand up to any scrutiny. Brian did, however, decide that he'd have to search elsewhere for his next purchase.

"Yes, we stock ether, and isopropyl alcohol is the same as rubbing alcohol," replied the chemist's assistant in Fletcher's Pharmacy of Dundrum. It was only the third try since leaving Cornelscourt. Brian had been surprised to learn that a bottle of ether could be bought legally, without prescription, provided you could find someone who stocked it. "Will there be anything else?" asked the clearly uninterested lady behind the counter.

"She's not even asking me what I want the ether for," thought Brian with some amazement. He had his story ready, had it been needed. He was going to say that he was a science teacher, and that his classes were preparing displays of all manner of insects, butterflies and moths found in the Dublin area, for an impending science fair. He would have explained that the most humane way of killing these bugs, while still preserving them for display, was to put them in a glass jar with a cotton ball that had been soaked in ether, and leaving them there for 10 minutes before pinning them to the styrofoam display boards.

Now Brian was sorry he'd even gone to the bother of fabricating that tale, and even a little annoyed that he hadn't been able to use it. He was tempted to tell her anyway, but she had already put the two brown bottles into a white paper bag containing the pharmacy's logo, and was now clearly interested in nothing more than getting paid, moving on to the next customer, going home at 5:30, and soaking her aching feet.

So Brian took his purchases and moved on to the hardware store. When he returned to his car after a further fifteen minutes, he was actually whistling to himself. It was Thursday evening, two days after he had watched Geoffrey Staines walk the streets, a free man.

"Roll on Friday," thought Brian, and the whistling stopped. The cold returned.

The following day, the plan that had been growing in Brian's mind like a baby grows in the womb of its mother, was born. It became a living thing that, like any newborn, is born completely dependent on its parent. After awhile, that dependence vanishes, to be replaced by wilful independence, and then nothing--not despairing parents, nor authoritative figures--can choose the direction this creature travels. Often, the path chosen is the right one, if not the same one the parent would have chosen for his or her offspring. Other times, there is no end to the damage, hurt and carnage to which the chosen path leads. Nothing can prevent this. And only death can ultimately stop it.

And so it was with Brian's brainchild, his plan of how to cope, in his own mind, with the man who had killed his son, destroyed his marriage, and taken away the meaning of life itself. He faced himself in the mirror the morning of Friday, the 14th of June, and knew that he cared little for the person who returned his blank stare. After all, he thought, the man was a virtual stranger. So he went about his chosen task with no fear as to the consequences, for his victim and more importantly, for himself. And it was this state of mind that made Brian more lethally dangerous than any animal stalking its prey. Even wild animals have care for what happens if the hunt goes wrong. To what happens to the young they might leave behind, or the painful death they might themselves be facing should prey suddenly turn and become violent predator. Brian had neither fear nor concern. This was something that was going to be done, regardless.

At 8:30 a.m., Brian phoned the office and reported that he was feeling decidedly unwell. He assured Carol at reception that it was almost certainly a 24-hour thing, and that he would be in on Monday without fail. Brian had missed only four days through sickness in the seven years since Danny had died, and he had never once during that time taken his full quota of annual leave days, preferring the routine of work to his own company. So no one at Business Solutions questioned his absence on that day, and company policy dictated that, unless he missed three consecutive working days, he wouldn't need a doctor's note to confirm his illness.

After hanging up the phone, Brian dressed in light brown casual slacks, Nike sweatshirt and Puma running shoes. He threw on a full-length rain mac, as dark clouds were heralding another wet summer weekend. Stopping in the kitchen on his way out the door, he grabbed the small brown envelope that contained the powder of six, crushed rohypnol tablets, and placed them in the pocket of his coat. Walking calmly to his allotted parking space, he opened the back of the Nissan estate and lifted up the flap of the spare tyre compartment. The never-used spare was there, and resting in the middle of the wheel were the two brown bottles of ether and alcohol.

Brian left them there, and noted that the plastic bag containing his purchases from the hardware store were still in place, stuffed under the back seat.

Satisfied, he climbed into the car, drove away from his apartment building, and out onto the Cabinteely bypass. From there, he drove east, past Loughlinstown and Shankill, and into Bray. Superquinn, on his right, was already busy with shoppers stocking up for the weekend. Carrying on straight ahead, he passed the Royal Hotel on his left. At the next set of lights, he turned left, passing the cinema, then the boulevard housing small, tastefully designed offices and various enterprises.

Further down, No. 279 Quinsboro Road stood tall and still proud, in spite of its demotion from glamorous private home to a dozen bedsits with shared bathrooms. Brian pulled his car into the curb and switched off the engine. Even though he had no intention of leaving the car, he scratched the relevant numbers on the Bray Urban Council parking disk he'd purchased in the newsagents, and displayed it in an appropriate place on his dashboard. The last thing he wanted was some gestapo-like traffic warden coming along, telling him he had to move on. He had chosen this location carefully. It allowed him an excellent view of No. 279, and, regardless of which way Staines turned when he came out, Brian could easily follow.

Now all he had to do was wait, and he didn't give a damn how long that would take.

As it turned out, he had quite a long wait. Staines had slept in, again. There was no meeting scheduled with the P.O., and he had reported for the first time to the garda station on Wednesday. Work was not high on his list of priorities; money was laughably abundant, by his own standards. Besides, Staines' head was fuzzy and sore, his eyes bloodshot, when he finally deemed it time to pry them open at two in the afternoon. The previous afternoon and evening had been spent at Sullivan's, which he'd been delighted to find still occupied its spot on Bray's promenade. Most of the establishments lining that thoroughfare are high class, well-designed and well-lit restaurants and nightclubs. With its poor lighting, hideously painted raspberry exterior and torn, imitation leather seating, Sullivan's was to Bray's promenade what a large blister is to otherwise flawless skin, an ugly reminder that nothing is as perfect as it seems.

Dragging on his jeans, T-shirt, denim jacket, and trainers, Staines thought a "hair of the dog" would be just the start to the weekend he needed. He had no other plans, no one to meet and nothing else that he particularly wanted to do. "Sullivan's it is, so," Staines said aloud, making the decision official and not caring that no one else was around to hear. He instantly decided to forego breakfast. A pint would take the place of a fry-up.

Exiting the house, Staines turned right at the end of the footpath, and walked down past the Dart station, turning right along the seafront. Within ten minutes of leaving his bedsit, he was sliding into a chair near one of the unwashed windows of his favourite pub. He didn't like sitting at the bar. There was always the chance that someone would try to strike up a conversation; Staines preferred to drink alone. In fact, he preferred to do most things alone. Ordering a pint of draft Miller, his back was to the window as the Nissan slid slowly past outside, the driver looking into Sullivan's before parking almost directly outside the pub, and placing yet another parking disk on his dashboard.

At 3:30, Staines ordered his fifth pint, and enquired of the barman whether it would be possible to get a cheese sandwich to go with it. Even with the bloated feeling brought on by the lager, hunger was finally making itself felt in Staines' belly. The disgruntled waiter said that they'd stopped serving lunch an hour previously, but that he'd go to the kitchen and see what he could do, since it was quiet. The evening rush wouldn't start for another two hours. Staines thanked him, with sarcasm dripping from his voice, for going to such extraordinary lengths for a good customer. Taking a long, greedy drink from the fresh pint, he drained nearly a quarter of its contents in one pull. Then he decided it was time to visit the gents. His bladder was threatening to burst.

Placing the pint on the table, Staines walked, only slightly unsteadily, to the back of the pub, past the cigarette machine, through the swinging doors, and into the smelly WC with a row of stained urinals against one wall, two leaking sinks, and two stalls, one of which had a toilet whose seat was hanging off to one side, holding on by a single hinge. The other cubicle had no toilet seat at all.

While he relieved himself, and the barman grudgingly slapped one slice of processed cheese between two slices of bread covered with thick margarine, neither could have noticed the man in the rain coat pass by Staines' unguarded drink. The only other occupants, two men sitting at the bar, had their backs to Brian, making his task almost ridiculously easy. As he walked past the table, he removed the brown envelope from his pocket and quickly dumped its contents into the three-quarter full glass, then quickly swirled the contents once before replacing the glass on the table. He achieved this almost without breaking stride, and then continued on to the cigarette machine, where he purchased twenty Benson & Hedges. Brian didn't smoke. He was using the cigarette machine as an excuse in case any of the staff wanted to know why he was there.

As he picked the pack from the machine, Brian stood up and came face to face with Geoffrey Staines. In that single instant, and for the only time from then until it was done, Brian's heart skipped a beat. Would Staines run this time? Would he attack? Make excuses? Apologise?

"S'cuse me, man, you mind if I get past?"

He hadn't even recognised him! Brian couldn't believe it. Staines' face had haunted him from the day he'd found Danny dead to the present moment. It was a horrible, sick truth that Brian could have described the features of his son's killer more easily than he could have done Danny's. Yet this man had come within inches of the father of his victim, and there hadn't been a single spark of recognition. It was true that they had only met on four or five occasions; Bridget had had most of the dealings with the window cleaner.

The two men had not come face to face in seven years and seven months. But Brian had mistakenly believed that the drugged lunatic who had shattered his world would surely have known him, if and when their paths next crossed. In a bizarre way, Brian felt insulted, in the same way he knew one of his customers had felt when they met on Grafton Street just before Christmas. The man, who had purchased a laser fax machine just weeks earlier, had greeted Brian cheerfully, only to find that Brian couldn't even remember his name. Brian was like that. He could have returned to the man's office in five years, and by associating the place with the man, recalled his name without reference to notes. Take the man away from the location, and Brian wouldn't recognise him if he'd stepped on him. In this case, the customer, after a very brief, awkward conversation, had walked away feeling almost cheated.

And that was how Brian felt now. Cheated and insulted. He felt very strongly that Geoffrey Staines should have known his face.

"By God," he said to himself as he returned to his car to wait, "he'll know more than my face by the time I'm finished with him!"

SEVENTEEN

After returning to his seat, Staines had a brief moment of uneasiness. He'd forgotten to ask the barman not to use margarine on his cheese sandwich. It was too late now to ask him to take it back and make another. Staines was pretty sure that, if he did, he might find more than margarine had been spread on the bread. And the creep would probably charge him another €3 for the sandwich and soggy crisps on the side. So he took a big bite of the stale bread and plastic-tasting cheese, and washed it down with a large gulp of his beer. This process was repeated until, within a short span of time, both the sandwich and the pint had disappeared.

Sitting quietly for a few minutes, Staines was trying to decide whether to have another pint of Miller, or if he should switch to Budweiser. The last pint just hadn't gone down as well as the first few; he put it down to the sandwich and decided to stick with the Miller.

But the instant he stood up to walk to the bar, his stomach lurched, and his head began swimming, feeling sickeningly heavy, as though his weedy neck were insufficiently strong to hold it upright. The weak lighting in the dingy pub appeared to Staines' eyes to be failing altogether, and his legs were also beginning to betray him. Spotting the inevitable, the barman shouted across, "Don't you dare get sick in here. If you do, you can bloody well clean it up yourself!"

"Fuck off, ya tosser," Staines sneered back. "Your poxy sandwich was poisoned." His words started to slur now. "I'd get the health inspector after you, but he'd probably be afraid to come in here—might catch something nasty!"

"You'll catch something nasty in about two seconds, pal," the barman warned. "Now clear off, and don't bother heading for the jacks. You can get sick outside — you're as green as grass already."

"As green as the cheese you put in my sandwich," Staines offered as a parting insult. "Ya big bollocks!" he got out, as he staggered through the door.

The sky was spinning in one direction, and the ground in the other. It was worse than any hurdy-gurdy ride he'd ever been on in any carnival. There wasn't a chance in a million that he'd make it back to his bedsit before passing out. A tiny part of his mind was confused. "I only had five pints," he thought. "Why do I feel so shitty?"

He staggered barely a dozen paces up the footpath, uncertain if it was even the right direction. The legs and head gave up at precisely the same instant, and as he fell, Staines wondered whether he'd feel much pain when he landed on the concrete. Then a strong arm reached around his waist, catching him as effortlessly as if he was a stuffed animal. He tried to say, "Thanks, bud," but it was mostly incoherent mumbling. Then he passed out.

Brian found it very easy to keep the unconscious man upright, even though he was now totally limp.

Dead weight.

He half dragged, half carried him to the waiting Nissan, then noticed the two youngsters on their way home from school, looking curiously at him. Brian just smiled. He had anticipated virtually every possible scenario. "Nothing to worry about," he said reassuringly. "My friend here has just had too much to drink. I'll get him home before he does himself any damage." He opened the rear door of the car, and deposited Staines like a bag of laundry onto the back seat. The kids moved on, discussing whether they'd have time to stop at the amusement arcade before heading home for their tea. Neither noticed that the Nissan pulling away from the curb had no number plates.

Brian reached the old cottage in less than fifteen minutes, and he hadn't come close to breaking the speed limit in doing so. The green gates were closed, so Stevens must have moved some sheep into one of the adjoining fields. This neither pleased nor bothered Brian. It was just something he was aware of, but which was ultimately a matter of complete indifference to him. He opened the gates, drove through, and closed them again, before driving up to the stone house. He discovered that he could pull the car around to the far side of the building, shielding it still further from view.

When he got out, he put the number plates back on the car, then took several bags of "supplies" into his little hideaway, before returning to the car, where he looked into the back and saw the monster who had shown his son no mercy, sprawled on the back seat, mouth wide open, drool running disgustingly down the side of his face and into his ear. The man was helpless, totally incapable of defending himself. Looking around, Brian knew that, if he wanted to, he could pull the limp figure out of the car, snap his neck like a chicken's, and bury him that night in one of the surrounding fields. The likelihood of him being found — and that was if anyone was bothered looking for him — was so remote it didn't bear thinking about. He could kill him all right. No one would ever know. No one would care.

He reached into the car and grabbed the collar of Staines' denim jacket. He pulled him from the car and carried the unconscious form straight into the cottage. Killing him would be far, far too easy. Too easy for Brian. And way too easy for Staines.

While he waited for his "guest" to regain consciousness, Brian boiled up a pan of water, and added a pinch of salt and some tagliatelle noodles. While they simmered, he made up, in a small saucepan, a portion of hollandaise sauce, from a packet, of course. Brian was no gourmet chef.

He was in no hurry. He rightly assumed that the rohypnol would keep Staines unconscious for three or four hours, and not having eaten all day, Brian was hungry. Into the gently bubbling hollandaise, he added some chunks of pre-cooked, skinless chicken, and stirred the contents together until all were piping hot. He drained the tagliatelle noodles, put them into a large soup bowl that Mrs. Stevens had left in one of the kitchen presses, and poured the chicken and sauce over the top. He ate hungrily, and drank deeply from the bottle of sparkling mineral water he'd brought along for the meal. When he'd finished, he washed up, dried the lot with a clean tea towel, and put everything back where it belonged. Old habits die hard.

At 7:30, Brian went outside the house for a little walk. He wasn't interested in the healthy aspect of a good stretch of the legs after a large meal. He just wanted to make sure that no one was in the immediate vicinity. To the east, he could see a small section of the dual carriageway, bumper to bumper with commuters making their way home after another day doing whatever it was they did to put bread on the table, or Dubliners heading to their weekend/holiday homes in Courtown, Kilmuckridge and Ballymoney. By late Sunday evening, and from very early Monday morning, the traffic would have reversed, back in the direction of the capital city, and people would be cursing the countless thousands of cars in front of them, their weekend's rest and relaxation forgotten.

"All right, let's give it a shot and see what happens," Brian mumbled. Then he filled his lungs with air, and bellowed with every ounce of strength he had, "HELLOOOOOO!" He listened for any response. None was forthcoming, though he did get a curious glance from a dozy looking sheep. Satisfied, he strode back into the house, and as he walked through the door, he said firmly, "Let's get started then."

Just after eight o'clock, Staines opened his mouth and vomited down the front of himself. The massive dosage of sleeping tablets, combined with the effects of the alcohol he'd consumed, had poisoned his system; his stomach simply wanted no more to do with such carry on, and took the necessary action to signal its displeasure. It took Staines a few moments to realise a number of things. First, he was upright, which confused him straight away, because he was quite sure he couldn't sleep standing up. Secondly, he couldn't see anything, although he was now alert enough to figure out that this was because something was covering his eyes.

The next two things that worked their way through the foggy swamp that was Geoffrey Staines' brain were more worrying to him. He couldn't move, and his feet were absolutely on fire with pain.

It would have been the perfect time for an out of body experience. Had he been able to achieve such a feat, Staines would have realised that the reason he couldn't see was because he was blindfolded. The reason he couldn't move was a bit more complex. He was standing, all right, against a vertical wooden beam, stripped naked except for his boxer shorts. A very large, studded dog collar cinched tightly around his neck and the beam held his head in place. His hands had been pulled behind his back, and a large amount of industrial packing tape wrapped around his wrists ensured they would stay there. His ankles had been taped as well, but that didn't explain the pain in his feet. Again, an out of body experience would have been a very, very good idea, if for no other reason than to avoid what was already in the process of happening to him.

"You're awake, then," a voice whispered from somewhere around his feet. "Good. Tell me. How do you feel?"

"What? Who...? Where am I?" Staines was fully awake now, and well and truly frightened.

"Did I say you could ask questions?" the whisper was angry now. "No. I did not! So let's start again, and maybe this will help you answer."

With that, Brian took the sheet of coarse sandpaper and recommenced rubbing it violently over the tops of Staines' naked feet. The blindfolded man screamed like a fatally wounded animal. He'd never imagined such pain was possible. Desperately wishing he would pass out, yet knowing he wouldn't, Staines cried and begged and cursed at his assailant. When the skin had been mostly removed from the tops of both feet, Brian worked up to the tender skin at the inside of the ankles, stopping only to remove a fresh sheet of sandpaper from the hardware store bag. He'd already worn the first one nearly smooth.

After the first ten minutes, Brian stopped. "You think that hurts?" he whispered to the writhing, pitiful creature struggling, without any chance of success, against his restraints. "Now, I'm asking you again, how do you feel?" Through the heightened sensitivity that accompanies intense pain, a new horror sliced into Staines' consciousness. His assailant wasn't even breathing hard. Staines was sure of it, and somehow this fact terrified him as much as the prospect of the imminent, inevitable torture that was sure to soon follow. The man he couldn't see was...what? Staines tormented mind grappled for an answer. He was...doing...a job. But he didn't seem to be taking any pleasure from it. It was more as if his attacker was swatting flies, or emptying dead vermin from a mousetrap.

Stupidly, he forgot to answer the ridiculous question again. "Christ, man, what do you want from me?" Staines sobbed.

"More questions. You just don't learn, do you?" came the whispered response. "All right, let's try one more time." With that, Brian turned the sandpaper loose at the back of Staines' knees. Anyone who has experienced sunburn in that area can testify as to just how sensitive that part of the body is, and Staines nearly came unhinged as the coarse paper shredded the outermost layer of skin.

"I'll tell you! I'll tell you, please God, stop, and I'll tell you!" Staines begged.

"How do you feel?" The whisper was barely audible.

"It hurts. Please don't hurt me any more," Staines whimpered.

"Oh, does it really, really hurt?" and Staines could hear the mockery, even in the whisper. "Well, let me see what we can do about that."

Staines heard the man retreat a few steps, then come back towards him. He then could make out what sounded like a safety cap being unscrewed for the first time from a bottle, like a medicine bottle. Terror gripped his heart like a falcon's claw. His breathing was made up of a mixture of short gasps and garbled sobs, and his heart raced until he could feel it beating behind his eyes.

"See if this helps, then," came the whisper, and again Staines noted with rising fear that the voice was utterly calm. He smelled the liquid as Brian began to pour, straight from the bottle, onto the ghastly wounded, raw flesh.

"No! Don't!" Staines screamed, as he realised what the bottle contained. The rubbing alcohol splashed onto the tops of Staines' feet, and the sound coming from his throat now was less than human. Brian's pulse rate still hadn't risen by a single beat. He let the clear liquid run down the back of Staines' thighs, from where it trickled onto the backs of his knees, burning the flesh worse than could any flame. The ankles got the same treatment, and at last, Staines' mind offered blessed release. He passed out, and knowing he was doing so, wished at the same time that he would never, ever wake up. Death would be so much better than what he'd been through.

Seeing his victim black out, Brian re-capped the bottle of isopropyl alcohol, and made himself a strong cup of black, instant coffee. He wished there was a fridge in the cottage. He would have liked to keep his mineral water and soft drinks cold, or even to have ice to put into them. He supposed he could bring out one of those little refrigerators designed for use in caravans.

It would be there for the next time.

With that thought, he took the only sharp knife in the house, and approached the motionless figure. After a moment's hesitation, he cut loose the taped wrists and ankles, but left the dog collar fastened. Then Brian walked out the front door, around to the back of the little cottage, and sat into his car.

EIGHTEEN

Staines came round slowly, as if he was willing himself not to; the pain he felt was unlike any agony he'd experienced in his miserable life. He had no idea what time it was. He could see through the window next to the front door that there was still some light in the sky — or was that the beginning of dawn? Given that it was nearly mid-June, and he had not the slightest idea of whether he was facing east, west, or otherwise, daylight only meant that it was somewhere between 4:30 a.m. and midnight.

It only slowly dawned on him that his hands and legs were free. The realisation made his pulse race, and he was actually startled when he was able to reach up to his eyes and find that his blindfold had been removed. He clutched at his throat, unbuckling the dog collar. He had to practically choke himself to do the latter; he would have done that, and chewed through his leg if necessary, to be free of this nightmare, this place, this…

Where had he gone?

There was no sign of the man who had tortured him for what had seemed an eternity. Had he just gone away? With a shudder, Staines wondered in the next instant, "Would he be back?" He wasn't going to wait around to find out. The first step he took away from the upright wooden beam that he'd been strapped to during his ordeal caused such excruciating pain that Staines had to clamp his jaws shut to avoid screaming out. He was further sickened when he realised that he'd ground his jaws down so hard, he'd literally cracked one of his back teeth. The flesh on his feet, ankles, and behind his knees was shredded, not enough to bleed like a deep cut, but oozing semi-clear blood, like that which comes from a really bad graze or carpet burn. Only this was a thousand, no, ten thousand, carpet burns, paper cuts and steam scalds rolled into one. The scabs would be thin and mucousy, and anything touching the area of the wounds for weeks to come would cause horrible pain.

But Staines did not cry out. He did not want to alert his captor, if the man was still around, to the fact that he was awake and about to make a limping dash for freedom. The second step was every bit as painful as the first, but this time, Staines had expected it, and braced himself. He tried taking one or two steps stiff-legged, to keep from bending his legs at the knees, thereby scrunching up the skin behind them, as he walked. Anyone watching would have found him almost comical. It looked as if he was parodying the old Nazi goose step. Tears streamed down his face, but he made his way to the door, fully expecting to find it locked and bolted. On the contrary, it had been left slightly ajar. Clearly, the man who had imprisoned him had made a run for it, having accomplished what he set out to do. Maybe he'd thought Staines had died, and got frightened. Or maybe the sick, twisted bastard had just had enough fun and games for one night, Staines thought to himself.

Only later would Staines wonder as to the nature of the attack. If whoever it was had wanted him dead, then, Staines would eventually admit to himself, he'd now be dead. Likewise, no bones were broken, his eyes hadn't been poked out, no obvious permanent damage had been done. And while his clothes and wallet were gone, robbery certainly hadn't been the motive. But on that night, he still hadn't made the connection between what he had just been put through, and what he'd been thrown in prison for more than seven years previously.

Even had he thought of little Danny Sykes' parents, he would never have equated the monster who had just put him through hell with the quiet, professional family whose windows he had once cleaned. So he assumed that he had well and truly ticked someone off in Mountjoy, that maybe they had connections on the outside, and this

maniac was someone who knew someone who owed someone else a
favour.

As he peeked out the front door, he could see the laneway, leading
away from the house and up towards the set of gates. Quiet as a
mouse, he stepped out into semi-darkness and started in the
direction of what he hoped would be a road he might recognise, or
on which he might be able to stop a passing motorist. Even if he
couldn't get a lift, which he knew to be an outrageously remote
possibility, given he was out in the middle of what appeared to be
nowhere, in just his boxer shorts, Staines thought he could possibly
get a driver to stop long enough to ask them to alert the gardai to his
predicament. That would be enough.

He'd covered more than three quarters of the distance, every inch
of it in agony, from the house to the gate, when he heard footfalls
behind him. A freezing cold shudder started in his brain, ran
straight down his spine, and into his bladder, causing a major
malfunction of that particular organ. Urine ran down his left leg,
and the salty liquid might as well have been pure acid for the
burning it set off when it reached first his ankle, then the top of his
foot. Looking back, he saw the shadowy figure jogging in his
direction, and knew without doubt that his attacker was coming after
him. Trying to ignore the pain, he hobbled to the gate, and
awkwardly clambered over it, at the same time glancing back to see
that his pursuer had closed the gap between them to about fifty
metres.

"Stay away from me!" Staines screamed at Brian. "Help!
Somebody, help! This man is trying to kill me!" Broken and
bruised, he limped out onto the tarmac road, turning right, since it
looked to be downhill, and the thought spun crazily in Staines' head
that this fact might help him build up some speed in his flight to
freedom. Being barefoot didn't help. Every second or third crippled
stride meant stepping down on a loose stone. By the time he'd gone
another hundred metres, the soles of both his feet were punctured
and bleeding. His chest was on fire from the exertions. He couldn't
stand the thought of going back into that cabin and what might

happen to him when he got there, and, just for an instant, he wondered if there was any way he could kill himself, right there and then, on the dark, deserted road. He looked over his shoulder, hoping with every fibre of his brain that he had somehow managed to put distance between himself and the mad man.

"Nice night for a jog," whispered Brian. He was just three feet behind his prey, and making no attempt whatever to catch up. Horribly, he wasn't even panting from the exertion of covering the quarter mile between the cottage and the spot they'd now reached. Only then did Staines realise that the whole thing was a set-up, and he was right. Brian could have run all the way back to Bray without breaking sweat, and certainly at a much faster pace than they were managing now.

This part of the plan had been hatched during one of Brian's countless sessions on the treadmill. He had wanted Staines to think he might get free, knowing the devastation to his victim's mind that would be caused by his re-capture. And every painful step that Staines took would multiply the anguish of the inevitable failure of his attempted getaway. So after Brian had cut Staines' restraints, he had gone outside, leaving the door slightly open, and waited in his car for his victim's fruitless dash for liberty. It was as close as a cat toying with a mouse before killing it as a human could possibly get. To Brian's mind, it was an exquisite punishment.

Staines stopped dead in the middle of the road, realising that further flight was pointless, crying pitifully, holding his arms out in front of him as if to ward off Brian's advances. Brian just stood and looked at the quivering mass that stood before him, and wondered if Danny had held his arms out in the same manner. That single thought was enough to spur Brian on. He reached into the pocket of his tracksuit top and pulled out a large handkerchief. From the other pocket came the bottle of ether. Soaking the cloth with the horrible-smelling liquid, Brian grabbed Staines' wrist, jerked him around with no apparent effort, and placed the anaesthetic over the trembling man's mouth and nose. As he felt him begin to go limp,

Brian whispered in his ear, "We're only just getting started, you know."

He threw Staines over his shoulder as he would a bag of potatoes, and carried the limp form back up the hill, through the gates, and into the stone cottage. The dog collar, packing tape, blindfold and wooden beam were all re-employed, though Brian was careful not to tighten the collar too much. He also checked for a weak pulse and other signs that his quarry might go into shock. He had no desire to send Geoffrey Staines to the hell that surely awaited him. Not yet.

While he waited for the effects of the ether to wear off, Brian stretched out on the small, single bed. Setting his alarm on his mobile phone for six a.m. the following morning, a quick glance at his watch told him he could still get about five hours of sleep. He admitted to himself that he was tired. It had been a long day, but he couldn't ever remember feeling as alive as at that very moment. Enjoyment would be too strong a word to describe how he felt about what he was doing. No pleasure had been gained, nor had it been expected. The best word, Brian thought, to describe how he felt about all of the events of the day just gone was "satisfied."

As Saturday dawned, Brian came awake without the aid of his alarm. Light streamed in through the small bedroom window as the sun rose quickly above the Irish Sea.

He walked into the kitchen, and ran the tap until the well water coming out was icy cold. Brian took a long drink, then refilled the glass and walked out to where Staines appeared to be either asleep or still under the affects of the ether. Brian threw the ice cold water onto Staines' naked chest, and watched impassively as the man gasped with the sudden shock. "You miserable bastard!" Staines screamed, not caring for the moment that he was completely at the mercy of the man he was cursing. "What do you want from me, you psycho?"

"I told you last night," Brian said, still whispering, "In the words of an old Carpenter's classic, 'We've Only Just Begun.'"

"Take this blindfold off me," Staines growled, trying to sound menacing. "I saw you on the road last night; there's no point in leaving it on now. I can describe you, mister, so you do what you have to, because someday, people are going to come looking for you."

Staines' reasoning was that he might as well brazen it out. He didn't think his tormentor was going to kill him, because he could have done that a dozen times already. And, he admitted to himself, he'd rather antagonize the man into killing him than go through what he'd been submitted to the day before.

"Describe me, then. If you can, I'll take the blindfold off. As you say, it wouldn't really serve any purpose. Go on. You have my word."

"You're about six feet tall — medium build," Staines offered, bluster already diminishing.

"Hmm, that doesn't narrow it down very much, does it?" Brian mocked. "I'm afraid you'll have to do better than that. Go on. Hair colour? Eye colour? Any distinguishing marks you can identify? What about my teeth? Straight or crooked?" Brian had correctly guessed that a terrified man running down a reasonably dark road in fear for his life wouldn't be in the best mental state to notice specific details, even about the man chasing him. That, coupled with the fuzzy state his mind would have been in from the chemical "cocktail" of beer, rohypnol and ether, meant most of Staines' recollections of the previous day would have centred on the pain endured, not the person causing it.

"Fuck you," Staines said, but he was beaten and knew it.

"Now, that's not nice, is it?" Brian admonished. "You know, we only worked on the lower body yesterday. How does it feel, by the way?" Brian observed the wounds and thought it unlikely that any infection would set in. But he knew there weren't enough ointments and gauze in all of Dublin to soothe the violated tissues on Staines' lower limbs.

When no answer was forthcoming, Brian went to the kitchen, brought back the electric kettle, and poured a few ounces of freshly boiled water onto the top of Staines' right foot. He listened to the screams and watched the face of his son's killer turn purple.

"Don't fuss," he whispered when the screams subsided. "You'll be glad to know that we're nearly out of the rubbing alcohol."

"No more! Please, just kill me," Staines sobbed.

"Why, because we're out of alcohol?" Brian feigned stupidity. "Aw, don't worry about that. I've got a couple of large tubs of salt here someplace. I'm pretty sure that will work nearly as well."

And so it went on, all day Saturday and Sunday, and for all but the four hours that Brian slept Saturday night. During the daytime hours between 11 a.m. and 6 p.m., Brian played loud music on a portable CD player he'd brought along on the trip, just in case picnicers or backpackers happened to be in the area. He set the little stereo just outside the front door, facing up toward the gates, and turned the volume to the maximum. He needn't have bothered. A misty drizzle moved in from the sea Saturday morning. On Sunday, it just plain rained hard all day. No one wanted to walk or picnic or collect wild flowers in that weather. No one heard Staines' screams.

As Brian had hinted, the soft skin just below the armpits received the same attention as had the lower extremities of Staines' body on the first day. The wrists had been considered by Brian, but dismissed due to the close proximity of large veins to the surface. He didn't want to accidentally shred one of those and have Staines bleed all over the floor. That just wouldn't fit into the plan. So he concentrated on areas that had a bit more padding, like the side of the body, below the rib cage and just above belt level, or those that would cause the most pain through movement. The very base of the spine, right down at the end of the tailbone, was sanded, then salted as well. The middle knuckles of Staines' right hand were roughed up until it looked like he'd put his fist into a meat grinder. Brian knew that Staines wouldn't be able to sit down for six weeks, or bend his fingers even slightly without causing himself, at best, horrible discomfort.

Brian never once lost control, never scrubbed so hard with the sandpaper that the damage being done would cause an injury severe enough to warrant hospitalisation. In his own mind, he was able to shut out the screams, the sobs, the curses, and concentrate on the task at hand much as if it was a DIY job at home. He gave Staines' limbs no more thought than he would have a skirting board or a windowsill being prepared for painting. It was an appropriate analogy, Brian thought to himself. When using sandpaper, the painter just wants to prepare the surface for further treatment; he doesn't want to do any real damage to the wood.

Staines was never allowed to go to the toilet, nor was he fed or given water. Brian told him to do whatever it was he had to do, where he stood, and by Sunday evening, urine, vomit, and human excrement were making the little stone house stink worse than any abattoir. The man strapped to the wooden beam moved closer and closer to the mental edge. He passed out with increasing frequency. He began babbling like an imbecile when Brian took a handful of salt and rubbed it vigorously into still another oozing sore. When, late in the day, he heard the by now familiar rustle of the plastic bag from the hardware store, indicating that Brian was getting out another fresh sheet of sandpaper, he actually broke into hysterical laughter. He hadn't yet been driven completely insane, but he was very, very close.

NINETEEN

"Wake up, you stinking bum!" Staines heard the words as though they had come from a great distance, but in fact, the man was standing directly over him. In an instant, terror gripped his brain.

"No more!" he screamed without having even opened his eyes. "Leave me alone, you bastard!"

"Shut your mouth, sick-o. I haven't touched you. Just get your ass up off the street."

"What?"

Staines forced his eyes open with tremendous effort, and looked up into the grizzled face of Charlie Walsh, Litter Warden. "Uh, right, thanks. I mean sorry, or…where the hell am I?" Staines asked, trying desperately to reconcile the events of the past few days with his current surroundings. Looking down, he noticed that he was in the very same clothes he'd been wearing on Friday. Even his wallet was still in the back pocket of the jeans. He made an effort to get to his feet, as Charlie looked on with equal mixtures of curiosity and disgust. The pain caused just from his clothes moving against the wounds he received made Staines cry out; he wilfully held back the tears, abandoning for now the attempt to stand.

"How do you morons let yourselves get into this state," Walsh asked with no sympathy whatever in his voice. "You must have been out here all night." With that, he moved off, shaking his head at the thought of the man he'd just seen, and at the vision of crisp bags, sweet wrappers, soft drink cans and beer bottles strewn along the street.

Slowly, Staines developed a picture in his mind of the last moments he could remember before waking up...where? From his sitting position, he looked back over his shoulder and saw the hideous paint job that only Sullivan's Ale House would allow the outside world to see. Though it was light, it was clearly very early morning. There was no one around at all, bar Charlie; not even the newsagents or coffee shops were open for business.

He had been begging. He remembered, already beginning to loathe himself, begging for a lot of things-- for his attacker to stop, for death, for a glass of water or a mouthful of bread. For...

The glass of water, that was it, only he hadn't been given a glass of water. "Maybe you'd like something a little stronger," the hideous, hated whisper had suggested.

"Anything," Staines had pleaded. His mouth was so dry, he couldn't even generate saliva to swallow. He'd heard the liquid being poured, and he smelled the whiskey before the glass was put to his lips. He didn't care, and gulped greedily, coughing and spluttering just once, before nodding his assent when asked if he wanted more. A second glass followed, and again, Staines received it almost gratefully, uncaring as to why his "host" had suddenly relented.

He'd then immediately felt violently ill. Twelve ounces of Bushmills on an empty stomach, inside a tortured body, was not a healthy thing, and his stomach threatened once again to evacuate all its contents.

"I think you've had enough," came the whisper, but Staines didn't know whether it was whiskey or torture to which he'd referred. In the next instant, a cloth had been slapped over his face, and Staines recognised the same sickening smell he'd noticed on the road, when he'd tried unsuccessfully to get away. "See you soon," was the last sound he'd heard before blacking out.

With horrible difficulty, Staines slowly, painfully, made his way to the Bray garda station. The trainers on his feet now felt like they were lined with the same sandpaper with which he'd been tortured. After a few excruciating steps, he could feel the wounds had already started to ooze. Likewise, his jeans sent spears of pain through him, just by brushing against the insides of his ankles, or simply touching the raw backs of his knees.

His theory about keeping his head down while in prison didn't stand up now. At the same time, he couldn't believe that he was actually going to go to the men in blue to file a complaint. For a long time, it had been his belief that the police were people to be avoided—not necessarily that they were bad, just a different breed, and different breeds don't mix. But this was different. The weekend he'd just been subjected to was inhuman. Someone had to pay. No way was he going to let this go.

Finally, he reached the station, and pushed open the front door. To his left was the enquiries counter. Sitting behind a desk on the other side of that counter was Garda Liam Shortt, who was coming to the end of a long graveyard shift, and who was in no mood for extra work ten minutes before he was due to go home. "Can I help you?" Shortt asked, hoping, but not expecting, that this was about nothing more serious than a parking fine.

"Yes," answered Staines. He was exhausted, every inch of him felt like it was on fire, and he was totally unsure how to proceed. Intelligence not being his strongest suit, he motored ahead, "Someone has just spent the weekend kicking the shit out of me, and I want to file a complaint!"

"Now let's start again," said Shortt, with a warning tone in his voice. "And this time, let's see if we can do it without using bad language. So once more, can I help you, sir?"

"What? That is absolute bullshit! I've been attacked. I've been tortured, and you're worried about my language? Once more," Staines was now mocking the policeman, "that is complete and utter bullshit!"

Pushing himself away from the desk, Shortt stood, revealing that his name wasn't exactly appropriate. His six-foot-six frame moved towards the counter separating him from the jerk on the other side. "You know, sir, they say the use of foul language to make your point is a sign of very low intelligence," he said quietly. Then, leaning across the counter so that his face was only inches from Staines', he said even more quietly, "And if you do it once more, I'm going to come across that counter, break off one of your arms, and beat you over your stupid, foul-mouthed head with the sticky end. Got that?"

Just what Staines needed — more pain. He instantly retracted his insulting remark. "Sorry, Garda, but I'm serious," he said in what was now a pleading voice. "I was attacked on Friday night, and this lunatic tortured me all weekend."

Shortt was more than a little skeptical. "Who did? Who tortured you?"

"I don't know," Staines admitted.

"Well, what does he look like?"

"About six feet tall, medium build...." Staines was beginning to worry. "I didn't really get a good look at him. He had me blindfolded most of the time."

"Right. Most of the time."

"Well, I got away once and tried to run, but it was dark, and he caught me, but when he caught me, I didn't really get a good look..." Staines was beginning to babble.

"Run where? Where did all this take place?"

"I don't know. Out in the country somewhere."

"How did you get away? How did he catch you the second time?"

"Well, I got away, sort of--I'm not sure how, because I think he let me go on purpose so he could catch me again." Staines was reaching the point of utter despair. He could see that Shortt didn't believe a single word of his story. "I couldn't run very fast, because I didn't have my clothes on and I was barefoot, and..."

"You were out in the country naked? So where did you get these clothes?" Shortt was on the verge of throwing him out.

"Oh, these are my clothes, all right, the ones I was wearing when he took me. He must have put them back on me when he let me go."

"I thought you said he caught you again."

"He did, but then he must have let me go again." Staines was beginning not to believe his own story. It just didn't make sense!

"So he took you on Friday, then let you get away, but he caught you again, but then he dressed you and let you go again?"

"Yes!" Staines said in desperation.

"And you got back to Bray from somewhere, but you don't know exactly where, out in the country? How did you get back?"

"I don't know. He drugged me, I think, and dumped me."

"Why would anyone want to do this to you?"

Staines didn't want to answer this question. He was fervently hoping to avoid having to admit that he had just been released from prison, and his suspicion that he had annoyed a fellow inmate at Mountjoy who was now seeking retribution.

"Well," Shortt asked again, patience dwindling by the second.

"I don't know," Staines mumbled.

"You know, don't you, that all of this is totally unbelievable?"

"But it's true," Staines protested.

"Right. Let's start one last time," Shortt said, emphasising the word last. "Where were you on Friday when you were attacked?"

"At Sullivan's, on the promenade," Staines admitted, and he couldn't fail to notice the clouds of doubt gathering in Shortt's eyes.

"You'd been drinking? Hmm, and where was it this man dumped you when he brought you back from wherever it was he tortured you for the weekend?"

Staines knew what the policeman was driving at, so he fudged his answer, "On the promenade," he said.

"Outside Sullivan's?"

"Well, near it, I suppose."

"Would anyone have reported you missing? Should I check the log book?"

Staines shook his head in the negative.

Shortt took out his notebook. "What's your name, sir?"

"Geoffrey Staines. Geoffrey with a 'G', and Staines with an 'e'."

The name didn't ring any bells with Shortt, but it didn't matter. He faced the smelly little man on the other side of the counter.

"Mr. Staines, it is my opinion that you have been drinking for the weekend, and that you probably have a wife or girlfriend, God help them, waiting somewhere for you. You have invented this story to keep yourself out of trouble, and you think that by reporting it to the gardai, they might substantiate it for you if questioned by your partner. All I can say is, if this woman, whoever she is, is gullible enough to believe the complete rubbish you've just put before me, then she deserves you and all that goes with you."

"No, it's all true!" Staines protested loudly.

"You stink of whiskey, and your story stinks worse," Shortt said, making no effort to hide his disdain. "Now get out of here, before I arrest you for being drunk and disorderly."

"But I'm injured," Staines cried, first waving his raw knuckles in the air, and then he actually started to pull down his jeans so he could show the garda his knees and ankles.

"Don't even think about it! You drop those trousers, sir, and I will arrest you for indecent exposure!" Shortt warned. "It's clear that nothing is broken. If you're injured, it's my guess that you either fell down drunk coming out of Sullivan's, or you've given yourself a couple of knocks to help back up your ridiculous story."

"Please," Staines begged. "I'm really, really hurt."

"This is not a doctor's surgery, and you've got three seconds to drag your miserable, lying carcass out that door!"

Defeated, and miserable to the depths of his being, Staines pulled himself away from the counter, out the door, and in the direction of Quinsboro Road. He should have known better than to expect a flatfoot to help. "Oh, hell," he muttered to himself, "I wouldn't have believed me, either." He tried to make sense of it all, and wished momentarily that he hadn't come out of prison at all. With that thought came the realisation at which most clear thinking people would have long since arrived. Whoever had written him the notes his last three months in Mountjoy must have been the psycho that had just put him through close to three full days of pure hell. But that was as near to understanding as he could get. He still couldn't make the final connection as to who had written those notes, or why.

His pre-prison past was too far away, too shrouded in the mists of
alcohol and drug abuse to have any recognisable substance.

As he pulled the trainers off his raw, scarred feet, back at his bedsit,
the tears began to flow in earnest. How could any person do this to
another human being? His dingy white socks were caked in dried
blood. Standing in the shower would bring fresh waves of searing
pain. One thought, though, gave a grain of comfort. He was sure
that the man wouldn't come back, and he vowed to keep watch, be
alert, and never be taken to the little cottage again. It was surely all
over, he thought.

He couldn't possibly have been more wrong.

TWENTY

The PULSE computer system used by the Irish police force was a well of information that never dried up. Contrary to public belief, once any name enters that system, it is there for life — and beyond. The acronym stands for "Police Using Leading Systems Effectively." One of its main functions is to allow all garda units around the country access to shared information. As criminals had become more mobile, it had become necessary to detail and track their movements, subjecting their activities to the highest degree of legal scrutiny, while at the same time taking care not to infringe constitutional rights. PULSE allows the gardai in Dundalk to source, or supply, information with their Dingle counterparts.

Any system of such a nature, of course, is only as good as the data put into it. Garda Liam Shortt hadn't believed a single word of Geoffrey Staines' story, but he knew one thing for certain. If he exposed his backside by not filing a report, something, somewhere, at some time in the future, would bite that uncovered backside, and hard. So rather than going home, as he dearly wanted to, he sat back down at his desk, opened up the relevant files on his PC, and logged his notes. Where it said "Name of Complainant," he typed in "Geoffrey Staines." Through the miracle of technology, before he could take another sip of coffee, information that Staines had chosen not to share came flashing up on the screen. A click of a mouse here, and a press of the return button there, and Liam Shortt could read for himself a detailed dossier on the man who had been cursing and whining in front of him just a few minutes earlier.

The electronic file included the date of Staines' arrest, alongside which was listed the name of the arresting officer, Detective Michael McCann. Shortt made a mental note to forward a separate report, by internal post, to the relevant detective unit. He wouldn't forget. Sending such reports is standard procedure, and Shortt was a diligent policeman.

He read further, noting that Staines had recently been released after serving seven years of a 14-year sentence, after killing a young boy in nearby Dun Guaire, that he was on the Sex Offenders Register, and that he was due to report to this very station every second Wednesday.

"What a creep," Shortt muttered to himself. He continued typing in the bare bones of what Staines had reported. "Alleged kidnap. Assault. No witnesses. No description of alleged assailant. No suspects." He added at the foot of the report his observation that Staines' breath had a strong smell of whiskey, that no serious injuries were visible, and that the complainant had admitted to being in Sullivan's Ale House before the alleged assault took place. Under the section headed, "Follow-up Activity/Response:" he typed, "Complainant cautioned re: drunk and disorderly. Nothing further anticipated." He left out the bit, though recalling it brought a smile to his face, where he had threatened to break off Staines' arm.

In the top left corner of his PC screen, he clicked on "File," then "Print." He would attach a copy of what he had just produced to the written report being forwarded to the detective unit. Once that was done, Liam Shortt stood up from his computer, signed off in the logbook, and headed for the door. He noticed the weekend rain had ceased, and that the sun was threatening to break through the thin grey clouds. Since he wasn't on again until Wednesday night, he decided to get in nine holes of golf before going home. It was only Monday morning, after all; surely the course would be nearly empty.

Sandyford Industrial Estate was far from empty. Thousands of cars, hundreds of trucks and dozens of buses crammed into this particular centre of business and commerce every weekday morning. The ninety minutes between 7:45 and 9:15 were always the worst, and Brian particularly didn't want to be late this day. The less attention he could draw to himself, the better.

The weekend over, Brian was, in spite of his supreme fitness, bone tired. He hadn't slept since the couple of hours he'd grabbed on Saturday night, and he'd only gotten three hours the night before that. Sunday night, sleep was a luxury he felt he couldn't afford. He'd sedated Staines just after midnight, pulled his clothes back on, and bundled him into the Nissan for the journey back to Bray. He again removed the licence plates from his car before setting out. That had been the easy part. Once in Bray, he wanted to make sure that absolutely no one saw him dump his unconscious cargo outside Sullivan's. As it had transpired, this was trickier than he'd imagined it would be. June was the beginning of the summer holiday season, and some people, Brian observed, just wouldn't go home to bed, even on a Sunday night. He'd expected the occasional pairs of young lovers, walking arms-around-waists, up and down the seafront, and the late night drinkers staggering towards their respective homes. But it had gone on and on and on. At one point, he'd heard Staines stirring in the back seat, forcing Brian to pull quickly into the roadside to anaesthetise his captive once again.

As the night wore on, the Nissan made no less than nine circuits, using various routes, around the whole of Bray. At one point, Brian had considered pushing Staines out of the car in one of the quiet residential neighbourhoods, or at the entrance to one of the factories on the Boghall Road. He mulled over the idea, thinking he could ring the gardai and tell them he'd been driving home from a party and noticed this strange looking man skulking around a house, or trying to get into a warehouse facility. He dismissed these notions almost as soon as they came into his head. He wanted to stick with the plan. A phone call to the police would mean questions being asked, and, for all Brian knew, his voice being recorded or his mobile phone number traced. He wasn't absolutely sure how advanced the garda technology was, but he knew he wasn't willing to risk finding out for the sake of maybe getting a small amount of sleep. He would continue driving until the opportunity he was looking for presented itself. Finally, just after 3:30 a.m., he'd taken his chance. Driving, once again, slowly toward Sullivan's, not another living soul could be seen in either direction. There were no faces in any windows, no couples pawing each other down by the sea, no drunks making zig-zag steps up the footpath.

Brian quickly stopped the car, with the passenger side nearest the curb, directly in front of the pub. Opening the rear passenger door, he unceremoniously pulled the motionless figure from the back seat, dropping him with a thump on the narrow grass strip between the curb and the footpath. Without looking around, Brian quickly jumped back into the driver's seat and sped off. Rounding the corner, he pulled into the parking area opposite the train station and reaffixed the number plates to the Nissan. Seeing that the area was deserted, he took a black plastic bin liner that contained the empty bottle of alcohol, the half empty bottle of ether, several used, now mushy and red-stained, sheets of industrial grade sandpaper, and wads of used packing tape, out of the rear compartment of the estate car and deposited the entire contents into a skip standing at the edge of the car park.

From there, he'd driven back out to the cottage, where he'd spent the next two hours cleaning, particularly the floor area around the wooden beam. He hadn't much to work with, just hot water and some Fairy Liquid, and, now that his prey was gone, his mind took on a more "normal" setting. The smell made him gag. By the time he finished, Sherlock Holmes himself would not have been able to find a single clue that anyone other than Brian had spent the weekend at the stone house. Everything was where it should be. Everything, to Brian's mind, was as it should be. The plan had gone, more or less, like clockwork. He not only expected that Staines would go to the police, he wanted it to happen. Had he witnessed the conversation taking place at that very moment between Staines and Shortt, Brian would have found it very difficult not to laugh with pure delight.

The sun was fully above the horizon by the time Brian got back to his apartment in Cabinteely, and the clock on his kitchen wall announced that it was ten minutes past eight when he walked through the door. Brian took a very quick, piping hot shower, then turned the water to ice cold just before he stepped out, in an effort to force himself wide awake. Dressing with almost frantic haste, he was back in his car by half past eight, and while he didn't get to Business Solutions by the hoped for nine o'clock deadline, he was only seven minutes late walking through the main entrance. Carol looked up from the reception desk, and gave Brian a sympathetic smile, assuming he was still fighting the affects of some virus.

"Do you feel all right?" she asked. "We kind of thought you might not make it in today."

Brian instantly wondered whom she'd meant by 'we,' but decided not to worry. It was widely rumoured in the company that Carol had the ear—at the very least—of the managing director, but Brian felt that he was safe enough on this occasion. He doubted that Carol and the M.D.'s next "pillow talk," if indeed there ever was any, would include him.

He continued on up the stairs, into the sales office, where he next bumped into Kevin Whyte. As was the norm, Kevin made another attempt at friendly conversation. "How you feeling, Brian? We (there was that word again) missed you on Friday. You ok? You look tired, all right; maybe you're still under the weather. Do you think you could do with another day off?" It was typical of Kevin to fire off three or four questions without waiting for a single reply. Brian didn't know if he was like that with everyone, or if he just did it with Brian, to get in as many words as possible before Brian cut the conversation short.

"Thanks, Kevin; no, I'm sure I'm fine, but thanks for asking," Brian said with more friendliness in his voice than Kevin had heard in years. "In fact, I actually feel pretty good—great even." Brian meant the words.

"Excellent," Kevin replied, wondering if the sudden talkativeness was a side effect of some prescribed medication. "I suppose a weekend in the bed can work wonders."

"Believe it or not, I didn't spend the weekend in the bed," Brian said, knowing he was bordering on recklessness, but not really caring. "I, umm, got started on a project I've been meaning to have a go at for awhile. Very therapeutic, you know; does wonders for your head."

"What kind of project? I didn't know you had any hobbies," Kevin was genuinely interested.

"You know what? It's kind of a secret thing—a surprise for somebody that I've, well, just recently gotten close to."

"Brilliant," said Kevin, who hadn't the slightest notion of what Brian was talking about.

"Yeah, it is, really. In fact, you could say that this...this project...could get to be even more than that. I'd go so far as to say it could become my passion."

As he sat at his desk, sipping his cup of black coffee with one sugar and a good drop of milk, he marvelled at the world of stark, incredible contrasts in his life. Not one of the nearly hundred people working in the building would have thought Brian capable of a single one of the many savage acts he had committed in the weekend just past. Why would they? Kidnap and torture just didn't fit into most people's idea of weekend rest and relaxation.

Then there was this job, selling photocopiers, to other civilised business people, dressed in suits, or to school principals in charge of hundreds of students. Contrast that with what he now considered his other mission in life. The first three days on that "job" had just been successfully completed. There had been no suits and ties in the stone cottage, no sales targets, no team meetings and no manager looking over his shoulder. Did that make it less real, less important, Brian wondered. Or more so. He was pretty positive where Staines' vote would be. He was less sure of his own. The other differences, between the traffic-choked city and the seeming wilderness just down the road, between the cottage itself and his comfortable apartment in Cabinteely, teased his brain over and over again. Which was better? Which was easier? Where would he rather be? He thought it unlikely that he could remain jumping from one set of realities to the other on an indefinite basis. Would he one day have to make a choice? Or would the choice be made for him?

Finally, there was the undeniable fact, and it had to be faced, that he was in a very good mood this morning. He didn't want to think that he could have enjoyed the weekend's events. He reasoned that maybe it was the excitement of the pursuit, the thrill of the capture, and then the massive relief of not being discovered or caught in the act, that had his spirits up. Surely, he tried to convince himself, he wasn't actually pleased with himself, or happy with what he had done. What he didn't want to admit to himself was that, if he had taken any pleasure from the torture he'd inflicted on a helpless human being, he was no better than Staines had been when he killed Danny.

If he had been feeling good, the thought of his dead son quickly put pay to any happy thoughts. It only took a moment. His eyes darkened, and the coldness returned to his core. Now there was no satisfaction from having executed his plan to perfection. If anything, he felt guilty that he'd allowed Danny to stray from his thoughts, even for a short time. As he had done countless thousands of times since the last night at Tarpey's Funeral Home, Brian closed his eyes, picturing his eight-year-old lying cold and still in a small white coffin. He worked out again, to the day, how old Danny would be now, and tried to picture what he would have looked like. Tall and skinny, probably, even gangly, was how Brian painted him, with no foundation on which to base that vision. He'd have been 16-and-a-half, though Brian didn't imagine the half years would have been as important to Danny at 16, as they had been at five, six and seven. Cars and girls would have replaced Danny's interests in toy guns and dinosaurs. He'd probably have tried cider or lager with his mates; Bridget would have been mortified. Brian would have tried to talk sternly about the "evils of alcohol" but would have instead ended up sharing stories of how he'd gotten sick on drink for the first time at an illicit poitin party. Brian knew it wouldn't have all been smooth sailing and happy families. He didn't delude himself that they'd live as harmoniously as the Waltons, or the Ingles family in "Little House on the Prairie." But they would have done their best, given a chance. And that chance had been ripped from them by an evil, depraved, sick beast.

And Brian hadn't been able to stop it from happening.

Brian mouthed the words again, "Sorry, son." That done, he took out his personal diary, the one in which he kept track of all his business appointments, contact names and phone numbers, and opened it to the Notes section at the back.

"Time to get back to work," he muttered. He wrote down a few words, to help crystallise in his own mind the direction he next wanted to take. He knew that Staines would be on the lookout, at least for awhile, and in spite of his inability to give an accurate description, there was no guarantee that Brian wouldn't be recognised the next time they came within close proximity of each other. A physical confrontation was of no concern whatever. Brian knew he could subdue Staines, and any three others like him, without breaking sweat, but it was way too early to bring their "relationship" to that kind of a head. Besides, if Staines did spot him in a public place, he might start screaming, possibly even attracting a garda, or worse, an innocent member of the public who might be convinced to lend a hand. Brian had no wish to drag anyone else into his dealings with Geoffrey Staines. So he worked on another angle.

"You can't fight what you can't see," he said to himself as he closed his diary.

Brian switched on his Toshiba laptop computer, one of which had been issued to all senior sales staff, to perform "in the field" demonstrations to potential customers of the versatility of digital multi-function office devices. The old days of the "photostat" copiers were long gone. Now, a single machine could perform the work that once required several expensive, independent units. Brian's personal favourite was the CFi4060, so-called because it could produce forty full colour, or sixty black and white images per minute. These could be copies or prints, because the CFi4060 could be linked directly to a computer network for use as a printer. In addition, it could scan documents, send e-mails or faxes, and, Brian always said with a wink at the conclusion of his demonstrations, deliver a lovely gin and tonic, but only after six o'clock.

Using the Adobe Photoshop software loaded into his laptop, Brian created, on screen, what looked to be a very official looking document. He then took out his mobile phone, which had an integrated digital camera, and holding the lens facing back towards himself, snapped a quick picture which he instantly downloaded into the Toshiba. He cropped the image so that it fit perfectly into the corner of the page. He also made sure that the picture showed just enough of his shoulders and neck so that his sports coat and tie were plainly visible. Walking out to the showrooms, Brian quickly connected his laptop, via a standard parallel print cable, to the CFi4060 currently on display. If anyone had asked, he would have told them he was preparing for an in-house demonstration. No one asked.

In less than fifteen seconds, the machine had delivered a high quality, full colour reproduction of what Brian had produced on screen. But he wasn't done. Brian re-adjusted the settings on his laptop, and clicked for another print. This time, the image that was produced filled no more of the A4 sheet of glossy paper than would have a large business card. "Bingo," Brian said aloud.

Moving to the stationery and supplies display, Brian switched on the laminating machine, and fished out an A4 pouch from under the table, into which he inserted his colour copy. Running the pouch through the laminator, Brian then trimmed the plastic coated page using the guillotine at the end of the table, until it was the exact size required. Inspecting the finished product, he was well satisfied with his result.

Unless someone had an awful lot of inside knowledge, they would never know, looking at the "I.D. card" just produced, that its owner wasn't genuinely Brian Fitzgerald, Health Inspector.

TWENTY-ONE

"Mick, this one's for you," said the clerk at Shankill Garda Station. Liam Shortt's follow-up report arrived in Thursday's internal post, with Detective Michael McCann's name at the top.

In the normal course of a detective's career, barring any screw-ups, fist fights with Superintendents or other serious indiscretions, it would be considered normal, after five or six years in plain clothes, to apply for a promotion. The next step up would be sergeant; after that, Detective Sergeant. What's more, any detective who solved, or greatly assisted in solving a murder, would find it difficult enough to avoid being promoted. As the man who had "cracked" the Danny Sykes murder case, which concluded in what was deemed a successful prosecution, trial and conviction, most of his colleagues assumed that it would only be a question of time before McCann was back in uniform, as is required when the promotion to sergeant takes place.

It hadn't happened. The Superintendent of the district, the man who sent recommendations regarding potential promotions to Garda Headquarters in the Phoenix Park, had let McCann know on more than one occasion he would look favourably on any application for a higher post. The detective was highly thought of, and well liked, admired for the no-nonsense way he approached his job. After a few years, some members of the force began to wonder why McCann remained a plain-clothes detective. True, a promotion would, ironically enough, mean taking an actual cut in pay, since sergeants didn't generally have access to anything like the overtime pay that detectives did. But it was the next step up the ladder, and no one who knew him doubted that Michael McCann could travel a long way up that ladder indeed, should he choose to make the climb.

In truth, McCann hadn't made the decision not to eventually apply for promotion. Like any policeman, he had notions of moving his career forward. At one time, he'd considered asking B-Branch for a posting on the Drugs Enforcement Unit, or the Immigration Unit, or even the NBCI, which is the Irish equivalent of the American FBI. But the characteristic drive that had marked him for such an early appointment to the rank of detective, while not missing altogether, had certainly been somewhat diminished. He was still an excellent investigator, finding clues where there appeared to be none, and often, when clues were seemingly non-existent, using reason and logic to great effect.

Single cases don't change a man like McCann, but some incidents undoubtedly have more affect than others. Danny Sykes had never really left McCann's mind, and he wondered often if the little boy was the reason he and his girlfriend, Angela, had never gotten married. Angela wanted children. McCann had, at one stage in his life, thought he wanted them, too. That had all changed the day he'd walked into No. 41, Fr. Cullen Terrace, and found the body of an eight-year-old boy who had been murdered. Murdered, and — the thought still made McCann shudder — far, far worse. He had known, from that day on, that he couldn't in good conscience willingly bring an innocent child into a world inhabited by the likes of Geoffrey Staines. Angela hadn't understood. She reasoned with McCann that he must have known there were bad people everywhere, or else there wouldn't have been any point in becoming a policeman. He could see the logic in what she said, but it couldn't change what was in his heart. Eventually, Angela gave up, and moved out of their shared apartment. She loved McCann, and they remained friends, but her desire to have a family of her own would never be realised if she stayed with him, so she moved on.

Had the judgement handed down in the case completely disillusioned McCann? No, but it would be fair to say he viewed the judicial system with a more jaundiced eye after the event. He wasn't completely cynical, but he didn't have the same blind faith that justice would prevail, as he'd naively believed whole-heartedly when he left the Garda training facility at Templemore.

In this state of mental limbo, McCann himself had made the decision to stay where he was, in the detective unit, trying to do what was right and best for the public he served, while he sorted out in his own mind what was right and best for Michael McCann.

He read through the report that Shortt had sent him, and as soon as he saw the name of the complainant, he froze. It was a full minute before he could read another line; he just kept staring at the name. Unlike Brian and Bridget, and Governor Dempsey, McCann hadn't been notified of Staines' release from prison. It shouldn't have come as a shock to him; he saw prison sentences cut in half every day of the week, sometimes in spite of garda protests.

But he was shocked. In one way, it seemed only yesterday that he'd supported Bridget Sykes when she fainted in the courtroom in Wicklow. On the other hand, it was like a century had passed. "He couldn't be out, not yet," McCann thought, but there it was, in black and white, and it wasn't as if there could be more than one Geoffrey Staines, parolee, sex offender, walking around the streets of Bray. A John Smith, maybe, or a Jim Connors, or just about any Murphy you cared to mention. But in his entire career, McCann had only met one Geoffrey Staines, and he dearly hoped never to come across another.

Forcing himself to read the remainder of the report, McCann's first instincts were that the whole thing was a fantasy created by Staines, possibly drug-induced. Second, if Staines had been attacked, then he almost certainly deserved it; like Staines himself, McCann figured someone on the inside was probably settling a score. Fair enough.

But something wasn't right. It didn't sit well with McCann that Staines had willingly walked into a garda station, drawing attention to himself in the process. That didn't fit the profile he'd normally associate with someone like Staines. Even if he'd gotten a good hiding from a paid thug, it surprised him that a complaint would be filed. Anyone, even someone as dim as Staines would realise that trying to bring the law down on a hired "heavy" who'd slapped him around a bit might backfire badly. Staines would also surely know, or at least suspect, that just about any garda on the force would feel he'd gotten exactly what he deserved, and not half enough, at that.

Reading through the remainder of the sketchy details, McCann decided he wanted more information than the report was giving him. He picked up the phone and dialled the Bray Garda Station, asking for Garda Shortt.

"He's on nights this week," McCann was told. "Went home about two hours ago. You might catch him on his mobile, though, or you could phone back tonight. He's on again at ten o'clock."

"Can you give me his mobile number, please," McCann requested, identifying himself when asked to do so. "Ah, Mick, how are you? Sorry, I didn't recognise the voice." Most of the force in Bray and Shankill stations knew each other. McCann wrote down the number he was given, and dialled it immediately. After seven rings, and just as he was about to hang up, Shortt answered.

"Hello." He was whispering.

"Hello. Is that Liam Shortt? This is Detective Michael McCann calling." Shortt was relatively new to the force, and McCann hadn't yet met the man.

"Yes. Sorry. You're ringing from Shankill Station, right? I recognised the number coming up on my phone, or I wouldn't have answered," Shortt said, still in a very low tone.

"Why not?" McCann wanted to know, slightly perturbed.

"Because I'm on the seventh fairway at Kilternan, and mobile phones aren't allowed out on the course!"

"Right, I see." Now it was McCann's turn to be slightly perplexed. He even found himself speaking in a lower tone. "Sorry, I just wanted to ask you about a report you sent me on a complaint filed on…" he checked the date on the report "…Monday morning. Guy named Staines. If you like, I can ring you later, or maybe you could give me a bell after you finish your round."

"Yeah, fine, that would be grand, if it's all right with you. I'll ring you in a couple of hours. Give me your mobile number, in case you've left the station. I'll write it on my scorecard. It'll just about match some of the other numbers I've been writing down!"

"Sorry to hear that," McCann said, grinning widely. "Having a bad day?" he asked after reciting his number.

"No, a typical day."

"What's your handicap?"

"My driving, chipping and putting. Only for those three things, I'd be giving Tiger Woods a helluva run for his money. Hey! Don't you curse at me!" McCann realised that Shortt was directing his comments elsewhere, no doubt to a perturbed golfer on the seventh tee box. "I'm just checking the yardage! ...No, I am NOT on the phone to the club pro! How'd you like a seven iron wrapped around your fat head?"

He came back to McCann, who by now was holding his sides and choking back laughter. "Listen, I've gotta go, but I'll talk to you later, ok? Christ! That dirty bastard teed off and nearly hit me!"

As he hung up, tears of hysterical mirth streaming down his face, McCann could make out the first few words of abuse that Shortt was showering on the offending golfer.

As promised, Shortt rang him back just before lunchtime. "How'd you get on?" McCann wanted to know.

"Don't ask. But I'll bet that gobshite on the seventh is still fishing his clubs out of the water hazard!"

McCann started to laugh again, not caring whether Shortt was serious or not. This guy was genuinely funny, and a sense of humour went a long way toward making what could sometimes be an ugly job more bearable.

"Serves him right," McCann said, then, almost grudgingly, moved on to the reason he'd phoned Shortt in the first place. "What can you tell me about Geoffrey Staines?" he asked.

"He's ugly, and he smells bad."

McCann cracked up yet again. If ever he got the chance, he'd love to partner with Shortt someday. "Anything else?" he said, still chuckling.

"Yeah, he came in with some crazy story about how he'd been kidnapped, by aliens or something. No seriously, he said that he'd been taken out to the country, tortured and beaten for three days; that he'd escaped once or twice but only because the guy who'd taken him had wanted him to. I checked the logbook yesterday. There were no missing person reports over the weekend. Anyway, he didn't know who this lunatic was, how he'd gotten out to the countryside, or how he got back, and he couldn't describe his attacker to me, because he'd been blindfolded—part of the time—except when he was running down the road naked! The thing was, except for some grazed knuckles, I couldn't see a mark on him. He wanted to drop his pants to show me his "ouchies," but hey, I'm still young and impressionable. I see enough really ugly things in this job without having to face the Staines family heirlooms, you know what I mean? He'd been drinking, that's for sure. He owned up to that himself—whiskey it smelled like. I couldn't guess if he'd been using anything stronger, but it wouldn't surprise me."

"Is that it?" McCann asked, thoroughly enjoying Shortt's description of the event.

"Yeah, I think so. I suppose he seemed upset enough. My guess is he'd been on the sauce for the whole weekend, and his old lady was waiting at home with a frying pan in her hand. He was desperate for a cover-up, but his story was weaker than my golf game, and that's saying a lot!"

"Thanks a lot, Liam," McCann said, already feeling comfortable enough to address Shortt on a first-name basis. "We'll have to get together for 18 holes someday."

"Not if we're going to play for money," Shortt replied. "But yeah, other than that, it would be fun."

Reluctantly, McCann hung up. He digested what Shortt had told him, and niggling doubts began worming their way into his brain. For starters, he'd remembered that Staines was a complete and total loner. It was unlikely he'd found a female companion while serving his sentence, nor in the short time since his release. So Shortt's theory about inventing a wild tale of kidnap and torture, to appease some woman, didn't add up.

What possible motive could Staines have for inventing such a fairytale? The more he thought it through, the more he kept arriving at the same one-word answer: none.

Unfortunately, this only led to more questions, the answers to which were even more elusive. Why were there no visible signs of serious injury? A hired goon would happily break a bone or two without thinking twice about it. What about the time span of Friday to Monday morning? It didn't make sense. Most contract jobs were quick, savage assaults, and the recipients were seldom left in any doubt as to who was responsible for the punishment dished out. It was also highly unusual, except in kidnap-for-ransom cases, for the victim to be "delivered" back to where the whole thing had started. That was too risky. If they were dumped, it would normally be in an isolated spot, giving the assailant plenty of time to make a clean getaway. None of it fit, and only two people had the answers that would help McCann piece this particular jigsaw together. One was the man who carried out the attack. McCann couldn't talk to him, because he hadn't a single idea as to who it might be. The second was Staines, and McCann wasn't at all sure he ever wanted to occupy the same breathing space as that man again. The detective was only human, after all. He wouldn't swear that Staines belonged in the same category, after what he'd witnessed first-hand more than seven years ago. Even the idea of interviewing the ex-con, with a view to gathering information that would help to capture his tormentor, was anathema to McCann. He had to admit to himself that, whoever the attacker was, he'd rather salute him than arrest him.

So, for the time being, he made observations in the private notebook he still carried with him, and decided to do nothing. Nothing at all.

TWENTY-TWO

Sarah Guilfoyle answered the door to No. 279, Quinsboro Road, and peered out at the man standing on the doorstep. "Can I help you?" she asked. He was well dressed, in shirt, jacket and tie, and a rain mac. The last wasn't particularly necessary, Sarah thought, as the weather was quite reasonable at the moment. Still, in Ireland, the sun could be shining when you walk out the door, and you could be soaking wet by the time you got to your car. She supposed this man, whoever he was, lived by the same philosophy.

"Brian Fitzgerald, Health Inspector," said Brian, briefly displaying the ID card he'd produced at the office. He was amazed that he felt no nerves whatever; he was already enjoying this particular round of role acting.

"We didn't receive any notification of an inspection," said Sarah, miffed at the unexpected intrusion. She wasn't unduly concerned. While residents were responsible for their own quarters, Sarah looked after the hoovering and dusting of the halls and corridors, and she also cleaned the shared toilet facilities three times a week. "Has there been some kind of complaint?" she asked, still not inviting Brian to step into the building.

"No, not at all. This is purely routine," said Brian, keeping his tone offhand and friendly. "I have to do this all the time; you do know that we're entitled to make up to two unannounced inspections per year, don't you? You can ring my office if you'd like to check. Do you have the number?" It was a bluff. If the landlady had made the call, Brian would have been gone the instant she turned her back to pick up the phone.

"Of course I know," said Sarah, not wanting to appear ignorant of the regulations. The truth was, she hadn't a clue as to whether such inspections were legal or otherwise. "I suppose you'd better come in then."

"Thanks very much. I hope I'm not putting you to too much trouble."

"No, it's no trouble. Would you like a cup of tea or coffee?" Sarah asked, deciding that it would do no harm to get on the inspector's good side.

"Not just this minute," Brian said. "Maybe later."

He asked Sarah if he could see the toilets, and the cooking areas. As they went through the house, Brian made quite a display of making tick marks and circles in his official-looking notebook. And the more time they spent in the house, the more he complimented Sarah on the wonderful job she was doing. He said he could find absolutely no fault with any aspect of her work, and that he was sure his glowing report would give the house a clean bill of health. She might even be exempted for two years from further inspections, the place was obviously that well run.

"Well, thank you very much. I do my best, you know," said Sarah, feeling flattered and proud.

"I can see that. Now, one last thing. Would you mind if I had a quick look at some of the bedrooms?" He saw her frown slightly, and rushed to reassure her. "I know you're not responsible for whatever state the rooms might be in. I'm just spot checking for things like structural damage, making sure that window latches are all right, access to fire exits, that kind of thing. I wouldn't have to see all the rooms, just one or two. How about we start with this one here," he said, casually pointing to the door on his right. "Is the tenant in?"

They were back at the front part of the house. The door at which Brian had pointed was the entrance to Geoffrey Staines' room. He knew this because, from his vantage point parked outside the previous night, he had clearly seen Staines through the window. He was also well aware that Staines was not in the room, because he'd

seen him hobble off ten minutes before Brian had knocked on the
door.

"I guess it would be all right," Sarah said, somewhat reluctantly.
"Hold on, I've got a set of keys in my bag." She disappeared for just
a moment, returning with a large key ring. Each of the keys had a
small square of white adhesive tape stuck on, with the room
numbers clearly marked. It took just a few seconds to unlock the
door to Staines' little flat; it was unremarkable in every way. Brian
hadn't known what to expect. "What would the room of a child
killer look like?" he'd wondered to himself. Had he expected to find
an altar to Satan, complete with red candles and incense? Maybe
some blood on the walls, a dead sacrificial goat in the corner? What
he found instead was just an untidy room, completely ordinary in
every way.

Pretending to test the window latch, and making another tick mark
in his notebook, Brian turned to Sarah and innocently said, "Yeah,
look, I'm not going to find anything wrong, I can tell. You run a
great house — is it all right if I call you Sarah?" She nodded her
assent, blushing ever so slightly, self-consciously putting her hand to
her hair. She was quite sure Brian was flirting with her. "I'm just
about done here," continued Brian. "I don't suppose that offer of a
coffee is still open."

"How do you take it?" Sarah asked without hesitation. "And
would you maybe like a little slice of apple tart to go with it?" She
was in no hurry for Brian to leave.

"Milk and one sugar, but I'm going to have to pass on the tart,"
Brian said. He was eager to finish what he was doing and leave,
unsure as to how long Staines would be away. He was also cutting it
fine to get back to the office before 5:30. Noting Sarah's obvious
disappointment, he added, "I'll take a rain check on that tart. Next
time, ok?" knowing full well there would never be a next time.

"That would be nice," said Sarah, leaving the room to make the
coffee, and desperately hoping that there would be a next time.

The instant she'd left the room, Brian removed a plastic jar from the
pocket of his raincoat. He threw back the covers on Staines' bed, and

quickly removed the jar's lid. Holding it upside down over the mattress, he shook the contents out onto the sheet, tapping the bottom of the container to ensure everything came out. That done, he replaced the lid, rearranged the blanket and quilt much as he'd found them, and left the room, waiting in the corridor for Sarah to return.

She brought him his coffee in a fine bone china cup. Brian thanked her and took a sip. She had added way too much sugar, for some reason thinking he'd like it better that way. "Is it all right?" she asked.

"Perfect," Brian said. He choked down the remainder as quickly as he could, all the while making small, polite conversation. He hadn't done the lady any harm. To the contrary, he'd brightened her day considerably, albeit under false pretenses. For that, he felt a small pang of conscience. "These things have to be done," he thought silently.

By 5:15, Brian was back at his desk, dutifully awaiting the appointed going-home time. "Close any deals today?" asked Kevin Whyte as he walked past.

"No. But I think I set up a nice one."

While Brian was in Fit 'n Trim that evening, Staines was in Black Joe's, his new pub of choice. While Brian curled heavy dumbbells to his chest, Staines curled pints of lager to his mouth. When Brian finished his four-mile run at 9:30, Staines finished his eighth Miller. An hour later, Brian had polished off a small steak, green salad and small bottle of mineral water at Buckley's Restaurant. Staines had polished off a kebab and curried chips from Gino's Takeaway. By 11:30, both were ready for bed. Brian slept soundly; Staines slept heavily.

At 7:30 the following morning, having decided to forego his early morning workout, Brian woke to the sound of his alarm, feeling fresh even before he stepped into the shower, wondering what the day would bring. At about the same time, Geoffrey Staines was opening crusty, bloodshot eyes, hours earlier than he normally would.

He didn't feel fresh, though. He felt...uneasy. He felt ......
uncomfortable. No, it was worse than that. Staines itched all over.
He wondered dimly if his scabs were tightening, and he was dying
to scratch them. As the fog slowly lifted from his brain, he knew it
was more than that. He started to claw at his chest and arms, then
his thighs.

"What the...?" Staines said aloud, suddenly leaping from the bed.
Looking down, he could see that he was covered in dozens of red
welts, from his neck to his still hideous-looking feet. He turned back
towards the bed, pulling back the covers, and was disgusted when
he saw the telltale spots of blood, hundreds of them, staining the
sheets.

"Fucking fleas!" he said loudly. He'd been bitten by fleas before,
but where on those occasions he might have found three, four or five
bite marks, he couldn't begin to count the number on his body this
day. "There must have been an army of the little bastards," Staines
muttered, furiously jerking the sheets and blankets from the bed. He
knew that he would itch for many days, the discomfort multiplied by
revulsion and concern of infection. How they got into his bed, he
had no idea. He also knew that if he complained to the landlady,
she'd accuse him of having infected the building himself, so he made
an early decision to say nothing.

The irony was delicious. Brian had hoped that Staines would file a
complaint with Sarah Guilfoyle. He could imagine her furious
indignation, and her bitter words when she informed the greasy
tenant that only the day before, the Health Inspector-- a very nice
man-- had given the building a clean bill of health! What Staines
couldn't have possibly guessed was that the nice "health inspector"
had taken a fine comb, like that used to gently scrape cradle cap from
a baby's head, and run it meticulously through the coat of a friendly
spaniel dog he'd seen furiously scratching and nipping at himself in
the car park of his apartment building. Sure enough, Brian had
managed, after twenty minutes, to remove from the grateful dog's
coat, and secure in the plastic bottle, no less than twenty ravenous
fleas.

But Staines chose to say nothing. Instead, he wrapped all his bedclothes into a bundle, including the polyester quilt, and limped down to the launderette, selecting boil wash and using three times the normal amount of detergent. He sat for hours, as the sheets and duvet soaked and spun, rinsed and spun again, before going through two full cycles in the large industrial drier. He was utterly miserable, constantly scratching, trying not to, imagining flea bites even where there were none. He saw people looking at him, some shaking their heads, as he continually clawed his chest through his T-shirt, or rubbed the heel of his hand hard on the thighs of his jeans, trying desperately to alleviate the horrible itchiness that would go on and on and on. He stopped at the chemist on the way back to the bed sit and spent almost €30 on ointments for his tortured skin, tar-based shampoo for his hair, and a de-lousing powder for his mattress. He was becoming a regular at the pharmacy. Enough gauze bandages and antibiotic creams to patch up a small battalion, paracetamol tablets for pain, and Disprin, which he found an excellent hangover remedy, had all been purchased by Staines in the past fortnight. He was annoyed to find that not one of those items was covered by his medical card; his cash was dwindling much faster than he'd hoped. At the rate he was going, he'd have to start looking for work by September. To him, that meant cleaning windows, and in his current physical condition, he had about as much chance of climbing up and down a ladder as he did of becoming a jet pilot.

He limped back to the bed sit, noticing as he went through the front door that the landlady was humming to herself as she swept the wooden entryway floor. "Good afternoon, Mr. Staines," she said brightly. It was the first time she'd greeted him in such a manner, and Staines wondered what on earth she had to be so happy about. With no more than a nod as a reply, he went into his room, dumped his bundle of wash on the floor next to the single, velour-covered lounge chair in the corner, placed his bag of supplies from the chemist's on the small coffee table, and slumped into the chair. For several minutes, he stared at the wall, wondering why things were going so terribly badly. He could make no sense of any of it.

Geoffrey Staines didn't actually consider himself a bad person. He knew he'd done some not-nice things in his time, but he didn't think of himself as some monster.

The reasoning behind the bizarre attack was still a mystery to him. Try as he might, he couldn't match a name or a face with anyone who might want to inflict the kind of pain to which he'd been subjected. Every step he took, every time he sat down, any time he rolled over in his bed during the night, caused him to wince with pain. Granted, nothing had been broken, and no infection had set into the horrible, raw wounds. But why would anyone want to torture him with sandpaper? Why not just kick him around, beat him with a baseball bat, even kneecap him? He would have found any of those things preferable to what had happened at the cottage. What he didn't realise was that, precisely because he'd have chosen those other punishments, given the option, his attacker had taken the chosen course. There was also the danger that a severe beating involving broken bones, smashed kneecaps, or bullets, would certainly have attracted far more attention from the police.

And now he had an infestation of fleas? He knew (or thought he knew) that the two were unrelated — one a sick, deliberate act of horrible cruelty, performed by a psychotic sadist -- the fleas just some freak of bad luck. Looking up at the ceiling, he sighed, "I guess someone up there just doesn't like me."

It would have been more accurate to say, 'out there.'

TWENTY-THREE

On Wednesday, June 26th, just a day more than two weeks since
Staines had walked out of his prison cell a free man, he reported to
Bray Garda Station, as required under the terms of his early release,
for the second time. He was not at all overjoyed to see the long
figure of Liam Shortt in the same chair he'd occupied on Staines' last
visit, and Shortt wasn't particularly pleased to be there, either. The
young policeman actually preferred night duty. Usually, it was
quieter, except for Friday and Saturday nights; he got extra money
for shift work, and he could work on his golf game during the hours
when most "normal" people were at their 9-to-5 jobs.

Shortt looked up from his desk, instantly remembering the balding,
weasel-like man across the counter. "Ah, look who it is," he said,
feigning pleasure at seeing his unexpected visitor. "Don't tell me.
Let me guess. Today you were set upon by Spiderman! Am I right?"

"I'm just here to sign on," Staines grumbled. He had no appetite
for an argument, especially with the giant in blue who was openly
mocking him.

"What?" Shortt pretended to be shocked. "Nothing at all to report?
Maybe Barney the Dinosaur trying to steal your bicycle, or Big Bird
making lewd, unsolicited advances? Come on, man, give us
something to protect you from — we've damn all else to do, don't you
know! How are the scratched knuckles, by the way?" He had an
excellent head for remembering details.

"Can I just please sign the book and go?" Staines wouldn't rise to the bait that Shortt was deliberately dangling before him. He scratched his neck, then his chest and under his armpit.

"You got the mange or something?" Shortt enquired. "Desperate dose, that, but it might help if you could use your back legs to scratch behind your ears."

"Flea bites, if you must know, and I probably picked up the damn things in here," Staines answered angrily, knowing full well he should just keep his mouth shut.

"Fleas?" Shortt chuckled. "Hey, do you want me to file a report that you've been assaulted by them? We could put out an all-points bulletin. Keep an eye open for any suspicious-looking fleas. I suppose we could put pictures up in the Post Office. You couldn't give me a decent description this time, could you?"

"Oh, you are hilarious — a real comedian," Staines jeered. "Why don't you join the travelling circus and become a fuc......," he saw Shortt's warning look, and remembered his previous threats regarding the use of foul language, so he quickly amended his sentence. "......become a clown, then loads of people could laugh at you all at once, instead of one at a time, like now."

Shortt could take insults as well as he could dish them out, but after reading the file on Staines, he had nothing but contempt for the man, and he certainly wouldn't accept any abuse from him.

"Why don't you sign your name here and go," Shortt said, and now there was no humour in his voice, "before you have a nasty accident. You wouldn't want to slip on that freshly-mopped tiled floor and fall head first through the glass door, would you?" He was truly menacing. Looking around, Staines saw the floor hadn't been mopped at all, but knew that wasn't the way the story would pan out if he didn't heed the garda's thinly- veiled threat. He signed and dated the book to prove that he had indeed attended the station on the requisite day, then turned and limped towards the door.

Shortt put on his best J.R. Ewing accent. He'd grown up watching
"Dallas," and was devastated when it had gone off the air. "Y'all
have a real nice day now, y'hear!"

As he watched Staines go, Shortt remembered the conversation
he'd had with Detective McCann six days previously. Thinking
back, there'd been something odd about the call. After all, McCann
had been the officer who arrested Staines for the murder of that little
boy. Surely he would know just about everything there was to know
about the killer. Yet when they had spoken, it had been McCann
who had been pumping him for information, not the other way
around, and he'd never said why. "What can you tell me about
Geoffrey Staines?" Shortt remembered him asking. Now Shortt
wondered why. He hadn't thought anything of it at the time. He'd
been too tied up in his golf game.

Picking up the phone, he dialled from memory the number for
Shankill Station. Asking for Detective McCann, he was put on hold
for a matter of seconds, then "McCann here," came down the line.

"Liam Shortt here. Listen, I've just had your friend Staines in with
me again, and I remembered our little chat last week."

"Yeah, I remember," McCann answered, already grinning as he
recalled some of the conversation. "Did you hear we had the sub-
aqua team out at Kilternan, looking for a 'Wilson' family? We had a
tip they might be found somewhere to the left of the seventh fairway.
Never found a sign of them, but we did recover two
Dunlops......and a Titleist!"

"Well done," said Shortt good-naturedly. "The two Dunlops both
have to be mine; I get them cheap every time I buy petrol, but I
couldn't afford Titleist golf balls on my salary."

"Right. Now, how can I help you, Liam?"

"I was just wondering what led you to call me. Why the interest?"
Shortt wasn't implying or insinuating anything, McCann knew, and
he answered as honestly as he could.

"Well, first of all, I didn't know he'd been released. It came as a bit of a shock. But something didn't sit right with me when I read your report."

"How so?" Shortt was genuinely interested.

"The man's just out of prison. What's he got to gain by calling attention to himself with some cock-and-bull story about being attacked? He'd have more luck finding sympathy in the dictionary than any garda station."

"And you don't buy my suspicions about him covering up a weekend of debauchery to buy favour with his lady?" Shortt asked.

"It would surprise me, to be honest. He had no one--no friends, family, and certainly no wife or girlfriend — to testify for him at his trial. He's a lone wolf. I can't imagine him finding true love in the 'Joy,' or in the short time he would have had after getting out, though I suppose stranger things have happened."

"You can say that again," Shortt replied, not yet ready to abandon his theory. "Look at that Paul Hill fella. He met and married a Kennedy, for crying out loud, from inside a prison. Mind you, Staines is even uglier than Hill was!"

McCann let out a little chuckle, and then became serious again. "It doesn't add up. None of it does. Let's say he was attacked, for the sake of argument. The most likely candidate to carry it out would have been someone from inside, right? Why? Money? Drug deal gone bad? Whatever it is, Staines' hands couldn't be whiter than white. Any ex-con I ever met would have just taken their beating and crawled back into a hole to lick their wounds. And then I was kind of wondering why anyone would make up a story that ridiculous in the first place; he must have known that kite wouldn't fly. Kidnap, torture, release and recapture, come on!"

"So what are you driving at?"

"That's just it. I keep kicking it around, but getting nowhere. Listen, you still on for that golf game we talked about?"

"Always," Shortt answered instantly. "When?"

"How about this evening? You're finishing at six, right? Well, it's staying light enough to play until at least 10:30 these days. We could meet at Kilternan and come damn close to getting in eighteen holes. And maybe we can come up with some answers between us while we're at it."

"Done, but unless you spend a lot of your time in the rough, we probably won't see a whole lot of each other."

"I'll risk it," McCann laughed. See you there.

At the appointed time, the two men met face to face for the first time. They exchanged pleasantries, paid their green fees, and made their way to the first tee. Hole number one at Kilternan is a straightforward, relatively short par four, with a wide fairway all the way to the green, which is protected only by a single bunker on the left side. As the "visitor," McCann accepted the honour, opting to use a three wood as opposed to a driver. The hole measured only 335 yards; he didn't need a huge first shot. Something straight was more important. After loosening up with two practice swings, he addressed the ball, drew the club slowly back, and was satisfied to hear the resounding crack as his Top-Flite took off like a miniature scud missile.

"Nice shot," Shortt acknowledged, as McCann's ball landed on the left-centre of the fairway, some 240 yards from the tee. He then took out his own driver, a standard-length club that had definitely not been designed for a man of Shortt's considerable height. Standing awkwardly, far too bent over, Shortt took an almighty swing, using all arms and no technique. The ball started in the same direction as McCann's, before suddenly slicing wickedly off to the right, and disappearing into three-inch rough when it came down.

"Yup," said Shortt resignedly. "Normal service has been resumed, ladies and gentlemen!"

McCann's second shot was too strong, flying over the green and landing off the back. He chipped on, the ball rolling to within ten feet of the flag. Two putts gave him a bogey five—a satisfactory start for an 18-handicapper. Shortt took a nine, and that didn't take into account the ball he'd lost into even deeper rough with his second shot. "Why do I love this game?" Shortt moaned. "To think, I pay good, hard-earned cash to do this to myself on a frequent basis! I'm a sick, sick man."

As the game progressed, it became clear that Shortt's game wasn't going to improve much. Three times, through a combination of a favourable, trailing breeze, and pure, blind luck, the younger man hit "monster shots," straight and unbelievably long. "That's what keeps me coming back," he admitted after a 320-yard, laser straight drive. "That's the shot I'll see when I close my eyes tonight, not the two I dumped in the lake on that last par three."

"So what have you come up with since this morning?" Shortt asked out of the blue as he lined up a putt on the third green.

"Not much," McCann admitted. "You?"

"Well, I have been thinking about what you were saying, and I did come up with one idea. Staines was put away for killing that young boy, Sykes, right? Maybe the boy's family are having a go. You couldn't really blame them, could you?"

McCann thought this over, then shook his head. It was something he had momentarily considered himself. "No, it still doesn't fit. I went to check up on the family about a year after the funeral. They took the whole thing badly, naturally enough. First the murder, then the light sentence, it was a really bad scene. I remember the father, Brian, had a right go at the judge at the end of the trial. Between you and me, I agreed with most of what he said. Anyway, I found out they'd split up right after the funeral; sold the house, and sometime after that, I heard the mother had moved back to the midlands."

"What about the father?"

"Brian's still in Dublin someplace, I think." McCann paused, thinking back, remembering the fire in Brian's eyes, and the look of pure hatred on his face when he'd tried to attack Staines. Again, though, he shook his head. "No, Brian might have it in him to run the guy over with his car, or even take him on with his bare hands; he can be pretty intense. But three days of torture out in the middle of nowhere? He's basically a civilised guy, and hey, we still don't know for sure that Staines was actually attacked, do we?"

"No, but if he was, maybe this Brian guy hired someone to do the job for him," Shortt offered.

"I don't know…maybe. But it still doesn't feel right, you know? How many hired muscle men do you know of who would work someone over for three days, without breaking any bones, and then give the guy a lift home? A good, sound beating is one thing. What Staines described to you, if it's true, was personal."

"Well, you don't get much more personal than killing someone's kid, do you?" Shortt said matter-of-factly. "And that brings you back to the father."

"Yeah, I guess it does."

They finished their round just as the approaching dusk was making it difficult to track the flight of the golf balls, especially in Liam Shortt's case. McCann declined the offer of a pint. "Thanks, though. We'll have to do it again," he said as he loaded his golf bag and shoes into the boot of his new Toyota Camry.

"I'll try to give you a better game next time," Shortt said, then, thinking out loud said, "Who am I kidding? No, I won't. My game will still be rubbish the next time we play, I know it will. Hope I didn't hold you up too much," he apologised, referring to the amount of time they'd spent in the rough looking for balls after another of his wayward shots.

"Not at all. Seriously, I enjoyed it."

"God, wouldn't it be lovely to be able to say that after a round of golf, and actually mean it?" Shortt said.

Laughing, McCann got into his car, and with a wave and a beep of the horn, exited the car park. As he drove, he considered the discussion he'd had with Shortt. Without waiting till he got back to either the station or his apartment, he suddenly pulled the Toyota over to the side of the road, and took his notepad out of the glove compartment. In short sentences, the detective outlined and summarised everything he knew about the events surrounding Geoffrey Staines' complaint. It didn't take long, but writing it all down helped McCann, as it had through his whole career, get a clearer picture, a sharper focus, a better understanding of the mystery unfolding before him. Rather than have twenty or thirty thoughts flying around inside his brain, bumping into each other and making a muddle of everything, committing those individual thoughts to paper brought an order, a sense of structure, on which he could build various theories. If the structure wasn't strong enough to support that theory, he could easily tear it down and begin again. But the foundation and the building blocks remained until, eventually, inevitably, he fit them together into something so solid it couldn't easily be torn down. This method had worked for him time and again. It was working now.

   After twenty minutes of writing, studying, thinking, then writing some more, McCann finally closed his notepad and locked it away. As always, no one else would ever see the things he'd just written. He checked his rearview mirror, flicked on the right turn signal, and pulled easily back out into mercifully light traffic. As he drove, he suddenly gave voice to what was now seriously worrying him.

   "Damn it, Brian, what are you getting yourself into?"

TWENTY-FOUR

Sarah Guilfoyle was an emotional wreck. She had been trying to talk herself out of making the phone call since the notion had first come into her head. It couldn't be helped, she finally admitted to no one in particular. She had what amounted to a schoolgirl crush on the handsome health inspector. He had just been so darned nice, and he had hinted that he wanted to see her again, she reasoned. Wasn't it he who had asked for a "rain check" when she'd offered him the apple tart? In her own mind, Sarah had turned that polite rejection into a promise that he'd be back to see her, and not because he was fond of apple tart.

Her plan was to phone the department where he worked, and ask him for a copy of his report, for her own files. She would then suggest that maybe he'd like to bring it by personally, and take advantage of her earlier offer of something sweet. Simple! And not too forward, she told herself, depending on how she delivered the word 'sweet.' She imagined the conversation they'd have over and over again, carefully reciting her responses to virtually anything he might say to her, laughing coyly at just the right times, pretending to be cross that he hadn't returned sooner. By the time she picked up the phone, she'd totally convinced herself that he was just too shy for his own good, and that he was probably dying to call back, but unable to bring himself to take the plunge.

Having finally steeled her nerves enough to dial the number she'd found in the green pages at the front of the phone book, Sarah was mortally disappointed when she was told that there was no Brian Fitzgerald at that number. "Well, could you by any chance tell me where he's based then?" she asked the lady at the other end of the phone.

"No, I'm sorry, I ..."

"Why not?" Sarah interrupted impatiently. "Don't you even have a list of contact numbers for each of your inspectors? I mean, what if it was an emergency or something?"

"If you'd be good enough to let me finish," came back the unseen voice, now distinctly cooler, "I'm trying to tell you that there is no Brian Fitzgerald working in this division."

"You must be mistaken," Sarah said, concern rising up slowly at the back of her mind. "Maybe he's new, or is it possible he's attached to one of the other health boards?"

"Not if he's carrying out inspections in this area. If you'll hold, I'll just check the complete listing to see if he's attached to another service. But you're saying he told you he was a health inspector?"

"He showed me his ID," Sarah said, now genuinely worried.

"Please hold a moment." After what seemed a half-day, but which in reality was less than two minutes, the health board lady came back on the line. "I'm sorry, but there are no Brian Fitzgeralds at all working with the Eastern Health Board, and I've also checked the listing of health inspectors in other regions, just in case someone got transferred or something. Nothing."

"But, he was here...he..." Sarah struggled mightily to find something intelligent to say.

"I'm sorry I couldn't have been more help," but the lady didn't sound sorry at all as she hung up before Sarah could reply.

Dropping the phone back into its cradle, she immediately ran from room to room, trying to think what in the world a bogus health inspector would want to steal from a house full of bed sits. She checked the imitation paintings were still in place on the hall walls. They were, and the inexpensive ornaments dotted here and there around the building appeared not to have been touched. She even checked her handbag, counting the money in her purse.

"But I was with him the whole time," she said aloud, then instantly remembered going for the coffee. She'd left him in that Staines fellow's room, and when she'd come back, he'd been waiting out in the hallway.

What to do? She didn't really want to upset Staines unnecessarily, by suggesting he might have been robbed. What purpose would that serve? If anything had been taken, surely he would have reported it to her by now. She was being only half-truthful with herself. Had she been honest, she would have admitted she was loathe to reveal to a tenant that she had allowed a stranger into his room without his prior knowledge or consent. What had she been thinking?!?

Then she moved on to the next set of questions in her mind. If robbery wasn't the motive, what was? Had he been "casing" the place, checking it during daylight hours to see where anything valuable might be kept? That was plausible. He'd seen virtually the entire house. Or was it something more sinister? Maybe he was some pervert, and he'd wanted to check the windows and doors so he could find an easy way to break in during some dark night, after which he could stalk the house, looking for her or some other unfortunate woman. Again, this seemed like a very realistic explanation to poor Sarah. She even put her hand to her mouth and gasped when she remembered how he'd checked the window latch in Staines' room.

"Checking for fire exits, my ass!" she said loudly. "Dirty bastard!" she continued, not even recognising the ease with which, in her mind, he'd gone from a shy, handsome, tart-loving civil servant one minute to an evil, skulking burglar-cum-rapist the next.

She decided on her next move at once. Going back to the hallway, she found the number she wanted on the sheet of "Emergency Listings" she kept blu-tacked on the wall next to the phone. Her face now flushed with temper as opposed to imagined potential passion, she rang the Bray Garda Station.

"I want to file a complaint," she said to the garda who answered the phone.

"And what's the nature of that complaint?" asked Liam Shortt, taking out a pen and paper.

Fifteen minutes later, Shortt was knocking on the door of No. 279, and Sarah Guilfoyle instantly ushered him in. As accurately as she could, she repeated the events of the day the bogus health inspector had called to her door, emphasising that she had asked him for ID before letting him in.

"I could tell right off there was something fishy about him," she sniffed.

After getting a very detailed description of "Mr. Fitzgerald," Shortt asked Sarah what, if anything, had been taken from the house, or if any of the residents had reported personal items of clothing, jewellery or money missing. He received negative responses on both counts.

Shortt then asked Sarah to show him around the rooms that she knew for certain this Brian Fitzgerald had been in, so she took him on the same circuit of toilet and shower areas, kitchen facilities and common hallways and corridors. When they'd finished the tour, Shortt asked the next, obvious question, "Do you know whether he was in any of the bedrooms?"

Sarah flushed again, cursing her own gullibility. She still felt uncomfortable with the fact that she had given a strange man access, unsupervised at that, to what was really a private room. But she wasn't going to lie to the policeman. "Just one," she admitted, waiting for an admonishment that never came.

"And which one would that be?" Shortt asked, still taking notes. When Sarah pointed at the door towards the front of the house, Shortt could never in a million years have anticipated the answer to his next question. "Whose room is that?"

"A new man," Sarah replied, "and he's only been here a couple of weeks. His name is Staines. Geoffrey Staines. Does he have to know about this, Garda?"

Struggling desperately to hide the shock he felt, Shortt shook his head. "No, not unless you think you should tell him, but he won't be hearing it from me...us...I mean the gardai."

"Are you all right, Garda?" Sarah asked, noticing how flustered the policeman suddenly appeared.

"Yes. I'm fine, thanks. But if there's nothing more, I really should be getting back to the station."

"But what are you going to do about it?" Sarah demanded to know. "I'm not sure I feel safe here anymore."

"We'll check it out, and in the meantime, I'll put in a request for a squad car to drive past this building at regular intervals during the night. If you see this man again, contact us immediately, but don't approach him yourself."

"Don't worry about that," Sarah said sharply. "It is my dearest hope that I never see that dirty little liar again!"

The instant he arrived back at the station, Shortt grabbed the phone and dialled McCann's mobile number, which he'd now committed to memory.

"Mick, it's Liam." The two had no further need of formalities. "You're not going to believe what's just happened. Well, it happened a couple of days ago, but I only just found out about it." Giving every detail of his conversation with Sarah, Shortt waited until the very last instant to deliver the punchline. It hit the mark.

"You're not serious," McCann said, genuinely stunned.

"Serious as a heart attack. Crazy, isn't it? What do you make of it? This Staines fellow seems to be popping up, one way or another, all over the place."

Shortt hadn't made the same connection that McCann already had, but the detective asked his younger colleague for a detailed description of this—hold everything!—"What did you say this inspector's name was?" he asked.

"Fitzgerald. Brian Fitzgerald. Except that's not his real name. Are you with me on this, Mick? You sound like your head's someplace else."

"Yeah, I'm with you all right. Brian, huh? Go ahead, give me that description again, would you please." When Shortt had finished, McCann said simply, "Sounds like someone I know, or, more to the point, someone I used to know."

"Really?" Shortt was surprised. He didn't have the benefit of remembering the name of the dead boy's father, which had at most been mentioned twice, when they'd had their earlier conversation on the golf course. "You think you might know the guy? Who is he, some con artist swindling widows out of their pension books?"

McCann saw no reason not to let his new friend and colleague in on his suspicions. After he'd done so, there was silence for a moment, then Shortt asked the simple question that only had complex answers, none of which McCann wanted to deal with, not yet, anyway. "What are you going to do about it, Mick?"

"I haven't got a clue," McCann admitted.

"You going to arrest him?"

"For what? Did this lady sign a formal complaint?"

"No," Shortt admitted, "but I think she would if we asked her to."

"Would you mind holding off on that for a few days? I'm not trying to put you on the spot. I just want to see where this thing is going, and try to head it off before it gets worse."

"No problem," Shortt replied. "You really think this Brian Fitzgerald was Brian Sykes?"

"I'm sure of it. The description you give fits him to a T. The age is right, hair colouring, height, build, professional appearance, the lot."

"What do you think he was hoping to find in Staines' room?"

"That one I haven't worked out," McCann admitted.

"Maybe he was hoping to find Staines himself there?" Shortt speculated.

"I doubt it. He obviously knows where Staines lives, and there's no reason he'd willingly involve any person who didn't have a part in his son's murder, and there was no one else. No, he could confront Staines any time, and anywhere he wants. It was something in the room he was after. I'd bet on it."

"What about this weekend of terror Staines reported to us? You think Sykes was involved, don't you?"

"I think there's a damn good chance of it, but we don't have anything like enough to arrest him for it, not even on grounds of suspicion." Deep down, McCann didn't want to arrest Brian, regardless, but he didn't admit this to Shortt.

"Weird," was Shortt's only comment.

McCann's response was equally brief. "Very."

With no small amount of reluctance, McCann called the file on 'Sykes, Brian,' up from his computer's database. He dialled the number listed behind "Last Known Place of Employment," and waited.

"Business Solutions Ireland, how may I help you?" came Carol's singsong voice.

McCann identified himself, doing his best to sound as casual as possible. He told Carol he was just making a follow-up enquiry, tying up loose ends as it were, and that he needed to speak with Brian Sykes. He explained that their records had given this listing as the last contact number, and asked if Carol by any chance knew where Brian was working at present.

"Mr. Sykes is still with us," she said, trying to maintain a balance of friendliness and professionalism. "He's not in right now, but I expect him back around five. Would you like to leave a message, or can I ask him to phone you?"

"Umm, there's no need." McCann made his decision there and then. "I'll pop around to see him. If I can't make it by — you close at 5:30? — I can catch up with him later. Look, do me a favour, don't upset him by telling him he's going to get a visit from the big, bad wolf. It's not like that — really--nothing to worry about, ok?"

"Yes, I suppose that's all right," Carol said after a moment's hesitation. She decided she wouldn't say anything to Brian. She might, however, have something interesting to tell the M.D. that night.

TWENTY-FIVE

The knock on the apartment door surprised Brian. He never had visitors, and it wasn't his birthday, so whoever was at the door, it wouldn't be Adam or Conor; the latter was still in Boston. Brian hadn't heard from him since Christmas, when he'd gotten a card containing a photo of his youngest brother, sitting in a Norman Rockwell-style setting, in front of a roaring log fire, beautifully decorated tree to the left, with his American wife and six-month-old daughter, Shania. Brian had chuckled when he'd been told the name with which the baby had been christened, Shania Nordberg-Sykes. Conor's wife had insisted on appending her maiden name, via the hyphen, to the married one, and had now passed the hybrid version on to her offspring. "Only in America," thought Brian, shaking his head.

Walking to the door, dressed in T-shirt and tracksuit bottoms, Brian decided that it was probably some poor door-to-door salesman knocking. It happened from time to time; usually ambitious young men operating under the delusion that they would make huge commissions if they only sold two sets of home encyclopaedias per night, or a half dozen sets of indestructible cookware per week, or just four life-insurance-with-no-medical-required policies per month. Brian was always polite to them, even though they were calling to his door uninvited. He'd been in sales a long time, and knew what a difficult career it could be, even in a relatively secure, salaried job like the one he was in at Office Solutions. Working unsociable hours, for commission only, trying to sell people things they mostly didn't want, could be soul destroying. So what Brian usually did was tell

the salesman that, whatever it was they were offering, he wouldn't
be buying, but that if they wanted to come inside for a cup of coffee,
he would let them practice their "pitch" on him. That way, they
weren't under any illusions, and Brian didn't have to feel guilty
about sending them away empty-handed.

Tonight, though, he was genuinely on his way out; he wanted to
get to Fit 'n Trim, and it was already nearly 6:30. So whoever it was,
they'd have to either call back in four hours, or forget it. He opened
the door, and the words were already halfway out of his mouth,
"Sorry, I'm just leaving...." He didn't finish the sentence.

"Hello, Brian."

"Hello, Detective." Now this was a surprise. Brian's mind was
racing furiously behind the impassive eyes with which he faced the
man he hadn't seen since that last day in court. He was in no doubt
as to why McCann was there. What he was grappling with was *how*
he came to be there. What had Brian done, or not done, to cover his
tracks? He was certain that Staines hadn't identified him to the
police and he'd left no paper trail, no evidence of any kind that he
could think of. This had to be a "fishing expedition." He decided to
brazen it out.

"Can I come in?"

"Sure," said Brian calmly. "Long time no see." They moved into
the small sitting room, and Brian motioned for the policeman to take
a seat in the comfortable lounge chair; Brian sat on the sofa opposite.
"So, how have you been?"

"Not bad, but Brian, we both know this isn't a social call," McCann
said, with no edge to his voice. "Though, I've got to say, you're
looking...fit."

It was an understatement. McCann was seeing what Brian's
customers and work colleagues never did. The tight-fitting T-shirt
revealed an almost super-human physique. Muscles rippled and
bulged, threatening to burst the cotton material covering Brian's
biceps and chest. Almost self-consciously, Brian threw on the
tracksuit top he'd had in his hand when he opened the door.

"Thanks," said Brian, "but it's not a crime to work out every now and then, is it? Or are you here because I forgot to pay my club subscription on time? That's a bit of a step down for you, isn't it, Detective?" The sarcasm was evident, though not yet openly hostile. McCann was saddened that they'd gotten off to such a bad start, particularly given the direction he knew their conversation was going to be heading.

"Listen, 'Detective' is a bit too formal for me, Brian," McCann was trying to take the heat out of the situation. "Call me Michael, or Mick, if you like."

"You mean like your friends do?" Brian asked. "But we're not friends. Detective."

McCann was disappointed, but wouldn't be dissuaded. "Have it your own way." Then he decided to make one last attempt to win Brian over. "I'm on your side, you know."

"Really? How's that, then?" Before McCann could even answer, Brian continued, his temper rising as quickly and ferociously as a sudden brush fire. "Let me tell you something. No one is on my side. No one! Not you. Not that judge, and certainly not those assholes in Justice that decided to set a child killer loose after not much more than a wet weekend behind bars!"

"What's that got to do with me?" McCann said, spreading his hands out at his sides. "I tried to do my job, to help you and your wife, and…"

"Well then, you did a pretty lousy job, didn't you?" Brian interrupted fiercely. "Help me? If you wanted to help me, you should have held down that scumbag while I smashed his sick head in, instead of pulling me off him! What do you want? What are you here for? Thanks from me? Forgiveness? Sorry, I'm fresh out. I'll tell you what. Go ask my son!"

McCann had no answer to that. The words had hurt him deeply, not least because he couldn't really argue with any of them. He'd pulled this man off the drug addict that had killed his little boy, because it would have been illegal not to, and because he'd have put his own career in jeopardy had he not done so. Many times since, though, he'd said to himself, "It was the correct thing to do, but was it the *right* thing to do?"

Now he looked at the angry man opposite him, and tried to take a different tack. "Have you been playing health inspector, Brian?"

"I don't know what you're talking about. I've been at work every day. You can check."

"That's good. I will check, since you mention it. So you wouldn't mind if I introduced you to a Sarah Guilfoyle then?" McCann probed.

"Who might she be?" Brian asked, feeling the trap's noose tightening rapidly. He wondered how in the hell they could ever have come to suspect him.

"She's the lady who looks after Geoffrey Staines' building. She got a visit from some bogus health inspector, and filed a complaint. She gave a really detailed description, which, I've got to say, matches you perfectly."

"Come off it," Brian blustered. "There must be hundreds, thousands of guys, that match my description."

"True," McCann conceded. "And guess what. This guy even used the name Brian. Brian Fitzgerald. If I'm not mistaken, isn't Fitzgerald your wife's maiden name?" McCann knew this to be so. It was all in the files.

"So?"

"Nothing, just bringing it up as a strange coincidence. Anyway, this can all be sorted out quickly. I'll just arrange a brief meeting between Ms. Guilfoyle and yourself at Bray Station. It won't take more than five minutes of your time, and we can eliminate you from our enquiries into this little matter." McCann could see from his face that Brian was beaten.

"Am I under arrest?"

"Maybe that won't be necessary. Nothing was taken; it appears no harm was done." Then it was McCann's turn to become fierce. "Damn it, Brian! What were you thinking?"

Brian looked back at McCann with eyes that suddenly turned as cold as steel. "I'm thinking I should have ended this when I had the chance."

"Bad idea, Brian, that's a really, really bad idea," McCann said forcefully. Now that he had Brian talking, he was determined to get more answers. He decided to use a little bluff of his own. "What do you mean, 'when I had the chance?' You mean a couple of weeks ago, don't you? Where did you take him? Where did you take Staines for those few days?"

"I didn't…I haven't seen him…been near him," Brian was now totally unsure how much information the detective had, and no idea in the world where he'd obtained it all.

"Yes, you did. Little place out in the country. Sounds like it was some picnic all right. We know all about it, taking him from outside Sullivan's, dumping him back there early Monday morning…" McCann was staring hard at Brian's face, looking for telltale signs, using the little bits of information he had in the hope that Brian might crack and own up to everything. But Brian wasn't ready to give in—not yet.

"I'm telling you, I haven't seen the creep. I was going to confront him at the bedsit," he lied. "I don't know what I'd have done if he'd been there. Probably nothing. You know how it is?"

The detective wasn't convinced. "Brian, you're playing with fire here. You don't know what you're getting yourself into." He spoke softly then, "We both know exactly what that man is capable of."

Sparks now flew from Brian's eyes. "What do you mean? You think I should be afraid of him? That little weasel? Take a really good look at me, Detective. I'm not eight years old—I don't think I'm his type. God, I wish I were. It would suit me nicely if Geoffrey Staines decided to come after me. I could break his back over my knee and plead self-defense."

"You can't go after him, Brian," McCann warned.

"Why not?" Brian snapped back. "Because I might get caught? Hey, here's an idea. I'll kill Staines, then get totally tanked up on booze and drugs. I'll get some slick, mouthpiece lawyer to tell a dozy judge that I was out of my brains at the time of the alleged crime. With a bit of luck, I'll be sentenced to two weeks in a home for the bewildered!"

"I'm going to do you a favour, and pretend I didn't hear any of that," McCann said gravely.

"Oh, right, you're doing me a favour. Gee, thanks for all your help," Brian mocked, pure venom dripping from each word.

"I didn't come here tonight to argue with you," McCann said evenly, then more pointedly, and looking Brian directly in the eye, "and I didn't come here to arrest you, but I could have."

That took a lot of wind out of Brian's sails. He deflated quickly, knowing that what McCann said was true. "What did you come here for...really?" he asked.

"To warn you off, to try and talk sense to you," McCann said earnestly. "Whatever you're planning, Brian, please man, give it up! Whether you believe me or not, I understand how you feel; I'm incredibly sorry for what's happened. It's over; it has to be over. Let it go and move on. It might not feel like it right now, but you've got to trust me that it's for the best."

"A man's gotta do what a man's gotta do," Brian said quietly.

"And you're forgetting one thing," came McCann's instant response. "I've got a job to do, too, regardless of my personal feelings. It doesn't matter that I think Staines should have been strung up for what he did. You and I don't get to make those choices. Maybe that's just as well. But like it or not, I've got to follow the laws as they're laid out, no matter how faulty they seem. I'm asking you now, please, don't put me in a position where I have to stop you from crossing the line."

Brian looked straight at him. "And if I do?" he asked.

"Then I'm telling you, I'll have to bring you down, even if it sickens me." McCann rose and headed for the door. As he reached it, he turned back and said, "I've got to live with myself, too, Brian." Then he was gone.

TWENTY-SIX

The first weekend in July finally brought the warm weather that had been so long awaited. People in their tens of thousands left the Dublin area — cars, minivans, motorcycles, jeeps — anything with wheels took to the roads, south to the beautiful silver sands of Brittas Bay, north to the lakes of Cavan, or west to the beaches and nightlife of Salthill in Galway. From early Friday afternoon, when it became apparent that the sun would burn hot and bright for at least the next few days, through lunchtime on Saturday, the highways, motorways and side roads were bumper to bumper with traffic, most of it made up of people who were just desperate to get away from bumper to bumper traffic.

Geoffrey Staines had no such plans, not to mention the fact that he also had no wheels with which he could transport himself to some seaside resort. His old Micra was long gone, scrapped while he'd been in Mountjoy. He actually missed the little motor and supposed that he might one day buy another, similar model. He had no idea where the money would come from, because he still had no job, nor any inclination to start working again. Reluctantly, he forced himself to set aside enough of the money he still had to go out and buy an extension ladder, bucket, squeegie and sponge when the time came that he could no longer avoid going back to work. A notice on the Superquinn message board would bring him enough cash jobs to keep him in the bedsit, and provide food and drink, and maybe the odd recreational "substance."

Of the latter, he'd found a regular, reliable supplier who frequented the Dart stations between Bray and Booterstown. The dealer called himself "Squeak." Staines knew of no reason why, except that it was a nickname he'd probably picked up as a kid, and which had just stuck to him when he moved into adulthood. Staines didn't care what he called himself; Squeak supplied pretty good stuff, and kept his prices reasonable.

Making his way along Quinsboro Road, Staines decided to see if Squeak was at the Bray train station. He thought maybe he'd have a little party that night—a party for one. He checked his wallet, deciding just what he'd splash out on, and how much he was willing to splurge. Carefully counting the notes, he calculated their value in "real money," as in pounds and pence. The single European currency, the euro, only came into use the month after he was sent down, and he still wasn't used to the red tenners, blue twenties, and brown half-tons. "Fifty of...these things," Staines muttered to himself as he walked, head down, towards the station. "Is that about forty quid? Or is it sixty? Damn this monopoly money!"

"Hello, Geoffrey."

Staines had been so busy concentrating he hadn't heard the man with the friendly voice come up behind him. "Damn, man, don't scare me like that," Staines said, laughing as he turned to see which of his few acquaintances had got the drop on him. He supposed it must be one of the barmen from Black Joe's. But the smile on his face froze when he looked up and realized that he did not know the man who had addressed him. Dressed in casual slacks, a short-sleeved shirt and a baseball cap, he could have been anyone—but no one that Staines recognised.

"Sorry, but how do you know my name?" Staines asked.

"We went to school together." This man was definitely not an old school pal. Staines had given up on education at fourteen, and even then, he had no real friends. Besides, this guy had the air about him of someone who had gone to school in Blackrock, or Foxrock, or one of those other 'Rocks--posh schools for kids with well-off parents.

"I don't think so," Staines said, turning to move away.

"Sure we did. Medical school—don't you remember? It only seems like, well, like last month," Brian said, moving closer.

"Medical school?" Staines snorted. "Man, whatever it is you're on, I wish I could afford to get me some." He didn't like the look in the man's eyes, and he became uneasy, turning again to walk off.

"Come on, you must remember! We were studying to be anaesthetists."

"To be what? Astronauts?" Staines hadn't a particularly wide vocabulary.

"No, anaesthetists. You know. They knock people out before an operation. You let me practice on you, a couple of times."

The penny dropped, and Staines felt his stomach lurch. In spite of the warm summer sun, he started to shiver, but tried to pretend he still didn't know what Brian was on about.

"You've got me confused with someone else, so if you don't mind, I'm on my way to meet a friend," he said, trying to sound dismissive.

"Maybe you're right," Brian said coolly, but he'd noticed the light of recognition dawning in Staines' eyes. "Maybe it wasn't medical school. Could it have been the technical college then?" Staines just shook his head, confused and frightened. "That's it, woodwork class! Aw, come on, you must remember! I know it wasn't much fun, in fact it was pretty hard work. All that sawing and hammering— *sanding and stuff!* God it was really torture, wasn't it?"

Staines wanted to run more than he'd ever wanted anything that he could remember, but he knew it was pointless. His injured feet and ankles had finally started to heal, but he remembered his doomed escape attempt, and the ease with which he'd been caught on the dark road that night. Running now was pointless, and looking at the man's biceps straining against the short sleeves of his shirt, a pre-emptive strike didn't seem like such a great idea, either.

"What do you want, you psycho?" Staines voice was close to a whimper.

"Oh, that's rich. You—you—are calling me a psycho. Well, I'll tell you what it is I want," and Brian's voice suddenly became dark as night and twice as frightening. "I thought I'd extend you an invitation to my little weekend retreat. We could have some more fun, you know. Get reacquainted, relive past times, maybe partake in some DIY." Staines started to back away, eyes wide with terror at the thought of the stone cottage and what had happened there.

"No! I don't want to go there again!" he shouted, as if he had a choice. "Who are you? What the fuck do you want from me?"

"Who am I? You still haven't worked it out, you thick, stupid slab of cow dung." Every step that Staines took backwards, Brian advanced an equal distance. "You know, I have to admit, you hurt my feelings. You really do. How could you forget me, a former employer?" Staines still didn't get it. "How could you forget my wife, and all the cups of tea she used to make you? No? Still can't remember? How about this, then? How could you ever, possibly, in your miserable, useless, godforsaken life, forget my little boy?"

"Your little boy.....?" Staines stammered.

"Danny."

At that moment, two realities hit Staines simultaneously. The first was that he was face-to-face with the father of the boy he'd killed. The second was that he was almost certainly going to die. Frantic, he looked about, and realised that people were everywhere. He'd been so intent on Brian Sykes it was as if the two of them were the only people in the world. They weren't! And he was incredibly relieved by that revelation. Brian, however, took another step forward, closing the gap between them to just inches.

"Help!" Staines screamed as loud as his lungs would permit. "Someone help me, please; this man is trying to kill me! Please, someone please, help!" As he'd hoped, he saw people looking curiously in their direction. Two male joggers in their early twenties, on the opposite side of the street, started to cross over, as Staines continued screeching for assistance. He didn't notice that Brian was giving him a quizzical look, hands buried in his pockets.

The joggers stopped a few feet away. "What's going on?"

Before Staines could say anything, Brian interjected. "Beats me," he said, as Staines mouth dropped open, a stunned expression all over his face. Brian pointed his right index finger towards his head, and made a looping motion, at the same time slightly crossing his eyes, indicating that the screaming man must be an escaped resident of some looney bin. "I don't know this guy from Adam. Never saw him before in my life."

"What?" Staines cried. "You did so. You just said you were going to attack me again, take me out into the country and torture me." He turned to the two would-be Samaritans. "Please, he really is trying to kill me!"

"Take you out to the country?" Brian mocked. "I don't think so. Frankly, I prefer redheads," he said. "You're not my type. Why would I take you anywhere?"

"You said I killed your son!" Staines shouted in desperation, and knew at once how completely ridiculous he must sound.

"Call the police, please!" Staines begged.

The joggers looked at the two men, one well dressed, well spoken and coherent, the other scruffy and babbling. "Call them yourself, whack-o!" the taller of the two said, and they moved off, laughing.

When they were gone, Brian gave Staines a smug look. "Want to try again? I think they especially liked that bit about torture in the country." He leaned very close, so that their faces nearly touched. "See you around. And that's a promise."

He turned to go, and Staines, frantic, grabbed him by the forearm, trying to prevent him from leaving. "We're going to the gardai!" he shouted. "You can't threaten me like this. I'll tell them what you did to me, and this time they will believe me."

Brian whirled, face etched with hatred, and grabbed Staines by the wrist, easily breaking the hold the smaller man had on his arm. He squeezed until Staines' hand turned purple; one twist and Brian could have snapped the joint like a twig. "Don't you ever, EVER, put your hand on me!" He hissed the words, and Staines winced from the pain of the steel grip. "I'm not Danny. I can fight back. In fact, I should break your rotten neck right now and claim self defence." He looked around. There were a lot of people still about, some continued to look in the direction of the disturbance Staines had caused earlier. Brian released the wrist. "But I'll save that for later. In the meantime, I swear to you, we're going to have some more quality time together." He turned and walked away.

Staines stared after him, forgetting his earlier plan of trying to find Squeak. In some ways, what he'd just experienced had the potential to be worse than what had happened to him on that weekend in June. The kidnap and torture had come out of the blue, totally unexpected. It had happened, and then, he had thought, it had been over. Were the episode never to be repeated, it would still have been a terrible thing, maybe the most awful thing in his lifetime. But he would have recovered. The wounds would have healed, and the pain would have faded into nothing more than a bad memory. Life would have gone on. Brian Sykes, though, had left a horrible sword hanging over his head just now. Staines knew that he'd meant it when he said he'd be back; it wasn't just an idle threat. Now every waking moment would be made up, in part, of horrible anticipation, wondering when Sykes would return, and what new horrors he'd inflict when he did. It was like a trip to the doctor's surgery for a tetanus injection, or to the dentist for a filling. The imagined pain beforehand was invariably worse than that which actually occurred. Staines was jumpy at the best of times, except when he was stoned on cannabis or spaced out on heroin. He knew that, from that moment on, any unexpected sound, or sudden movement in a crowd, would have his heart pounding in dread.

"Well, fuck that for a game of soldiers," Staines said, earning a disapproving look from a young mother out wheeling her two-year-old up the street in a push chair. He made his way, once again, to Bray Garda Station.

By an incredible coincidence, Liam Shortt had drawn the weekend shift. Looking out at the sun, he cursed the man who'd drawn up the rota. Eighteen holes, even thirty-six, and a couple of ice cold pints after would have been just the ticket. Instead, he was tied to the damn desk, dealing with the likes of............

"Geoffrey Staines, as I live and breathe," Shortt said as the ex-con walked up to the counter. "To what do I owe this incredible honour?"

"I know who attacked me."

"So do I," Shortt said, with mock sincerity. "It was one of the Power Rangers gone wrong, wasn't it? We've had reports of him, up and down the seafront; they're putting it down to a faulty battery pack driving him insane, but hey, I say 'hang the bastard.' That's if we can catch him. Slippery devil just keeps flying away every time we get close!"

"It was Danny Sykes' father?" Staines still couldn't remember Brian's first name.

This stopped Shortt in his tracks. The time for joking was over. "What makes you think that?" he asked, taking out a notepad and pen.

"He just told me himself."

Shortt stopped writing and put the pen down. "Sure he did, and exactly why would he tell you that?"

"To scare me," Staines insisted. "He said he's going to come after me again."

Much as he wanted not to believe what he was hearing, Staines' story had a ring of truth about it, and Shortt knew he'd have to follow up this time. "Go on, you better tell me everything, from the beginning."

When he left the building, Shortt filed his report of the story Staines had related. Hesitating, not wanting to disturb McCann on a Saturday afternoon, Shortt eventually decided that the detective wouldn't thank him for holding the new information until Monday, and he rang the mobile number.

"Mick, it's Liam again...no, you rotten bollocks, I am not on the golf course, and thank you very much for reminding me of that fact. I'm afraid I've got some more news for you, and I don't think you're going to like it."

He couldn't have been more right. It was McCann's turn to be angry. The detective walked straight to his car, and gunned the 2.2-litre engine to life, squealing the tyres as he pulled off. He wasn't on duty, but what he had to say to Brian Sykes wouldn't keep until Monday.

TWENTY-SEVEN

One seriously upset policeman was waiting for Brian Sykes when he arrived home after his workout. McCann was standing outside his front door, seething, when Brian, freshly showered and carrying a sport bag full of sweaty gear, walked up.

"Been waiting long?" Brian asked nonchalantly.

"Yes, as it happens," McCann replied through gritted teeth. He noticed the kit bag, and asked the outwardly calm man who was the current source of major irritation, "For crying out loud, Brian, don't you ever take a night off?"

"Not if I can help it. Do you want to come in, or are you going to arrest me out here?"

"I should," McCann admitted, "and I still might, if you don't stop this crazy vendetta you seem hell-bent on carrying out."

"Well, while you make up your mind, do you want to come in for a cup of coffee?"

Something had changed. There was no hostility in Brian's voice, no aggression in his manner. He was calm, and apparently rational. "Black, two sugars," McCann said, moving aside, allowing Brian to turn the key in the door.

When they entered the apartment, McCann went straight to the chair he'd occupied on his last visit; Brian went to the small, clean kitchen, boiled the kettle, and brought two cups of instant Maxwell House into the sitting room. "I'll bet I know why you're here," Brian said, as he sat on the sofa, taking a sip from the steaming mug.

"I'll bet you do, too, but why don't you tell me anyway," said
McCann evenly, much of his anger having dissipated. He'd expected
a bad-tempered encounter, and didn't rule out the possibility of it
still taking place, but for the moment, things were going better than
he'd thought they would.

"Did you or one of your comrades-in-arms have a visit today from
an hysterical little toe rag by the name of Staines?" Brian asked, but
in the same tone he'd have used if asking whether McCann had spent
the day at the beach. McCann nodded in the affirmative. "Did he
tell you I tried to kill him?"

"No. Did you?"

"Not at all, but that's not what he told two passers-by on
Quinsboro Road." McCann listened without interruption as Brian
related the events of the early-afternoon confrontation. When he
came to the part about the joggers' response to Staines' pleas, the
detective, in spite of himself, grinned, but managed to keep himself
from laughing, and he hid the smile behind his coffee cup.
"I never laid a finger on him, not today, anyway," Brian concluded.
"Well, except when he grabbed me and said he was going to take me
to the garda station. I...uhh...let's just say I persuaded him that
wasn't such a good idea; not in the best interests of his health."

McCann was confused by the sudden openness. He wondered
silently what exactly was driving the man sitting before him. What
made a middle-aged business man push himself, night after night,
until he developed the kind of physique Brian now had? What
motivated him to pose as a health inspector, risking his job, and
potentially his freedom? How far would he go? How far had he
already gone?

You said, 'not today, anyway.' You took him last month, didn't
you, Brian?"

"Do I need to phone my solicitor?"

McCann thought for a few seconds, then said, "Not yet. I'm going
to be honest here. If we get to the stage where I have to arrest you,
I'll caution you first. Until then, we're just two guys talking, trying
to work something out, ok?"

"By the way, what's the penalty in this jurisdiction for transferring fleas from one mange-riddled dog to another?" Brian asked, and now he was the one trying to suppress a grin. "You've got to admit, it's true poetic justice, pure genius, if I say so myself."

"All right, now you've lost me," McCann said.

"That's what I was doing at the bed sit. I knew you'd want to know." He told McCann about infesting Staines' bed with the biting insects, how he'd persuaded Sarah Guilfoyle to let him check out one room, and how he knew which room to ask to see. McCann just shook his head, and didn't know whether to feel more admiration for Brian's imagination and initiative, or disgust at the deed itself.

"Brian, you've got to admit, that's pretty twisted," McCann said honestly.

"I can think of things that Staines has done that are far, far more twisted. And so can you, if you try hard enough," Brian replied.

McCann quickly changed the subject back to where it had been a few moments before. "You were going to tell me about that weekend. By the way, I'd better tell you, I spoke with a Mr. Carl O'Dowd at your offices yesterday afternoon. He told me that your level of absenteeism is practically non-existent — except for one Friday last month. Friday the 14th, the day Staines said he was taken. He also said you've been working really hard lately, that you're out on calls from mid-morning to late afternoon nearly every day. Quite complimentary, he was, but I'm afraid he wouldn't supply you with much of an alibi, if it turns out you need one."

"I won't need one," Brian said.

"Why? Are you telling me now you didn't do it?"

"Are we still just two guys talking?" Brian asked. McCann nodded. "No, I'm not telling you I didn't do it. You already know I did. You're just trying to fill in the gaps here, right?" Brian said, and there was neither fear nor remorse in his voice.

"Where'd you take him, Brian?"

"It doesn't matter. I won't be taking him back there again."

"If it doesn't matter, then you might as well tell me. Like you said yourself, I'm just filling in gaps here." McCann was anxious that Brian keep talking.

Brian took a deep breath, then told the detective every last detail, from his meeting with Albert Stevens, right down to the precise directions on how to get to the stone cottage. (A phone call to Mrs. Stevens the next day would verify that her husband had indeed rented the house to a writer, or an artist, she wasn't sure which, named Danny O'Brien.) Calmly, he related how he'd spiked Staines' pint, and used ether to subdue him on two or three other occasions. When he got to the point of describing what he'd done with the sandpaper and alcohol, McCann cringed as he imagined the pain it must have caused. Brian finished his story with the journey back to Bray, and how he'd had to wait for some time before dumping Staines outside Sullivan's. As he finished talking, he slumped back on the sofa.

"Why, Brian?"

"Why, what?"

"So many things. Why are you telling me all this now?"

"Because you asked me, and because the way events have unfolded, there didn't seem any reason left not to tell you."

"Why the sandpaper? Why not just beat him with a tyre iron, or a baseball bat?"

"You're the detective. You tell me."

McCann thought for a second, then said, "You wanted him to suffer. Not just for a few days, either, but for a long time after. You didn't want to knock him out, by clubbing him over the head, you wanted him awake, in agony, the whole time."

"Yes," Brian confirmed, "and if I'd broken anything, he would have had to go to a doctor or a hospital, and then your brethren in blue would almost certainly have taken the matter more seriously than I assume they did. Staines was — is — just out of prison. I didn't think he was as likely to get a sympathetic ear if he walked into a garda station without anything broken, no bruises on the face; in fact, with his clothes on, he didn't look like he'd been touched."

McCann shook his head in wonder. The amount of single-minded determination that had gone into what was almost a military-style operation was unbelievable. "Remind me never to piss you off," he said to Brian, and he was only half joking. "The thing is, you've left me with a real problem on my hands."

"Is this the part where I get the caution?"

"You don't seem particularly concerned about it," McCann said, still not understanding why that was so.

"You still haven't made up your mind?" Brian asked. McCann, looking down at the floor, shook his head.

"Let me ask you something," Brian said, and McCann raised his eyes so that they met Brian's steady, even gaze. "Why did I do it?"

"We've gone through that. You wanted him to suffer. You wanted to punish him."

"For what?"

"For what he did to Danny," McCann said softly, and now he had to look away.

"And?"

"And what?" McCann asked. Isn't that enough? What more reason could you need?"

"Precisely. When I said 'and,' I meant, 'and what's wrong with that?' You tell me what I did that wasn't right, that wasn't…justice," Brian said forcefully. "No one else got hurt. Even Staines is still walking around on a sunny day like this. Do you have any idea how that makes me feel? Him warming his face in the sun, Danny cold in his grave."

"I told you before," McCann said. "You've got to let it go."

"You said something else before," Brian replied. "You said, 'I've got to live with myself, too,' or words to that effect." McCann nodded. He remembered saying those exact words. "Well, I thought about that after you left. I can understand it. It's my turn to say that I know exactly how *you* feel. Because what I'm doing to Staines is what I need to do to live with myself. So you do what you have to do; I'll understand, but it won't change the way I feel."

"What are you saying?" McCann asked. "Do you want me to arrest you? Are you asking me to help you stop yourself?"

"No. That's just not on the cards. I'm telling you that if you have to arrest me, if that will help you sleep better at night, then that's what you should do. I wouldn't resist, and I wouldn't tell lies about our conversation in court. I've given you enough evidence to put me away for...how long...a few months, a year maybe? This would be my first ever offense, outside the odd parking ticket, and I think, given the circumstances, provocation, state of mind, call it what you will, it's not likely that any judge would put me away for very long, especially if I got that bleeding-heart moron Evans. But it won't stop me from doing what I have to do. It might put it off for awhile, but that's all it would be, a delay, more time for Staines to think about what's coming, and wondering when. That's what I was trying to get across to him in Bray today. What's going to happen is going to happen, regardless."

McCann stared, wide-eyed. Never in his career had he been confronted with a situation like this. "You're putting me in an impossible situation, Brian."

"Yeah, I can understand that, too," Brian said, "but it can't really be helped. I'm not much of a believer in fate, but this—this thing—has been mapped out, in my mind, from day one. Do you know something? I actually feel sorry for you." McCann gave him a questioning look. "You have to make a choice between stopping me, which I've already admitted would be impossible for you to do, to protect a filthy, inhuman child killer, or you have to let me get on with...whatever...and still be able to face yourself in the mirror every morning."

"It's not an easy choice," Brian continued, with total sincerity, " I know I wouldn't want to have to make it. You're probably sorry I told you everything now, aren't you? Having that much knowledge can be a real burden. Let me see if I can help you a bit. I promise you, as God is my witness, that regardless of what happens to Geoffrey Staines, no one else, not another human soul, will get hurt. When I'm finished with him, it's not like I'm going to move on to someone else. You'll never hear from me again, I swear. And the world will be just that tiniest bit better off."

"You're asking me to stand back and knowingly let you kill someone. I can't do….."

"I'm not asking you anything. I'm telling you what's on my mind, just like you said. We're just kicking this thing around, remember? But think about it. Since you came through that door tonight, have I asked you to do one single thing for me? I don't think so. For that matter, I don't ever remember actually saying that I'm going to kill anyone, either."

"Are you telling me you definitely won't?" McCann looked straight at Brian then, and Brian stared back, unmoving, and gave no answer. "All right, then I'm going to ask you something, and I want you to think about it carefully before giving your answer," McCann said. "What if Staines were to disappear? Would that satisfy you?"

"What do you mean?" Brian was momentarily confused, but then understood what the detective was offering. "Oh, I get it. You're going to pay the little man a visit, and warn him off. Suggest to him that he might find another climate more suitable for medical reasons. Make it clear to him that London is lovely this time of year. He's got no ties, no job, no family. No one would miss him, except maybe the odd publican and the drug dealers, so why not make a fresh start somewhere else? Is that what you're getting at?"

"Something along those lines," McCann admitted.

Brian didn't hesitate. "Forget it. I don't care if you send that pig to the North Pole. It's not good enough that I don't have to see him on the streets. I still have to see him in here," he said, pointing at his head. "And I'd spend a lot of time wondering if he was sizing up another young boy, wouldn't you?"

"I'm being honest here. You might be able to hide him away, and put me through a lot more trouble, and expense. But I've got nothing else to do with my money, and nothing else to do with my time. Job, car, apartment—all of it be damned—I'd find him anyway, and anywhere."

McCann knew he should arrest Brian on the spot. He clearly had no intention of stopping his one-man crusade. But he asked himself what good it would really do. In addition, thinking back over their entire conversation, McCann couldn't remember a single thing the other man had said that he could argue with. Brian had talked what, on the surface, was perfect sense. Most of the time, his voice hadn't risen above a level any school teacher would use. McCann closed his eyes and saw for the umpteenth time that tiny body, scarred and broken, lying on a filthy bed, and tried to imagine what life — what living — with that vision must have done to a man like Brian, and to his wife, Bridget.

He opened his eyes, and saw Brian staring at him, as if he'd known exactly what McCann had just been thinking. But something clicked inside the detective's head. It was clear he wouldn't be able to keep Brian Sykes from wreaking horrible, and ultimately illegal vengeance on Geoffrey Staines. No one could. Brian had said as much. Still, there might just be one person.

"I'm not going to arrest you, Brian, not today, anyway." He got up and extended his arm. Brian did the same, and the two men shook hands firmly. "I'm not saying I won't, and I'm not agreeing to stand by and do nothing, but I mean it when I say I appreciate how truthful you've been with me tonight. And one other thing. I'm going to have Staines put under constant surveillance. You've been honest with me, so it's only fair I tell you that."

"That's fair enough. Like I said, you do what you have to do," Brian replied, clearly unruffled. "Thanks for stopping by." He opened the door and let McCann out into the night air.

As soon as he'd pulled away from the apartment building, McCann turned on his mobile phone, using the hands-free kit mounted on the right hand side of the dashboard. He wanted to make a call, and he didn't want to wait till morning. He dialled directory enquiries, and when the operator asked which number he was looking for, he replied, "I'm looking for the number of the Fitzgerald residence, in Kilcormac, County Offally."

Within moments, the detective was speaking with Bridget. He felt a twinge of remorse when she first came on the line. She sounded terrified, and he realised she must have been frightened when told by her mother that a Detective McCann wanted to speak with her. Bridget had been expecting the policeman to tell her there had been a sighting of Geoffrey Staines in her area, or something along those lines. It was the only reason she could think of for him to be ringing her on a Saturday night. When she quickly realised this wasn't the case, she was relieved, and somewhat annoyed.

"Sorry, Mrs. Sykes."

"Please, call me Bridget. 'Mrs. Sykes' isn't…well…call me Bridget, ok?"

"Sorry. Bridget," McCann said, silently chastising himself for yet another indiscretion, his second in less than a minute. He'd already managed to upset the lady with thoughts of the monster who'd murdered her little boy, and then managed, in almost the very next breath, to remind her that her marriage had fallen apart, not that she needed any reminding. He could have kicked himself, and he began to wonder if his instinctive rush to make the call had been one of his less-than-brilliant ideas.

But he forged ahead. As briefly as he could, and leaving out many of the more gruesome aspects of the case, he explained why he had called. Brian was getting himself into potentially serious trouble, having become fixated on their son's killer, he told her. No one seemed to be able to talk him around. McCann said that he didn't want to see Brian get himself hurt. This was only a half-truth. Having seen both protagonists, the detective didn't have any fears that Brian might suffer physical damage at Staines' hands. He convinced himself that what he meant by "getting hurt" was what would happen to Brian, legally and psychologically after, not during any such confrontation..

"I'm not at all sure what any of this has to do with me, Detective," Bridget said. "What exactly is it you want?"

"I was wondering if you'd talk with him, maybe try to get him to see sense," McCann admitted.

"Me? Talk sense to Brian?" Now she was becoming annoyed. "Listen, Detective McCann, right now I'm standing facing my mother's kitchen wall, and I'm telling you straight, I'd have a much better chance of talking sense to it, than I would to Brian. Are you aware that he and I have not spoken a single word to each other since the night before Danny was buried? He didn't even talk to me—not once—the whole day of the funeral." She was becoming upset now as she recalled that horrible time. "I haven't seen him, or heard from him, other than through his solicitor, in more than seven years. And now you want me to...what...just pick up the phone and say, 'Hi, Brian, it's your wife, Bridget, remember me? Listen, I hear you've become a stalker and I just want you to know that I don't think it's a very good idea.' Is that what you're asking me to do, Detective? Or maybe I should call around to his place, give him a slap on the wrist and send him to bed without his cocoa. Do you think that might do the trick?"

"I'm sorry," McCann said. "I'm really very sorry to have troubled you. It's just that you were the last person, as far as I can make out, that your husband was ever close to; I've seen him. There's no one else, you know. And I was thinking—hoping really—that there was still enough—history—left between you......"

"There's nothing left between us," Bridget interrupted, surprised at her own, mixed feelings when she'd heard McCann say that Brian still had not developed a new personal relationship. She hadn't known, and hadn't thought she'd care, one way or the other.

"And you're wrong," she said. "I am not the last person that Brian was close to."

"What? Oh, you mean his brothers, or his parents. That's not really...."

She interrupted again. "No, I mean Danny. The last person who really mattered to Brian was Danny."

Then she hung up.

TWENTY-EIGHT

"I need something a bit different this time, Squeak."

"No, problem," the drug dealer said to Geoffrey Staines as they stood on the platform of Bray Station, mid-morning on Tuesday. "What are you after, a little Colombian? Maybe some LSD; that's making a bit of a comeback, you know. Whatever it is, man, you just tell Uncle Squeak, and he will provide. Might take a little time, and cost a tiny bit extra, but dude, your wish is my command. I live to serve."

"Can you get me a gun?"

There was an immediate and distinct change in Squeak's demeanor. "You planning a job, man? I mean, I can help you, but if this thing has to be totally clean — untraceable — it's gonna cost big. On the other hand, if you're just gonna use it the one time, then send it out there," he gestured in the general direction of the Irish Sea, "to go swimming with the fishes…"

"For fuck's sake, who are you, the Godfather? I just want a gun. Now can you help me or not?" Staines was uncomfortable having this conversation in a public place, but he hadn't wanted to ask the dealer around to his bedsit. Since Sunday, he'd noticed squad cars driving up and down Quinsboro Road, on an annoyingly regular basis, and he didn't want to risk an uninvited visit from one of the boys in blue when Squeak was around. Who knew what they would find? Being caught in possession of narcotics, or in the company of someone who was carrying, and a known felon at that, would be a serious violation of the conditions of his release. He could be back in Mountjoy before the day was out, serving the rest of his sentence, with maybe some extra time thrown in for good measure, as a result of a drugs bust. So he had called Squeak on his mobile phone and arranged to meet him at the station.

"Chill, man, take a pill or something." Squeak giggled childishly when he realised what he'd just said. "Take a pill, get it?" He saw the warning look Staines was giving him. "Yes, I can help you. I know a guy in Finglas who's reliable enough. What do you need it for anyway?" Squeak couldn't help sticking his nose in.

"It's a present for my niece," Staines said sarcastically. "What do you think I need it for?"

"Touchy today, aren't we?" Squeak sniffed. "Listen, I don't know what you need it for, but I'd like to know what I'm getting myself involved in. If you don't want to tell me, then go find your own damn gun."

Staines relented. He had no other contacts he felt he could approach to fulfill his current requirements. "Protection," he said. "There's this guy getting a bit heavy with me; fancies himself a real hard man. Likes to play rough, you know? So let's just say I'll sleep better with a little company under the pillow. And if Tough Guy comes calling again, he's gonna get more than he bargained for."

"How'd you get on the wrong side of him?" Squeak wanted to know. "You been eating at another man's table, is that it? Giving his ol' lady dancing lessons, the old Tom Jones bump and grind kind of thing?" Staines shook his head. "You owe him money?"

"Speaking of money, what's this...item...going to set me back?" Staines was eager to change the subject. He wasn't anxious to let the drug dealer know why Brian was bent on making his life hell. His choice of cash as the new topic of conversation was excellent. Squeak forgot all about why his customer might want the gun. The two men agreed a provisional price, which Squeak said he would honour barring exceptional circumstances and providing the piece he had in mind, a .38 calibre revolver, was still available. They agreed to meet back at the station the following morning.

Brian started the day like most others, pumping weights and pounding the treadmill before showering and making his way to the office. Before leaving his apartment, he threw his sweaty workout gear into the washing machine fitted underneath his kitchen sink. Then he walked around the apartment, opening various picture frames, removing the contents, and placing the photos into his briefcase. From a plastic bag he found on the top shelf of his wardrobe, he removed several dozen pictures—snapshots taken on family holidays, at weddings, anniversaries, nights out with old friends—picked out the few that he wanted, and put those in his briefcase as well. The rest he returned to the plastic bag, which he then took out to the kitchen and threw in the rubbish bin.

He'd been thinking a lot since his Saturday night meeting with Detective McCann. Brian knew that the policeman wouldn't...no, it was more a case that he couldn't...stand back and allow him to have his way with Geoffrey Staines. Brian had seen it in his eyes, and McCann had admitted as much before leaving. But for Brian, walking away, moving on, and "letting it go," as the detective had said, wasn't an option. The plan that had been his "brain child" at the beginning, now had its own life to lead, had become almost independent of Brian, if still physically reliant on him to see its way through to the end. Brian didn't mind. He had no fear of what would happen, nor any thoughts about whether what he was doing was right or wrong. To his mind, there was only ever going to be one outcome, regardless.

As he was leaving the office mid-morning, he dropped the very brief letter he'd just typed into the "Outgoing Mail" tray situated outside the door of the accounts department. Driving back in the same general direction he'd travelled to work three hours earlier, he called to the One Hour Photo shop at Cornelscourt, opened his briefcase, and pulled out the large stack of pictures he'd taken from the apartment. Placing his order, he enquired when the young shop assistant expected them to be done. "Do you need them in a hurry, sir?" she asked him politely.

"No, not particularly," said Brian. "Any time over the next few days will be fine. I'm planning to go away, and I'll need them before then. But I'm not going just yet." He took the receipt the girl gave him, and said he'd call back on Thursday or Friday. She assured him his order would be ready by then.

Returning to his car, Brian checked his appointment book. He drove to the offices of Phoenix Insurances in Blackrock, where he was meeting Stanley Fletcher. The meeting lasted ten minutes, Brian explaining to Stanley why using a digital copier as his main office printer made sound economic sense, in spite of the initial large capital outlay. "With a cheap laser beam printer, your main cost is in the cartridges you have to keep buying. In the lifetime of that printer, the average company spends one hundred times more on cartridges than on the hardware itself? And if it breaks down after the twelve-month warranty expires, what can you do? You've either got to get it fixed or replaced, and both are expensive options. And don't even talk to me about inkjet printers," Brian exclaimed. "Did you know, and I swear this is true, that for virtually all the inkjet printers produced by major manufacturers, it's a fact that one drop of ink used in their cartridges is more expensive to the end user than an equivalent amount of Chanel No. 5!"

"All right, you've given me your pitch, and I accept what you're saying," Stanley said. "But the machine you're trying to sell me is quite expensive, and I'm not sure we need all the whistles and bells."

"Well, as it happens, I'm in a position to make you a very special offer." Brian pulled the revised quote from his briefcase. "You can see that figure at the bottom of the page is almost twelve per cent lower than the one I sent you last week. And before you ask, the reason I didn't quote you that number straight away was because we only found out the manufacturer was putting out a special offer on this model yesterday. That's why I asked to see you personally this morning. As for the 'whistles and bells,' true, you might not need them today, but in a few months, or a year, when your employees see that every other company has those features, they're going to wonder why they don't. If you have to go out and buy another machine in that kind of timeframe, then it does become expensive, because the money you spend now on a machine with a lower specification will effectively have been wasted.

"Can I think about it?" Fletcher asked. "How long is this special offer going to go on?"

Brian's tone changed, almost imperceptibly. "Let's just say, Stan, I don't think I'll be in a position to hold that price for very much longer. If you want to deal with me on this, you should probably do it soon."

"I'll phone you, this afternoon or, at the latest, tomorrow," the purchasing manager promised. "I just want to mull it over."

"Thanks, I look forward to hearing from you," Brian said, shaking Fletcher's hand. "Before I leave, can you tell me if it's possible to check that my own policy's up to date? Who would I need to ask about that?"

"I can check it here for you. Do you mean your car insurance?"

"No, my life plan," Brian said. He saw the surprised look on Fletcher's face, and made an effort to put him at ease. "Nothing to worry about," he said, tapping his chest. "The old ticker isn't ready to pack it in just yet. I just want to make sure everything's in order, as long as I'm here, you know? It seemed like a good opportunity, and I'm always forgetting to get premiums and stuff paid on time."

A few clicks on his computer screen, a quick call to Customer Services with a policy number, and Fletcher was able to report to Brian that everything was up to date and paid in full. Bridget was listed as the sole beneficiary, and the straight life payout, in the event of Brian's death, would be €200,000.

"Thanks, Stan. I appreciate it. You know how it is, you can never be too sure about these things." And you never know when you're going to need them, he thought.

Brian went back to his car. As he sat in, he placed both hands on the steering wheel, and briefly rested his head against them. Closing his eyes, Danny's face suddenly appeared to him. Only, this time he was smiling and laughing. Brian clung to the vision, squeezing his eyes more tightly shut, lest the image escape from behind them. His mind showed him what he wanted to see. Danny, the way he'd like to remember him, running through the park, carefree, with Bandit nipping at his heels. Brian smiled, and without thinking started to open his eyes, then said "No!" and quickly closed them again. Too late. He could still see the park, but Danny was gone, having disappeared behind a stand of oak trees.

"I can't stand it anymore," Brian said, opening his eyes and seeing only strangers going about their own business, caught up in their own little world. A world that Brian no longer felt a part of, and with which he increasingly wanted nothing more to do. But he didn't cry. No tears had passed his eyes since the day he told Bridget he'd found their son, but not in time to save him.

What was he waiting for, he asked himself. It didn't matter that Staines was under virtual round-the-clock protection. American presidents had their secret service, film stars had their bodyguards, ultra-wealthy businessmen had private security. Yet presidents had been assassinated, celebrities gunned down, and wealthy men kidnapped from their bedrooms and held to ransom. There was no one who couldn't be got at, and Staines wasn't the type that the gardai would indefinitely spend huge resources trying to protect, of that Brian was sure. And in that, he was correct. When McCann had said he was putting Staines under 24-hour watch, what Brian hadn't realised was that it was being done for his protection, not the ex-con's. The detective was doing everything he could to, in his own words, protect Brian from himself.

No matter. Brian had had enough. McCann wouldn't back off, but that wasn't important now. He closed his eyes once more, but Danny had gone. Brian wanted to follow him, through the park, behind the trees, laughing and smiling. "I'm coming, son," he whispered.

It was time to end it.

TWENTY-NINE

Wednesday and Thursday came and went, to most people passing normally, relatively uneventful. McCann tried to turn his mind to other cases requiring his attention. An active, well-organised criminal gang, formerly based in Limerick, was now trying to establish a Dublin base, from which they could more profitably expand their racketeering and drugs empire. There had also been another murder in the capital. Two young men going home from separate pubs arrived almost simultaneously in a fish and chip shop on Grogan's Road. A violent argument ensued as to which of them was first in the queue. One of them pulled out a knife and stabbed the other seventeen times, twice hitting the heart. The dead youth was nineteen. His killer was seventeen.

McCann did his follow-up work, gathered evidence and basically went about his duties in a professional, if not highly enthusiastic manner. For him, it was like staring at black clouds gathering on the horizon, waiting for lightning to strike. All the signs that a massive storm was about to break loose were there, the atmosphere charged with electricity. He knew that sometimes, but not often, thunderheads gather, then, without warning or reason, dissipate and vanish, without ever unleashing the fury within. On those occasions, the sun comes out when least expected, when it looks as if there is absolutely no chance of fair weather. Mostly, though, the storm just explodes, lightning flashes, and there's nothing anyone can do to stop it. No one can predict where the lightning bolts will strike. The storm just takes its course, and the only thing anyone can do is pray that not too much damage is caused.

McCann had known since Saturday night that the storm known as Brian Sykes, wouldn't stay harmlessly out on the horizon. The roaring thunder inside the man had been building for seven years, and, no more than a storm cloud can hold itself back, that pent-up tempest was going to burst forth, of that McCann was positive. What made McCann all the more certain was the calmness with which Brian had spoken to him. If he'd ranted and raved, something like he'd done the first time McCann went to his apartment, the detective might still be holding out some hope. Generally speaking, in his experience, people who rant and rave eventually calm down and can be made to see reason, if rational arguments are presented to them in the right way.

Brian hadn't shouted and sworn. For crying out loud, he hadn't even seemed upset, McCann thought. Whether the policeman agreed with them or not, Brian's reasons were rational and well thought out, not spontaneous, half-crazy notions. His single-minded determination was evident, and McCann doubted that any cooling off period, regardless of length, would dampen that incredible willpower. His story had checked out. McCann had driven out to the stone cottage on Sunday morning. He saw the green gates, and when he went through them, up the lane to the house and looked in through the kitchen window, he could make out the upright wooden support beam standing in the middle of the floor. The sun was warm on his back, but McCann still got a chill when he thought of what had taken place there.

He'd phoned Bray Station, first speaking with Liam Shortt, then with the superintendent, and asked him if it was possible to have squad cars patrol the Quinsboro Road at regular intervals. He'd been told that everything possible would be done to accommodate his request, but that none of the patrolmen would be asked to put in expensive overtime, especially to protect an ex-con. McCann decided it would be a very bad idea to elaborate on his reasons, so he thanked the superintendent and asked to be reconnected to Garda Shortt. Giving the young officer slightly more information than he had the senior man, McCann asked Shortt to circulate descriptions of both Staines and Brian to the patrols. He had declined the offer of an evening rematch at Kilternan, but promised that they would play again soon.

Now, it was just a case of waiting. Every time he was called to the phone, McCann was sure it was going to be about an attack, or worse, on Geoffrey Staines. He had to ask himself what he would do when the call did come, as he was certain it would. He'd had plenty of time to think about it in the days since his meeting with Brian, and he'd made his decision. Actually, he'd known from the beginning what that decision would be, but it had crystallised since. As he'd said to Brian, he had to live, too. Live with himself. Be able to face himself in the mirror every time he shaved. As much as deep down he wanted to turn his back, he couldn't. If he did, the next time he wanted to bend the rules would be that bit easier, and the time after that easier still. He couldn't start playing judge, jury and executioner; down that path lay certain ruin. If Brian crossed the line, McCann thought sadly, he'd have to bring him down.

What was worse was that the detective knew he would cross the line, and he couldn't think of a single way to stop him. Arresting him for what he'd already admitted, was an option, and one McCann was still considering, but from which he was holding back. Even in the normal course of events, if he did bring Brian in, the man would make bail, and it would be weeks or months before his trial took place. And having the timeframe of an impending court appearance looming ahead of him might trigger Brian into action sooner than would otherwise be the case. McCann didn't think it would be a positive step to bring the situation to a head by creating a judicial deadline. It was very awkward, and he could see no obvious solution. "If Brian Sykes is a storm cloud," he said to himself, "then Geoffrey Staines is going to get very, very wet."

He was dragged from his deep thoughts by a voice behind him. One of the other detectives stationed at Shankill was calling him. "Mick, there's someone here to see you."

He wasn't expecting anyone, and was sure he had no appointments. He came out of his office and walked up to the public desk, pulling up sharply, stunned to see who was waiting for him.

"Hello, Detective McCann."

"Mrs........I mean, Bridget! What on earth are you doing here?"

The letter that Brian had posted from his Dublin office Tuesday morning had arrived in Kilcormac, Co. Offally, courtesy of Ger Simmons and an efficient postal service, on Wednesday morning. Simmons had noted the Dublin postmark, but the envelope was typed and there were no logos to give further clues as to its origins. Disappointed, he had pushed the letter through the Fitzgerald's hall door and moved down the road, reading a postcard from Ibiza as he went.

Bridget was equally bemused when she saw the unexpected letter. Patti still wrote occasionally, but didn't use a typewriter or word processor, and she always wrote her return address in the upper left hand corner of the envelope, so Bridget knew it hadn't come from her. Still standing in the hallway, she pulled out the single sheet of paper.

Immediately after finishing the letter, she ran into the kitchen, tears streaming down her face, and asked her mother to drive her to Dublin. Roisin, now in her mid-sixties, didn't like driving at the best of times, and the thought of trying to find her way through unfamiliar Dublin traffic terrified her. She phoned her husband at work. David wanted to know if it would keep till the weekend, and Bridget shook her head violently, no. He agreed to take the following day, Thursday, off work, and the two of them had left Kilcormac right after breakfast. On the way to the capital, Bridget had rung Shankill Garda Station; she'd written down the number McCann had given her when he phoned Saturday night. The policeman that answered the phone gave her precise directions on the easiest way to get to the station, coming in from the west side of the city. When he'd asked if Bridget wanted to leave a message, she declined, but did ask if Detective McCann would be on duty that afternoon.

Without preamble or pleasantries, Bridget handed him the letter.

"Dear Bridget," it read,

"I'm sorry. I didn't mean what I said that night. You probably don't even want to hear that, and it doesn't make things any better. The words were inexcusable, and you deserved better from me. You did nothing wrong, and I feel I did nothing right.

Now, it's time for me to put those things right, or as right as they can be. I needed to tell you that you were not at fault for what happened to Danny. I guess it's important to me that you know that, after the terrible things I yelled at you.

If anyone was to blame, it was me. I could have done so many things differently. I could have cleaned the windows myself, if I hadn't been such a coward about that ladder. If only I'd been able to do that one, simple thing, maybe we'd never have met Geoffrey Staines. You and I, and Danny, would all still be together, and I honestly think we'd be happy. You're a good person, and Danny was a good person, and when we were with each other, it made me feel like a good person, and that made me happy.

I don't expect you to forgive me, by the way. I've certainly never been able to forgive myself. I do hope that one day you can find, if not happiness, then whatever is the next best thing. If you can, you'll have proven once again that you're a better person than I am. Because I've given up trying. It's just too hard. You needn't feel sorry for me, though, and don't worry about me either. I have my own mission in life—a new goal. I'm nearly there, and even though I know accomplishing that mission won't make me happy, maybe it will give me some peace. That's really as much as I can hope for. Take care, Bridget.

It had simply been signed   *--Brian*

"What's he going to do?" Bridget asked McCann, worried to the point of desperation. "Is he going to kill himself? Is he going to kill that man, and then himself, is that what he means?"

"I don't know," McCann admitted. "When I spoke to him, it didn't sound like suicide was part of his plan. But this letter sure makes it sound like those plans might have changed."

At the same time Bridget and the detective were talking in Shankill Station, Brian was in Dublin city centre, in Capel Street. He put the Nissan into one of the many public car parks, and walked up the bustling thoroughfare, lined on both sides with shops, markets and boutiques of every make and ethnic origin. Finding the one he was looking for, he entered Johnny's A1 Security Shop. The Golden Pages ad had promised that, after a visit to their premises, anyone of any age, stature and gender could walk the streets of Dublin, New York or Shaghai without fear for their own safety. The bold print stated that Johnny's specialised in personal security devices of all sizes and shapes, suitable for all situations.

Surveying the glass showcases, similar to those found in a jeweller's, Brian could see there was indeed a wide selection on offer. Cans of pepper spray were the best sellers, but there were also alarms that came disguised as everything from key rings to pretty pendants. One touch of the right button, and any potential attacker would get an earful of high-pitched, incredibly loud, whistles, screeches or sirens, designed to attract attention from up to a quarter mile away.

None of it, unfortunately, matched Brian's particular requirements. He was still looking when a lady roughly the size of a champion Japanese sumo wrestler, with shocking red hair and a moustache to rival anything Brian could have grown in a month, came out of the back store room. Her voice was as deep as her hair was red. "Hi, I'm Johnny. Can I help you find something, or are you just browsing?" Momentarily, Brian wondered if anyone the size of this woman would ever need to carry with her the mace, foghorn aerosols or anything else on offer in the shop. It would take a very brave man to even consider causing Johnny any inconvenience.

"Hi, uh, Johnny," Brian said, clumsily trying to figure out how to build a rapport with this scarlet-headed mountain. "I suppose you hear this a lot, but when I saw Johnny's, I was expecting...someone else."

"You're right," said Johnny good-naturedly. "I started out as Joni, you know, like Joni Mitchell, the singer." Brian nodded, afraid to admit that he'd never heard of the woman. Music was most definitely not his strong point. "Anyway, even as a young girl, I was pretty big. Some of the girls in my class said it was only right the biggest pupil in the school should have a boy's name, so they started calling me Johnny, and it stuck," she said matter-of-factly, and with very little malice toward the offending girls. But then she said, "Girls can be real bitches, you know. I think they're ten times worse than boys when it comes to bullying, don't you?"

"Definitely," Brian agreed.

"I mean, boys just beat the lard out of each other, and then it's over. Girls mess up your head, and they can be so vicious about it."

Brian decided he'd made enough of a connection with the proprietor to risk making his request. "Look, Johnny, you've got a great range of stuff here, but there was something specific that I was hoping to get, and I don't see any of them on display. It's for my wife, actually, but she was too embarrassed or nervous or something to come with me," Brian said, shrugging his shoulders and giving Johnny a 'what can you do?' expression.

"What is it you're looking for...and what did you say your name was?"

"Sorry, Johnny. Crikey, where are my manners? My name's Brian." He hesitated, then figured there was no point in covering up, so he finished, "Brian Sykes."

"Nice to meet you, Brian," Johnny said, proffering her right hand, and shaking Brian's with a grip to match his own. "So what is it you're after?"

"You know, we were in Paris last summer, and these things were in every second shop we went into! The Champs Elysee is practically lined with these yokes, and I should have bought one then, but

Bridget, my wife, had other ideas about what we should be spending our money on. I'm sure you know what I mean." Johnny nodded. She liked to shop as much as any woman. "Anyway, it's one of those stun gun things," Brian said innocently. "Bridget has to walk home from the bus stop after work, and it's about four hundred yards from there to our house. I'd feel safer if she had one of those things; there have been three or four women mugged in our area this year already."

"I'd like to help you, Brian, I really would," Johnny said, and then she told Brian what he already knew, "but those stun guns, and tazer guns with the wires—all those things are illegal in Ireland."

"No way!" Brian said, wide-eyed, playing his part to perfection. "Why is that? I thought if stores could sell something in one country of the EU, any other country could carry them, too. Are you sure they're illegal?"

"Positive," said Johnny, believing every word that Brian was feeding her. Then Brian saw her glance, briefly, in the direction of the store room. He pretended not to notice.

"Damn," he exclaimed. "Johnny, is there any way you can help me out here? I mean, you wouldn't have a demonstration model or anything like that you could sell me, would you? I'd feel so much better if Bridget was walking home with one those things in her handbag. I'd pay full price, and I promise, it would just be between you and me."

She thought for a moment and grinned across the counter, moustache turning up at the corners. "You're not going to believe this, Brian, but I just happened to be in Paris myself last month. And well, I couldn't resist getting a couple of those, umm, items to bring home. I put them in my luggage, and when my return flight landed at Dublin airport, there was no one in the Blue Channel for me to declare them to, so I just kept going. Imagine that!"

"Imagine," Brian said, returning her smile. "Would you sell me one, Johnny, please?" he said, drawing out the last word for a full five seconds.

Johnny looked around. There was no one else in the shop, and trade had been a bit slow. She went back to the storage area, and returned a few seconds later with the stun gun, still in its original wrapper. It had a black handle, and two evil-looking prongs at the business end. In the middle of the handle was a built-in trigger. She explained to Brian that you could put the two prongs up against another person virtually anywhere, even on their clothing, and pull the trigger, delivering 25,000 volts and dropping even the largest man in his tracks. The electrical surge affected the central nervous system, not causing any permanent damage, but completely incapacitating the recipient for up to fifteen minutes.

"Perfect. I'll take it, and Johnny, you're a saint. How much do I owe you?"

"Three hundred," Johnny said.

"Three hundred?" Brian protested. "They were about sixty in the shops." He had no idea if that were true; it had been ten years since he had been in Paris, and that was to attend an Ireland vs. France rugby international. He actually had seen the stun guns on that trip, and it had struck him at the time that they were quite inexpensive.

"Then take a cheap Ryan Air flight to Paris and buy one over there," Johnny said, but not in a mean way. She was still smiling.

"No, I'll take it," Brian said, counting out the money, "and I take back what I said before."

"What's that, sweetie? Oh, don't tell me, I already know. I'm no saint, right?"

THIRTY

Friday dawned dry and bright, the seventh consecutive day of hot summer weather. For Ireland, it had been a highly unusual, if welcome, heat wave.

Bridget had gone to Dun Guaire, where she spent the night at Patti and Ted's. Her father had reluctantly driven back to Kilcormac, only after extracting a promise from Bridget that she'd call him if she needed him. She told him she'd get the bus home after she'd spoken with Brian, then kissed him on the cheek good-bye and sent him on his way. In the past, David had always liked Brian. He could see that the man made his daughter happy, and no father could wish for more than that. But he'd watched his little girl, which was how he still thought of Bridget, suffer in silence for too long now. He knew it was mostly down to what had happened to his grandson, but the marriage break-up had taken away from her any slim chance she had of getting over the tragedy and moving on. Now he saw her rushing headlong back to Dublin at the first word from Brian in seven years. She had chosen not to share the contents of the letter with him, other than to tell him she and Brian had some things to "sort out." To David's mind, she was just setting herself up for another fall, and more pain. He blamed Brian for the marriage ending, though Bridget had never once said to him it was Brian's fault.

"Things to sort out? Yeah, right," David snorted as he drove out of Dun Guaire. Mostly, he would have liked to find Brian and just kick his ass.

McCann had spent most of Thursday night on the phone, with very little success. He rang Bray Station looking for Liam, only to be told that Officer Shortt was on two days off, but that he'd be back on

Saturday. "Serves him right, I hope the sun's splitting the stones all weekend," Brian said to himself, before asking the garda he was speaking to whether there had been any reports of suspicious activity from the patrols on Quinsboro Road. He might as well have asked for the following Saturday's winning lottery numbers; he'd have had a better chance of getting useful information, or at least a semi-intelligent response from the man.

From six o'clock onwards, he tried contacting Brian at his apartment. Each time, the phone rang out. He wasn't sure what he'd have said if Brian had answered. There didn't seem much point in going over the same ground they'd covered the previous Saturday, and Bridget had asked him not to tell Brian she'd revealed the contents of the letter. Likewise, she didn't want to arrive at Brian's apartment unannounced. She wasn't sure what his reaction would be, and she wasn't emotionally strong enough for any unpleasant confrontation. For all she knew, Brian might have said everything he felt there was to say in the letter; she thought there was a very real chance he'd react badly, especially when he found out she'd shown the note to the police. She'd be willing to talk to him if, and only if, he agreed in advance to meet with her, and she was leaving it to McCann to organise. Bridget was struggling on several emotional fronts. Brian's letter had brought back some horrible, ugly memories that she had tried so hard to bury — and some nicer, now bittersweet, memories as well. The truth was, she'd never been able to bury them deeply enough; they were always there, just under the surface, constantly threatening to re-emerge, pulling her this way and that, when all she wanted was some peace.

Several times, McCann had thought about driving back to Brian's place. Each time, he stopped himself. He reasoned that if Brian was there, he'd probably answer the phone, so there was no point rushing over and waiting around when he might not come home at all. Just before ten o'clock, he tried for the last time, and again, there was no answer. "Where are you and what are you up to?" McCann asked the man who wasn't there.

The fact was, Brian was nowhere special. He'd finished work precisely at 5:30, and joined the throngs of people trying mightily to work their way out of Sandyford Industrial Estate, from where they made torturously slow progress home. Brian had already decided to forego his evening session at the gym.

The stun gun he had purchased earlier in the afternoon was hidden under the front passenger seat of his Nissan. He half smiled, half winced, when he thought again of the extortionate amount of money he'd paid. "What a woman," he said, mostly with good-natured wonder and admiration, thinking of Johnny. But he'd have to stop at the ATM machine before going on to Cornelscourt. He still had a few purchases to make, and Johnny had cleaned him out of cash.

Thursdays and Fridays at Cornelscourt Shopping Centre offer late-night opening hours, with none of the outlets in the centre closing their doors until ten p.m. during the bright summer months. So Brian was in no hurry. His first call was to the One Hour Photo shop, where his order, as the young assistant had promised him, was ready and waiting. The large bundle was wrapped in plain brown paper, and Brian paid the extra fifteen cent government tax for a plastic carry-bag. He then moved on to a gift store offering all manner of crafts, porcelain statues, paintings and posters. He walked slowly through the aisles until he came to the section where dozens of different types of candles were on display, and picked out sixteen, in a combination of pillar candles, scented-in-a-jar, and smaller night-light versions, all in red. Next, Brian went to the menswear section in Dunnes. He wasn't there for long, because he knew exactly the kind of jacket he was looking for and found it quickly. In the hardware store, he bought the tools he needed. Finally, the last purchases of the night were from the small home and garden outlet, where he found the bottle he was looking for in the pest control section, and the plastic ties near the checkout.

He didn't go into the main Dunnes Stores grocery area. Normally, he did his week's food shopping on a Saturday. He'd wait until then, he decided, to see if he needed to buy any messages. He frankly didn't think there'd be much point.

He carried his plastic bags out to the car park, the balmy night air making everything feel...well...all right, he thought. Suddenly, he felt hungry, but he didn't want to go back to his apartment for pasta and fruit salad, his normal Thursday fare. He drove instead to Killiney, where the excellent Carusoe's overlooks Killiney Bay. Sitting at a table for one, he ordered fillet steak, medium rare, with black pepper sauce. On the side, he asked for a tossed green salad with ranch dressing, a baked potato with sour cream, and a portion of cheesy garlic potatoes as well. From the wine menu, he selected a half-bottle of Chilean Merlot. Everything was cooked and presented to perfection, and he ate ravenously.

When he'd finished, Antonio asked if he'd like to look at the dessert menu. "No," said Brian. "I already know what I want. Do you still do that hot blackberry crumble, sprinkled with cinnamon and covered in loads and loads of whipped cream?" When the waiter answered in the affirmative, Brian said, "I'll have that, and a cup of whatever that special coffee is, just black."

Paying the bill, Brian was asked by the manager if everything was to his satisfaction. Brian looked him straight in the eye as he answered, "I can honestly say I can't remember the last time I had a meal that tasted so delicious, and it wouldn't surprise me if I never have one like it again."

Brian left Carusoe's just after 10:30, and drove home, reaching the Cabinteely apartment fifteen minutes later. Removing his purchases of the day from the Nissan, he took them into his apartment, and through to the bathroom, concealing them without much thought or concern under some towels in his laundry basket. "It's not like they'll be there for long," he said to himself. He didn't bother watching any television, opting instead to go straight to bed. Tomorrow, he knew, was going to be a very long day.

Geoffrey Staines, while not forgetting his promise to himself to be constantly on the alert, nevertheless managed to spend most of Thursday afternoon and right up till closing time that night at Black Joe's. It had been more than five days since he'd been accosted by Brian Sykes, and while he was still nervous and jumpy, particularly

at night, when he was alone in his bedsit, he'd already grown tired of
looking over his shoulder every ten seconds. As early as mid-week,
he'd started to convince himself that maybe the man had been
bluffing, and that he wouldn't be coming back. Or maybe the gardai
had paid him a visit and warned him off, Staines thought. Certainly,
that snotty Garda Shortt had had the smart-ass smile wiped off his
face; the recollection gave Staines a deep sense of satisfaction.

He was resting a bit easier for another reason. Squeak had come up
trumps with the .38. And he hadn't raised the price, though it still
pained Staines to part with the €200. His money was going so fast, it
stunned him. He'd thought five grand would last him a year, two
years maybe, considering he was also collecting the dole. There
wasn't a chance of that now, he thought. He hadn't worked out,
maths being yet another subject he was miserable at in school, that at
€4.25 for a pint of Miller, €6.50 for a packet of Marlboro Lights, as
well as the odd €30 here for cannabis, or €40 there for heroin, the
money he'd earned over seven years in Mountjoy would be gone by
October at his current rate of spending.

He didn't hesitate about handing over the cash for the gun, though.
It was still in his room, tucked between the mattress and box spring
of the bed. He'd have liked to carry it with him when he went out,
but it seemed to Staines like there were gardai everywhere he
looked, and he didn't want to risk getting caught with a concealed
weapon on him. "Christ, that's all I'd need," he said to Squeak. "I'd
be back inside before my feet could hit the ground." So until the
police made themselves scarce, the gun would stay hidden. As
Staines saw it, with so many of the boys in blue about, Sykes wasn't
likely to have a go at him on the street anyway. And if he did try to
break into the bed sit, Staines decided he'd rather shoot the man
dead and go straight back to Mountjoy than face another minute in
that hell-hole of a cottage at the hands of a sadistic madman.

He went back to his bed sit, full of beer, and collapsed into bed,
fully dressed. He slept straight through the night.

At 9:30 Friday morning, McCann's phone rang. The garda at the
front desk, who'd answered the incoming call, asked if he'd take a
call from someone named Bridget. "Put her through," McCann said
crisply, then, "Bridget, good morning. Listen, there's no real news."

"You haven't even been able to contact him?" Bridget asked, with
Patti standing beside her, clucking disapprovingly. Patti was one of
those who mistakenly believe every policeman on the force just puts
in his or her hours, trying their best to keep their heads down, doing
as little as possible until it was time to go home in the evening. Now
Bridget was becoming perturbed. "Surely that can't be good.
Shouldn't you be out looking for him, or something?"

"Looking where, exactly, Bridget? It's a pretty big city, and he
could be anywhere. Besides, the news isn't all bad. I just finished
speaking with someone at his office ten minutes ago; thought I might
catch him at work. It seems he came in at the usual time this
morning and went straight back out again."

"Well, that's good," Bridget said, relief in her voice. "If he's gone
to work, then he's not planning to do anything today, is he?" she
reasoned. "Wait a minute. He didn't--I don't know--turn in his
company car or anything, did he? That would be just like Brian,
trying to have everything in its place, right to the end." She was
instantly sorry she'd used the last two words.

"No, in fact the lady at reception said that he seemed to have a lot
on today," and now McCann was forced to admit to Bridget the bad
news. "She said he'd told her on the way out that he expected to be
on appointments right through to 5:30, and that he might not make it
back to the office before closing. He said he'd phone in if he wasn't
going to beat the deadline, and that he'd see her on Monday."

"You should have been at that office when he arrived in this
morning," Bridget said disapprovingly, "and taken him straight into
custody."

"On what grounds?" McCann asked, slightly exasperated.
"Writing an upsetting letter? Bridget, think about it. Nowhere in
that note does he say he plans to kill himself, or anyone else."

"But you know he's going to do it!" she wailed.

"Knowing something and proving it are, unfortunately, two entirely different things." He didn't want to go into a discussion about why he hadn't arrested Brian six days earlier. It would serve no purpose, and he hadn't changed his mind. "We'll find him, ok? In the meantime, you sit tight. I might need you at a moment's notice. Is it all right with your friend if you stay there today, and maybe again tonight? I'm hoping that we can sit down and talk this thing through with Brian this evening. If we haven't tracked him down by the end of the day, you and I can wait at his apartment, if you decide that's what you want to do. He's bound to turn up there at some stage."

Patti said that, of course, she could stay as long as she needed, and insisting that McCann call her the minute he had any kind of news, Bridget hung up.

Around 11 a.m., just after Sarah Guilfoyle had left the building to do some shopping, the courier knocked on Staines' bedroom door. For a man who'd consumed eleven pints of lager the night before, he came awake relatively quickly, still that little bit on edge.

"Who is it?" Staines asked, his mouth dry, his throat raw and scratchy from cigarettes and beer.

"Special delivery," came the reply, and Staines immediately sat bolt upright in his bed. He recognised the voice, he was nearly sure. He needed to hear more.

"I'm not dressed" he lied. "Just leave it there at the door, and I'll get it in a few minutes," Staines said, reaching under the mattress for the loaded revolver.

"Sorry, sir, you'll have to sign for it."

Staines was now positive. It was him; the voice was the same one that had threatened to return. It was Brian Sykes, and in spite of the fact that he had a gun in his hand, fear grabbed Staines and shook him as hard as any earthquake could. Jesus, what should he do? He couldn't phone the police. There were no phones in any of the bedrooms; the payphone for residents' use was at the end of the hall, and Staines didn't have a mobile. He couldn't jump out the window, either. It was near the door, and the man on the other side would surely hear him. Staines had a vision of himself, hanging half in, half out of the building while Brian Sykes waited on the ground, ether and handkerchief at the ready.

Another insistent knock at the door, and Staines' teeth began chattering. "Give me a second!" he called, trying desperately to steady himself. Taking huge, gulping breaths, he forced his feet to move, inch by inch, towards the bed sit door. When he finally reached it, he was faced with an unexpected dilemma. The door to his room, he suddenly realised, opened inwards, swinging from his right to his left. He was naturally right handed; if he wanted the gun to be instantly at the ready, he'd have to hold it in his left. Either that, or if he really wanted the gun in his right hand, he'd have to stand awkwardly to the left of the door as he faced it, and extend his left arm across his body to reach the handle. For a few seconds, he couldn't make up his mind, and to anyone watching, he would have appeared comical as he actually practiced the movements he'd make. Finally deciding that it would be best to have the weapon in his left hand, trembling all over, he opened the door and started to raise the gun.

He saw two things as he did so. The first was a man with a notepad, dressed in a brown jacket, very like the Federal Express couriers wear, and wearing a pair of mirrored sunglasses and a baseball cap. He was looking intently at the notepad in his hands, as though checking to make sure of an address. Secondly, he saw the stun gun, partly secluded under the top page of the notepad. Staines stared at it, horrified at the sinister appearance, then raised his eyes and looked straight into the face of Brian Sykes, whose features transformed instantly into a mask of unadulterated hatred.

Staines' moment of hesitation gave Brian his opportunity. Dropping the notepad, the enraged man lunged forward, pushing the door wide with his left hand, extending the stun gun, already making an evil, electric crackling sound, with his right. Staines was literally too frightened to scream. He fell backwards, raising the revolver as he did so, but having no time to take aim. No matter,

Brian was within a foot of him. Staines jerked the trigger. As the bullet slammed into Brian, his momentum carried him forward and he fell against his frantically back tracking intended victim. The two antagonists tumbled to the floor together. The menacing stun gun found its mark. In the horrible silence that followed what had been a two-second battle, neither man moved.

THIRTY-ONE

"McCann, there's another call for you. Lady on line three, says it's important."

The detective snatched up the receiver, punching the flashing extension button. It had to be Bridget. She must have heard something, or found him herself, he thought.

"What is it, Bridget?" he asked, without even saying hello first.

"I'm sorry, this is Sarah Guilfoyle, and I'm looking for a Detective McCann. I rang Bray Garda Station, and they gave me this number. They said Detective McCann would be there, and that he would know what this is all about. Is he there? I already told the officer I spoke with in Bray I don't want to leave a message."

"Sorry, Ms. Guilfoyle, this is Detective McCann," he said, mind racing. This couldn't be good. "How can I help you?"

"Well, I'm the landlady at No. 279 Quinsboro Road. One of the tenants here is a man named Geoffrey Staines." McCann's hand gripped the phone tighter, his knuckles turning white. "I've just come back from shopping—I was only gone for 45 minutes—and when I arrived in, I noticed the door to Mr. Staines' room had been left open."

"Go on," said McCann, pulse racing ever faster.

"Well, I thought it highly unusual, going out and leaving the door wide open for all and sundry to see. He's never done it before. So I went and knocked, but he wasn't in his room. I thought maybe it was just an oversight on his part, but, you see, I've been a bit nervous lately. We had a strange man pretending to be a health inspector around here a couple of weeks ago. I reported it at the time, but as far as I know, they haven't caught him yet, and I've been terrified he might come back."

"Was there any sign of a struggle? Was furniture smashed, or had the door been forced in any way?" McCann asked.

"Not that I could see, but...."

"Is anything missing, besides Mr. Staines?" McCann interrupted impatiently.

"Detective, I'm trying to tell you," and now McCann could hear in the woman's voice that she was well and truly frightened. Either she'd been trying to bravely cover that fear, or he simply hadn't noticed it. "There was blood on the floor, quite a lot of it."

"I'm sending someone over right away. Don't touch anything. In fact, please, Ms. Guilfoyle, don't go back in the room, and don't let anyone else in there, either."

Now that the call had been made and the information delivered, Sarah's steely resolve to keep a tight grip on her emotions melted away, and she began crying softly. "All right, Detective. What's the world coming to, anyway?" she whimpered. "What's this all about?"

McCann made the requisite calls to Bray Station, and asked for a forensics team to be sent immediately to what could possibly be a murder scene. Still, there was no body, and so, maybe, there was still time to stop this madness before it reached a disastrous conclusion. He ran out the door to his car, brain spinning wildly as he tried to piece everything he knew into something concrete that would help him find Brian, and hopefully a still-alive Geoffrey Staines. He wondered at the blood on the floor. It didn't fit with the pictures Brian himself had painted in McCann's mind. And if he had just walked in and stabbed or shot his son's killer, why take the body away? The policeman didn't think that Brian would run and hide. In a bizarre way, McCann felt Brian wouldn't like to cause him that much inconvenience. The letter sent to Bridget made him believe that suicide was a distinct possibility, but if that was Brian's intention, why not end it there and then, in the bed sit? The more he thought it through, the more McCann was convinced that Geoffrey

Staines was still alive. The blood had to have been the result of
something going wrong. The ex-con surely wouldn't have gone with
Brian without putting up a ferocious struggle. McCann wondered
momentarily how far he himself would go to avoid being captured
and tortured the way Staines had been; the detective decided there
was very little he wouldn't do to avoid it.

After the previous weekend, the element of surprise was something
Brian couldn't count on using to his advantage. Perhaps, thought
McCann, Brian had been forced to bludgeon Staines into submission.
Given the two men's contrasting size and strength, the policeman
never really considered the possibility the blood might have come
from Brian.

But where had he taken him? Only one place made any sense to
McCann. He made a bee line for the M11, pushing his Toyota as fast
as he safely dared. On the way, he rang Bridget, who answered the
phone after one ring.

"It's started," McCann said.

Traffic was light; the weekend rush to the southeast hadn't quite
yet materialised, and McCann's Camry topped one hundred miles
per hour going down the motorway. Retracing the route he'd taken
the previous Sunday, he turned right at Kilmacanogue, raced up
Rocky Valley Drive, past the Roadstone quarry, and continued on till
he reached the green gates, and just two hundred yards further on,
the little stone house. It looked impossibly peaceful and serene from
the outside. All around, birds were singing, insects hummed in the
hot early-afternoon sun, and today, a flock of Albert Stevens' sheep
was grazing the lush green grass all around the cottage. McCann's
mind couldn't reconcile what was happening outside the old stone
walls of the cottage with what, he feared, was currently taking place
inside.

He drove straight up to the house; there was no need for a surprise
entrance and quite likely no time to plan one. Only after he reached
the front door did the detective notice there was no sign anywhere of
Brian's Nissan, or any other vehicle. McCann was sure there was no
place within a half mile that would shelter a car from view, and he

doubted Brian would want to take the necessary time to carry an unconscious victim any great distance. McCann ran around to the back of the cottage. Nothing. He looked through each of the building's four windows. They weren't there! Now what?

He sat back into the Toyota, but this time, the detective was in no hurry. Where should he rush to, he asked himself. He'd missed something, of that he was certain. One of the more surreal aspects of this case was the amount of truthful information he'd been willingly given by one of the main characters involved. McCann knew beyond doubt that Brian hadn't lied to him at their last meeting. To the contrary, he'd knowingly given the policeman enough evidence to put him away, at the same time making it clear the consequences of his confession were a matter Brian viewed with relative indifference. He hadn't tried to con the detective. McCann's mad dash to the cottage came as a result of his own inaccurate assessment of what he knew.

Brian hadn't sent out the wrong signals; McCann just hadn't been tuned in.

So what, if anything, had he said that would help McCann now? The detective forced his brain to slow down, to recall as much of the fine detail of his last conversation with Brian as possible, rather than just the general thrust of what they'd discussed. It was agonisingly difficult. He started to open the glove box, reaching for his notepad. Then he pulled his hand back, slamming the compartment closed with a curse. Nothing in his little black book was going to help him now. He just had to think it through. "But there's no time!" his brain screamed.

One thing seemed certain. Brian wasn't going to show up at the cottage. McCann started the engine and pulled away, leaving the stone house in its picturesque setting behind, sheep scrambling to get out of his path as he sped up to and through the green gates. As he drove back towards the city, McCann asked himself again, "If not the cottage, then where?" It was inconceivable that he'd take the ex-con back to his apartment; still, he'd get a squad car from Shankill Station to drive by, just in case. He tried to think like Brian. If he was going

to torture Staines before killing him, which McCann was certain he
would do, then he'd need someplace relatively quiet, secluded. Why
wouldn't he take him back to the cottage? True, Brian would have
known that McCann would come looking, but he'd also have had to
assume there would be enough time to inflict some ghastly pain on
his helpless prey before concluding his "work." So there was
nothing to be gained, no point, in not taking him there.

Something stirred in McCann's brain. He pieced the thoughts he'd
just had back together, in a different order, out loud, only it wasn't
his voice he heard saying the words. It was Brian's. "…no
point…wouldn't take him back there again…."

"Damn it!" McCann shouted. Brian had told him straight out, and
he'd forgotten. The remark had been almost offhand, and McCann
had been so intent in talking the man out of what he was planning,
the words Brian used had gone straight out of his head until now.
All he'd really wanted to know was where Brian had taken Staines to
torture him, and when he'd extracted that piece of information, he'd
completely forgotten what had been said just prior to that admission.
"How could I be so stupid?" he wondered, silently cursing himself
yet again.

He'd asked Brian where Staines had been taken the weekend in
June. Brian had said, "It doesn't matter. I won't be taking him back
there again." Once again, he'd told the truth. McCann hadn't been
misled in any way. He'd just screwed up.

There was still one problem, and it was a big one. The detective
now knew for certain where Brian and Staines *wouldn't* be found. He
had absolutely no idea where they would.

THIRTY-TWO

Into the early hours of the evening, McCann had every unit in the Dublin area watching out for Brian's Nissan Estate. As it happened, it wouldn't be found, and it wouldn't have changed things in the slightest if it had. Brian had left the car parked round the corner from the Hertz Rent-a-Car agency on Leeson Street. He used his credit card, and told the man at the counter he'd only need the Ford Transit van for one day. Brian explained that there were some deliveries he needed to make, and his own vehicle was out of action.

From there, he'd driven to Bray, parking at the very top of Quinsboro Road. He knew he was faced with a number of difficulties. Watching the street from inside a coffee shop on Tuesday and Wednesday afternoons, he had noticed a squad car would drive slowly down the avenue, once every twenty to thirty minutes, past the bed sit, the officer inside the car definitely on the lookout. Brian felt he was pretty sure he knew what, or more precisely who, it was the police were watching for.

His next problem was Sarah Guilfoyle. Brian had no wish whatever to harm the lady. She had done him no wrong and was completely innocent of anything other than bad taste in the tenants she allowed to rent her rooms. Besides, he had made a solemn vow to McCann that no one else would get hurt as a result of his "activities." Even in his amateurish disguise, he knew Sarah would recognise him if he called to the door; she'd taken more than one close look, he'd noticed, when he'd posed as the health inspector. If that happened, he was in no doubt she would immediately call the police, rather than offer him a slice of apple tart. She'd already filed a complaint, and Brian thought it unlikely he could persuade her his intentions had been harmless.

Finally, there was Staines himself. Brian guessed that the little weasel would be expecting him. Confident that he could overpower the ex-con, his main concern was getting the stun gun to him before he could cry out for help. Once he'd been "zapped," Brian knew, he'd be unable to either yell or struggle. And after that, Brian would have no need for sleeping tablets or anaesthetic.

As it transpired, events worked out very much in Brian's favour. The weather being fine, each of the residents, bar Staines, was out of the building, enjoying the sun, heading for the park or the beach, or just for a walk up the Main Street, by mid-morning. This was good news to Brian; it meant that if Staines did have a moment when he could shout out, no one would be around to hear him. Then Brian saw Sarah Guilfoyle leave the building, shopping bag slung over her arm. He froze momentarily when she turned in his direction, eventually walking within a few feet of his van. He pretended to be studying the contents of his clipboard, and was mightily relieved when she walked straight past, not giving the white van, or the man sitting behind the wheel, a second glance.

It was time to move, and he started the engine, driving up Quinsboro Road and parking at the curb directly in front of No. 279. As he stepped out of the van, another patrol car came around the corner, slowing visibly when the officer saw the vehicle parked in front of the bedsit, and a man standing next to it who roughly matched the size and shape of the one for whom he'd been told to be on the lookout. Brian knew there was no point in running. He took a completely different approach. Smiling and waving, he flagged the officer down, motioning for him to stop.

"Is it okay if I park here for just a minute?" Brian asked, as open and friendly as he could be, even leaning unnecessarily close to the patrol car window, rather than making any attempt to hide his face. He checked his folder, taking great care not to let the stun gun be seen, and again pretended to scan what was actually a blank page. "I'll only be a second," he continued. "I've got just one letter to deliver, and...let's see...yup, one package to collect, as well. Do you mind?" He was utterly plausible, and the policeman was convinced. He'd been told to watch out for a businessman in a Nissan Estate, who might be acting suspiciously or hanging around the building, not a courier in a Transit van who was clearly just going about his job. But just before he answered, he made a note of the licence number.

"Don't leave it there too long, ok? I'll be back around in about twenty minutes, and I'll expect you to be gone by then."

"No problem officer," said Brian. "I expect to be long gone, well before that."

The police car drove away, and Brian went to the door. "Let's get started," he muttered to himself, as he walked into the entryway.

But it hadn't all gone according to plan. Brian had been unable to get to his target before the gun went off. The bullet had slammed into his right upper arm. Tearing through hard masses of muscle and sinew, it mercifully missed the bone and exited out the other side. The pain was unexpected and intense, and when they fell, Brian had been stunned, but he hadn't blacked out.

He rolled off the limp figure of Geoffrey Staines, and nearly cried out when his arm came into contact with the floor. "Bastard!" he yelled as he stood up. He kicked Staines in the ribs out of pure frustration, not knowing and not caring if, in his current state, the man could even feel it. He saw the gun still in Staines' left hand, and nervously kicked that away as well. Then Brian noticed the red blotches on the left side of Staines' T-shirt, and knew it was his own blood. No major arteries had been hit when the bullet passed through his arm, but there was a considerable amount of blood, nonetheless. Feeling light-headed, Brian feared he didn't have much time before he might pass out, and he moved quickly. All the strength he'd built up over the past months would be needed now. He pulled the plastic ties he'd purchased in the garden centre, like those used to secure young trees to wooden stakes, out of his jacket pocket. Within seconds, Staines' wrists were securely bound behind

his back, and his ankles were similarly restrained. A strip of grey
packing tape was stuck in place over the mouth.

Brian then took a sheet off Staines' bed, and completely covered the
still unmoving man. He saw again the gun that he'd kicked to one
side. Picking it up, Brian tucked the weapon into his waist band,
behind his back and under his jacket, much as he'd seen TV cops do
a thousand times. He switched the stun gun to "Safety," and put it
in his left jacket pocket.

With incredible effort, he hoisted what now looked like no more
than a bundle of wash over his good left shoulder. He was also able
to partly cover the right sleeve of his blood-stained jacket with a
loose corner of the sheet. When he stood up straight, everything
went very dark, and the room started to spin dangerously. Brian had
no choice. He let Staines fall to the ground with a loud thud, and
dropped to one knee, lowering his head, willing the spinning to stop.
"Come on," he said through clenched teeth, perspiration popping
out on his forehead. "You can't quit now!" He knew that either
Sarah, or the patrolman, or both, could return at any minute. It was
not the thought of getting caught, but rather of not completing what
he'd so single-mindedly set out to do, that finally spurred him on.
Again, he raised Staines from the floor, and this time, when the room
started to spin, he ignored it. Taking small, quick, half-steps, he left
the building, and walked down the footpath, struggling with all his
might to make it appear, in case anyone should be looking, that he
had nothing heavier than a load of commercial laundry thrown over
his shoulder.

Reaching the back of the van, Brian stretched out his right hand to
open the rear door. Sheets of searing pain were his reward, but he
did his best to ignore it. Swinging the door open, he dumped Staines
into the back of the otherwise empty cargo area. Looking quickly
around, Brian could see that, while there were plenty of people
about, no one seemed to be paying him a blind bit of notice. It was
as if he were invisible, he thought, but the truth is, most people
would find it inconceivable that such events could be taking place, in

their presence, in broad daylight, on a busy street. Things like that just don't happen to ordinary citizens, or so they thought.

He got into the driver's seat, started the engine, and drove to the corner, where he turned right. At the next intersection, he turned right again, effectively doubling back towards the Main Street. Sweat poured down his face, stinging his eyes, and he knew he was in trouble—all kinds of trouble. If he passed out and crashed the van, gardai would be on the scene within minutes; Brian's "cargo" would be discovered, and that would be that. Even if he didn't black out, Brian had no way of hiding the blood that by now was soaking half the right sleeve of his jacket. Should he be stopped for any reason whatever, it would be noticed, and again, he knew, the authorities would be summoned. He was also well aware of the fact that he was in no shape to take part in a high-speed chase, should one ensue, so his options were becoming worryingly limited. Driving out to the Boghall Road, Brian pulled the van around to the rear of a now-deserted IDA factory, once the home of an electronic components manufacturer he'd first spotted the night he brought Staines back from the cottage. Making every effort to ensure the Ford was shielded from the view of passing traffic, he pulled it up tight against the back of the building, parked it, and switched off the engine. He then promptly fainted.

When he came to, the afternoon had turned to evening. The sun was beginning its slow descent in the western sky, and already the air was becoming chilly. Brian's shoulder had stiffened, and the agony was something he hadn't imagined possible. Much of the blood on his sleeve had dried, turning crusty and dark crimson, but there was still more seeping out of his wound. He knew he'd have to do something to stop the bleeding, or he would soon pass out again, maybe even go into shock. It wasn't the horrible pain that had forced him back to consciousness, however, nor the sudden drop in temperature. A slow, steady banging sound had wormed its way into his head until he had finally started to come round, momentarily unsure of his whereabouts.

He thought, as he struggled his way back through the darkness, that opening his eyes would surely make the thump-thump-thump he was hearing stop. He forced his lids to rise, when all he really wanted was to leave them closed; he wished for nothing more at that moment than to sleep for days on end. But the noise grew louder, and Brian suddenly came back to reality with a sharp jolt, no longer disoriented. He turned his head, looked into the back of the van, and saw Geoffrey Staines, fully conscious, kicking the back door of the van over and over again, trying desperately to attract attention. Brian could see the side of the pathetic little man's face was torn; Staines had been rubbing his face on the floor, trying to remove the heavy packing tape from over his mouth, so he could scream as well as kick. He'd been unsuccessful and after twenty minutes had given up, concentrating on smashing his feet against the door and sides of the Ford, hoping that someone, anyone, would hear and come to his assistance. His wrist and ankle restraints were still firmly in place. He couldn't have broken free of them if Brian had been out for a month. Not realising his captor was now awake, Staines jerked from fright so hard when he heard Brian's voice, he banged his head off one of the side panels.

"You trying to make me lose my deposit?" Brian asked Staines, alarmed to hear that his own words were slurred, as if he'd been drinking for the afternoon. Feeling there was nothing to lose, Staines resumed frantically kicking, increasing the intensity until he was thrashing wildly on the van's floor, like a fish out of water.

"Hey, give it up!" Brian reached into his left jacket pocket, removing the stun gun. "Or do you want another bite from my little friend here?" he asked, brandishing the hideous looking weapon as a snake charmer might a venomous cobra. Staines eyes grew wide with fright, and he shook his head violently from side to side, trying to plead through the tape still sticking fast to his face. The electric shock he'd received couldn't be described as painful, but he was nauseous and horrified at the paralysis it had induced in a split second. He stopped kicking and lay still, watching to see what would happen next. Brian looked at him with eyes that were still half-glassy, studying him like he would have a laboratory animal. Without warning, he said to Staines, "You hate me, don't you?" The ex-con again shook his head in the negative, thinking he might somehow placate this lunatic. "Yes, you do. It wouldn't be natural if you didn't." Still Staines shook his head "no."

"Let me make it easier for you to tell the truth," Brian said, voice quiet, but finding strength from some deep inner place. "You're going to die tonight, and I'm going to be the one to kill you. It's going to happen; there's nothing you can do to stop it. You know it was me who took you out to the cottage — of course you do. Well, what if I told you that those three days were a picnic, a walk in the park, compared to what I'm going to do to you over the next few hours, before I stick a needle full of something a lot nastier than what you're used to into you're heart and send you straight to hell — do you think you could admit to hating me then?"

Staines couldn't answer. The words he'd heard were horrible, terrifying, and worst of all, he knew them to be true. But he just stared into Brian's eyes.

"Answer me!" Brian bellowed, his voice exploding in the confines of the van. "You killed my son, and in a little while, I'm going to kill you, and you hate me for that, don't you? Answer!" he screamed again.

With death absolutely assured, Staines felt some of the fear inside him actually slip away. The inevitability of death, when it hits, has that effect on some people. And as some of that fear left him, it made room for other emotions. His face slowly changed. Yes, he hated this man. Staines thought back to the night on the road, the way Brian had taunted him, letting him think he was going to get away, then running him down like a naked animal. Slapping that stinking handkerchief over his face, the taste of the ether still on the sides of his tongue when he came round, strapped like a beast to the wooden beam; Brian had dripped boiling water onto flesh already scarred and torn, nerve ends so exposed that even the air brushing over his wounds had felt like it had come straight from a blast furnace. Staines began to nod his head, slowly at first, then more rapidly, and his eyes revealed the truth of what his mouth could not speak. Given even half a chance, he would take great pleasure in killing his tormentor.

"You hate me. Right. Good," Brian said, his voice now at a normal level. Then he turned and started the engine. "At last we understand each other."

When they reached their destination, Brian slowly climbed out of the van, fighting equal amounts of pain and dizziness. He opened the rear door, Staines straining to look around Brian, to see where his captor had brought him. "You remember how I said if you were good, I wouldn't use this on you again?" Brian asked, removing the stun gun from his jacket pocket. Staines nodded, terror in his eyes.

"Well, here's the thing," Brian said evenly, giving no hint of what was to come, "I lied." With that, he jabbed the crackling black weapon against Staines' neck, and pulled the trigger. Half carrying, half dragging the limp body inside, Brian secured him in place, before putting a blindfold over Staines' eyes. "No fair peeking," Brian said. "I've got work to do, and you don't get to see it until everything's ready."

THIRTY-THREE

Frantic. It was the only word to describe the way Michael McCann felt as the sun started to set. He'd tried everything he could think of to find Brian. Phoning Office Solutions twice during the day had done no good. The detective was told that senior sales personnel were not required to leave a list of their day's appointments with management. Likewise, when he phoned at 5:25, Carol informed him Brian had neither made it back to the office, nor had he checked in; she assumed he'd gotten tied up in a meeting or presentation someplace, and offered to take a message, which she assured McCann would be handed to Brian first thing Monday morning. "No message," he'd said, and hung up.

Forensics had found little that would be of assistance in anything other than a prosecution or an autopsy, when they called to Staines' bed sit. Certainly, no clues had been left behind that would help in ascertaining the two men's current whereabouts. Plenty of blood, but no clues. Except for one. A .38 calibre slug had been removed from the doorframe of Staines' room. That meant the gun had been fired from inside the flat, toward the door.

"Jesus, he got himself a gun," McCann muttered when given this information, but he was referring to Staines. It changed everything. He now knew there was a very real possibility the blood on the floor was Brian's. It didn't take a rocket scientist to figure out Staines was the most likely candidate as shooter. Had it been Brian, things would almost certainly have been much different. First, the bullet would have been fired from outside the room inwards, not the other way around. Secondly, there'd almost certainly have been a body to go with the blood. Had Brian decided to end things suddenly, with a bullet, he'd have finished the job and left the body in place, then either turned the gun on himself or given up to the authorities. To McCann's way of thinking, not one bit of that scenario felt right. It didn't fit.

It meant that Brian had been hurt, how badly was impossible to tell. He made a decision to share none of the information with Bridget, for the moment. Then, suddenly, another small break. "Mick, telephone, line two. It's Bray."

"McCann here," he answered, wondering if they'd found Brian's car, or better still, the two men. But the caller was the officer in the patrol car who had spoken to Brian outside the bed sit that morning. He explained, as briefly as possible, what had happened with the white Transit van, and the conversation he'd had with the man driving it. He admitted honestly that, when he returned to Quinsboro Road twenty minutes later, he'd seen the Ford turning right at the corner, and assumed the courier had gone on his way. With that, he'd completely forgotten to check the licence number he'd written down, and he'd been called off the patrol ten minutes later to a major disturbance at The Riviera Hotel in Greystones. An itinerant wedding had turned into a massive street brawl, with members of both families causing serious damage to the hotel foyer, some cars and vans in the parking lot, and, not least, to each other. He'd thought no more of the white van until he'd returned to Bray within the last hour, when he'd heard of the shooting incident at the bedsit. At that stage, he'd immediately checked with Motor Vehicles Division and tracked the licence number to the Hertz Rent-a-Car agency. Within ten minutes, the agency's reservations centre been able to confirm the Ford was indeed theirs, and that it had been rented out before noon of that very day from their Leeson Street operation. There was no record of the van having been returned as yet.

"Did they give you the name of the man who rented it out?" McCann asked, already suspecting the answer.

"Yes, sir," said the policeman. "The man paid by credit card. It was Brian Sykes."

Quickly writing down the licence number, McCann asked the officer if there'd been any recent sighting of either the Ford van, or Brian's Nissan. When he was told that neither had been seen, McCann asked that an immediate alert be put out to all patrols in the city, with any sightings to be reported directly back to himself. He wasn't confident the Ford would be found quickly. There were hundreds, if not thousands of them on the streets of Dublin, the proverbial needle in a haystack. "Check the area around the rental car place. My bet is you'll find the Nissan somewhere in the vicinity," McCann said. "If you do spot it, let me know, but don't touch it. We'll assign someone to keep watch from a distance; Sykes might still come back for that car."

The patrolman asked if he should put in a request for roadblocks or checkpoints outside the Greater Dublin region and received a negative response. McCann said he didn't believe Brian would chance leaving the area. He needed time for what he wanted to do, and hours behind the wheel moving away from the city would be time wasted. The gunshot injury he might have sustained would further reduce his capacity to travel any great distance.

Once again, McCann shook his head in wonder at Brian's determination, and the initiative to get the job done, whatever it took. But the situation was becoming critical. At least one shot had been fired, blood had been spilled; desperation was setting in, and the point of no return was rapidly approaching. And still, he had no idea where Brian could be going. He'd wracked his brains since leaving the cottage, and drawn a blank. He needed help, and he played his final trump card. Picking up the phone, he dialled the number that he already had memorised.

"Bridget, I'm coming over, if that's okay with you. I'll be there in less than an hour. No, we haven't found him yet," he replied to her urgent query, "but from everything we know, it looks like we need to find him quickly. I'll tell you everything when I get there, if that's all right. I don't really want to waste time discussing it over the phone."

Forty-five minutes later, he was back almost in the exact spot where it had all started, in Dun Guaire. The street looked the same to him, though the gardens were now more mature, the trees and shrubs had grown tall and thick in the years since he'd last been there. He drove past the Sykes' former family home, and noticed lights burning brightly through the window, the new occupants contentedly going about their lives much as Brian, Bridget and Danny had been doing until Geoffrey Staines changed it all in one night of drugged madness. Three doors further down, he stopped in front of Ted and Patti's home, leaving his car in the street rather than pulling into the driveway.

Patti opened the front door before McCann had time to knock. She led him into the sitting room, where Bridget was anxiously waiting, and took orders for coffee, leaving the two alone to talk.

Bridget had been wearing a lightweight pant suit when she'd called in at Shankill Station the previous day, having selected it, without much thought, for the trip to Dublin from Kilcormac. Now she was wearing a pair of jeans and a plain blouse she had stuffed hurriedly into an overnight bag just before leaving home, when it dawned on her that she might have to stay for more than a day. For the first time, McCann could see the toll Danny's death, and the subsequent years, had taken on Bridget. She was not just thin, now she was gaunt-looking, cheekbones protruding, eyes looking hollow and haunted. The detective thought she could pass for sixty, though he knew her to be much younger. Mental stress had brought physical consequences, and McCann wondered if the process that had brought Bridget to this stage could ever be reversed. He very much doubted it.

As quickly as he could, he outlined the events of the day, touching, but not elaborating, on the bullet that was found, the white van and Brian's failure to return to either the office or his apartment. Tears had come to Bridget's eyes when she realised that McCann was telling her Brian had probably been shot, but she held them back, not allowing them to flow. McCann also gave her a very sketchy outline of the events in June, when Brian had kidnapped and tortured their son's murderer. He spared her the details; she just didn't need to know.

"Do you think he's killed Staines?" Bridget asked.

"I think he's going to, if he hasn't already. It's my honest belief that Brian will finish it this time."

"Why this time? Why not just carry on making that monster suffer?"

"Because he knows I couldn't let him do that," McCann admitted. "I told him as much last Saturday, just before I phoned you. He's determined, more than any man I've ever met, Bridget, to finish this thing, once and for all. If he thought there was any chance I, or anyone else would be able to get in his way, he'd want to get the job done before we could stop him."

"I don't care if he dies, you know?" Bridget said, looking straight into McCann's eyes. "Staines, I mean," she added, in case the detective had misunderstood.

"I don't blame you."

"Can you help Brian?" she asked, and the look in her eyes had become one of pleading. "If you find him in time, can you help him? He sounds...like he's sick...he's not a bad man, you know?" and her voice trailed off.

"I'll try. I promise you that. If there's anything at all I can do on his behalf, it will be done, you have my word. But we have *got* to find him first."

For awhile then, there was silence between them. McCann thought of how she'd described Brian. 'Sick.....not a bad man....' He felt he knew Brian now, probably as well as anyone could. He didn't feel uncomfortable in Brian's presence; there was no sense of being in the company of an evil, diseased mind. Under different circumstances, he could easily have concurred that Brian was, indeed, a nice man. Then he had to ask himself if a nice man could spend three days inflicting unthinkable pain on a helpless man tethered to a wooden beam. Would a sick man be able to plan, months in advance, an

operation that required cunning, deception, and superhuman
willpower to see it through, then put that plan into action, in spite of
the inherent danger and increasing numbers of formidable obstacles
being placed in his path? In his head, the answer to both questions
came back, "No." Then his heart asked yet another question.
"Could a good, decent, law-abiding man be driven to deranged acts
of sickening depravity if he'd witnessed the dead body of his only
child stretched out on the murderer's bed, like a piece of meat on a
slab?" This time, McCann admitted to himself, the answer had to be
"yes."

I've got to find him, thought McCann, and he began concentrating
so hard his pupils contracted, as though he were staring into a bright
light. "Bridget, help me, please," he begged quietly. "I can't think of
any place he might be. By morning, Staines will be dead for sure,
maybe Brian, too. Have you got any, vague notion, some favourite
spot he used to go to, some place he liked to go to be alone? Any
idea, no matter how crazy — just say it. It doesn't matter how
ridiculous any of it sounds." He remembered saying similar words
to Brian, all those years ago, when he was trying to jar him into
thinking who might have taken Danny. Now, he was back at the
beginning, back where it all began, and he couldn't believe it could
be this way, the very same as last time.

"That's it!" He shouted the words as he jumped to his feet, startling
Bridget so badly she spilled coffee all down the front of her blouse.
Patti stuck her head into the sitting room to see what was going on.
"It's the very same as last time," McCann said, already moving
toward the door.

"I don't understand. What's the very same, who....?" Bridget
didn't get to finish her question.

"Brian's gone back to where it all started," the detective said,
reaching into his pocket for the mobile phone. He was going to need
backup.

"What are you talking about?" Bridget asked incredulously. She
was totally confused and becoming angry. "You don't mean our

garage? There are people living there, for God's sake! Are you
completely out of your mind?" she raged.

"Not your garage. Brian's gone back to where this whole thing
started for the two of them, for *him and Staines*! He's back at the
house, Staines' house, the place where we found Danny. That's
where it began for Brian, and that's where he is now, I'd bet anything
on it!"

"I'm coming with you, and don't even think about trying to stop
me!" Bridget said, following him out the door. Again, McCann was
struck by the uncanny parallels between this night and that other
day in April, all those years ago. Brian had insisted on travelling
with him on that occasion. It broke the rules, but McCann had
decided to make an exception, because of the circumstances on the
day. This time, he knew he might need Bridget there, to help him
pull Brian back from the edge, if he hadn't already gone over. He
remembered the air of desperate hope in the car as he and Brian sped
through the streets, only to find they were too late when they arrived
at their destination. He said a silent prayer that in this instance, the
similarities wouldn't hold.

McCann looked at Bridget. "Get in," he said, and they sped off in
the direction of No. 41, Fr. Cullen Terrace.

THIRTY-FOUR

"Don't come in, whatever you do, under any circumstances, until you get my say-so." The words were McCann's but they weren't directed at Bridget. He was on his mobile phone, and had been patched through to the nearest patrol car. He'd asked for two units to be sent to the scene, knowing he'd look incredibly foolish if all of them arrived to an empty, deserted house. The detective was sure that wouldn't happen.

It fit, all of it did, with what he'd been trying so desperately to piece together. Brian needed a location that was quiet, where he was unlikely to be disturbed, a place where a bit of torture going on was unlikely to attract too much attention, too soon. Knowing Brian's mindset, if that were possible, McCann felt he'd want something more than just an out-of-the-way setting for the final confrontation, something more....poetic...that was the word Brian had once used, describing the time he'd infested Staines with fleas. To Brian, finishing the job on Staines in the same place the man had killed Brian's son, and more than that, had effectively taken away Brian's life as well, would be true justice. It was like a long distance race in a track competition. The participants run and run, but the winners— and the losers—still end up right back where they started.

McCann shook his head; it all made such perfect sense now. He liked watching quiz shows on television, and like most people would often hear a question to which he just couldn't, for his life, think of the answer. Then the host gives that answer, and of course, he'd known it all along, but couldn't find the right words, because they were buried in his head under all the other little things he knew, things that didn't matter at that precise time because they didn't help. Now that this particular riddle had been solved, or so he hoped, McCann again shook his head in amazement; it was so obvious. Why hadn't he worked it out sooner?

In the years that passed since Danny Sykes ran and laughed, and played with his dog, Bandit, and who was then taken, brutalised and choked to death, decay and neglect had set in to Fr. Cullen Terrace. Most of the houses were boarded up now, covered in graffiti; street lights were broken. The local council despaired, and there was talk of tearing down the old terraces and putting in some new community service-type facility-- maybe a youth centre. But public funding was not available, money was just too tight, and after awhile, even maintenance on the empty terraced houses was put on the economic back foot. It was not a street down which many decent people would willingly walk after dark, especially if they were on their own. Brian had driven slowly past one night, months earlier, and seen first hand the disease that was already horribly disfiguring, and which would someday kill off altogether, Fr. Cullen Terrace.

"Perfect," he had said to himself.

McCann and Bridget saw the white Ford van parked on the street outside number forty-four, and the detective didn't need to check the licence number to know that it was the rental. Getting out of the Toyota, he could see what looked like dim light coming from around the edge of the front door. He thought that a bit odd; surely the electricity had long since been cut off. Moving closer, Bridget at his left and slightly behind him, McCann could see the front door had been forced open, as if with a crow bar, and had been damaged enough not to be able to close properly. He reached the front door, crouching slightly, and slowly pushed it open. "Oh, dear God.....sweet Jesus...."

The vision was straight from the depths of hell.

Sixteen red candles had been placed around the smoky room, casting eerie flickering shadows into dark corners, where anyone looking would have expected to see Satan's minions crouching, pitchforks at the ready. In the middle of the room, a naked Geoffrey

Staines sat in a rickety wooden chair, arms pulled painfully tight
behind his back, his wrists lashed with the plastic ties. Likewise, his
ankles had been secured to the chair's front legs. There was no
escape. An old, small kitchen table was to his right.

McCann nearly forgot Bridget was with him. From behind his
shoulder, he heard her gasp, "No! Brian? That can't be Brian." Her
voice was no more than a whisper.

Brian stood, stripped to the waist, behind Staines. He was covered
in sweat and his own blood, and Bridget saw for the first time the
impossibly muscled body the steroids, and Brian's own mindless,
obsessive determination had brought about. He had torn a wad of
cloth off his discarded shirt, placed it over the bullet wound and
wrapped the packing tape around his upper arm. This had slowed,
but not stopped, the flow of blood; it still trickled down his damaged
limb and had, through his exertions, been smeared over most of his
upper body. He stood straight and tall, like a black priest before an
unholy altar.

It was impossible to take it all in at once. One bizarre detail would
register in the brain, only to be superseded by another. This was an
evil place, Bridget felt. She knew unspeakable acts had taken place
in this house. Then, and now.

"What has he done?" she asked herself, when she finally noticed
the walls. In the half-light of the candles, it had taken a few brief
moments for both Bridget's and McCann's eyes to adjust.
Simultaneously, they saw Brian's grotesque handy-work covering
almost every inch of wall space in the small room. Bridget began to
cry, low moans coming from deep within her.

The pictures of Danny that Brian removed from his apartment had
been enlarged at the One Hour Photo shop—hundreds of them, each
blown up to twelve-by-eighteen. The little sweet, smiling image was
everywhere, laughing, making funny faces for the camera, dressed in
his First Holy Communion suit (the one he'd been buried in), and
sitting on the grass with Bandit. It was horrible, worse than any
gruesome nightmare, and Bridget wanted to turn and run, but she
couldn't. She was fixed to the spot, unable to move.

Brian raised a cigarette to his mouth, eyes staring straight ahead, unseeing, unaware even of the two intruders. He inhaled deeply, the orange tip of ash glowing menacingly. Bridget wondered in a detached, out of context way, when Brian had taken up smoking. Then he reached down and jabbed the cigarette into Geoffrey Staines' left ear, grinding it in, and the scream that came was like that from a mortally wounded beast. McCann could see Brian had also burned horrible red holes into Staines' neck, the tops of his shoulders and arms, and on his face, just under each eye.

McCann had watched, transfixed, for what had seemed like minutes. In fact, he'd only pushed open the door fifteen seconds earlier. Now Staines' scream acted like a catalyst, spurring the detective to action. He took a step forward. "Brian, stop it! It's over."

His eyes cleared, and he looked at the detective as though he was seeing him for the first time, and from a distance. With no expression whatever on his face, he said "But I'm not finished yet."

"He's out of it," Bridget whispered, but McCann knew that wasn't so. He'd seen Brian look exactly the same way the last time they'd been in the house together, just before he broke Fran Kennedy's jaw.

"Brian, what are you going to do? You know I can't let this go on. Come on, let's get out of here, go get a cup of coffee, sort this mess out," the detective said softly.

Brian shook his head, pointing to the table sitting next to his hostage and said, a bit more insistently, "But I've got all this stuff, and it has to be used up. It would be a shame to let it go to waste," as if he were talking about food he'd bought in for a company picnic.

McCann looked at the table. An assortment of tools had been laid out, side by side, at the ready. At the end of the line was a hypodermic syringe, already filled to capacity with strychnine. Then he saw the gun, and the detective became even more uneasy. Still, he didn't want to make any aggressive motions or threats. There were too many variables, too many ways to set off this time bomb. He'd have to defuse it, one step at a time. "Who does that belong to?" McCann asked, gesturing in the direction of the revolver.

"That? Oh, that's his," Brian said nonchalantly. "He hasn't got much imagination, has he? Not like me."

"That's for sure, Brian." McCann looked at the table again, and made another try. "You know, those things will keep till another day. Come on, what do you say, why don't we get out of here and....."

"Because I'm not finished! I have work to do, don't you understand that?" Brian bellowed the words. Snatching one of the tools up from the table, holding it aloft, he said with vicious menace, "See this? This is my all-new Black and Decker cordless, twin-action drill with rechargeable battery pack! It comes with a variety of bits, suitable for any DIY requirement." He sounded utterly insane. "For example," he said, picking up the largest drill bit from the table, "this one can bore holes through any hardwood, effortlessly. Now what I'm going to do with my little friend here," he continued, patting Staines on the shoulder, "is step around behind him and give him a small taste of what he did to Danny. I want him to know what it feels like," Brian hissed through gritted teeth.

"Then, you see this one?" He picked up another attachment. "This is a hammer action bit, designed for use on walls, masonry and concrete. I thought what I might do to our Mr. Stone Head—Stone, Staines, it's so hard to tell the difference—is just punch a little, bitty hole through his skull, and then, hey, we'll just look inside and see what we can see! Maybe something will ooze out, and we can send it to a lab in Switzerland. Maybe some scientist could find something in the slime that explains why a filthy, stinking animal like this can rape and strangle the most innocent, beautiful child that God ever put on this cursed planet!"

Still holding the drill aloft, Brian pulled the trigger, and for Staines, it was too much. Hearing the whirring sound as the tool was powered up, he gagged at the thought of what was about to happen, and he started to vomit. Looking down, Brian noticed this, and quickly reached out his left hand, painfully jerking the grey tape away from Staines' mouth, watching impassively as bile spewed and spluttered down his front. "No, no, no," Brian scolded, his voice quiet again. "We can't have you drowning in your own puke, though it's not the worst idea I've ever heard; wonder why I didn't think of that. Never mind, a plan is a plan, and you're going to stick around for the end, mister."

"You're fucked!" Staines screamed at Brian. Then to McCann, "What are you waiting for, asshole? Arrest him. Get this psycho lunatic bastard off me!"

"Shut up!" Brian yelled. He had dropped the tape to the ground, or he would have slapped it straight back over Staines' filthy mouth.

"You shut up! You're the one going to jail now, and I hope you rot there!" Staines was nearly hysterical. "You're an animal. You're worse than an animal, you piece of shit!" Hatred dripped from every word. He couldn't think of anything bad enough to screech at the man who had imprisoned, tortured and terrified him for more than a month.

"You're nothing but a coward!" Staines face was purple with fury. Then he said the words that sealed his fate.

"You're just a big sissy! You're as big a fucking sissy as your little whimpering shit of a son was!"

Bridget screamed in agony, like she'd been stabbed in the stomach. McCann gasped, then froze, stunned beyond words and action, and Brian, his muscles bunching into knots of steel, turned and stared into the face of the man he was going to kill.

"Yeah, that's right. I remember everything!" Staines sneered, eyes glinting and full of evil. "I wasn't that out of it; really wasn't a bad night, all-in-all, but fucking hell, could that little pup scream!"

Brian reached for the table, picking up the syringe. His face had gone blank again.

McCann spoke then. "Brian, listen to me. I'm not going to stop you."

Staines stared, wild-eyed and horrified. "Just hear me out, please," the policeman said, and Brian looked at him, his features betraying nothing of what he felt underneath.

"You do what you have to do. That's what it really comes down to, isn't it? And if you need to kill this man to bring you any comfort or peace of mind, or whatever it is you're after, then go ahead. This is no trick. I'm not going to lift a finger to stop you."

Behind the detective, Bridget was silently shaking her head, mouthing the word, "No."

"But I told you once before," McCann said, "I've got to live, too, Brian. So you do what you must, and then so will I. If you decide to kill him, that means I'll be taking you in, testifying against you and doing my best to put you away for as long as the law decides is fair and just. That's what I have to do. You've mentioned that word 'justice,' a few times. After what I've just heard come out of his mouth," he said, pointing at Staines, "I don't think it would be just of me to take this decision away from you, and I'm not going to do it. I'll have to live with that, whatever happens."

"Thank you," said Brian, raising the syringe in his left hand, turning back towards Staines.

"Brian, no, please don't!" It was Bridget, and they were the first words she'd spoken directly to Brian since entering the house.

"Hello, Bridget," said Brian strangely, as though he'd just bumped into an old friend. "Umm, maybe you shouldn't be here right now," and he faced Staines, raising his arm yet again.

Desperately thinking of a way to stop him, Bridget screamed out the words, unaware that she was going to use them until they were already out, "Please! I love you!"

Brian whirled around as though shot, "Well, don't!" he yelled, ferociously loud. "How could you? I don't! I don't love myself! I hate myself!" and for the first time in more than seven years, he felt an unfamiliar stinging behind his eyes. "How could you love me? I killed him! I killed our little boy as surely as this monster did!"

"No! You didn't. It couldn't have been helped. I know that now!" Bridget pleaded.

"Yes, it could. I could have done…something. I should have found a way to protect him, to save him!" Then, utterly resigned, "It's too late."

For the last time, he raised his left arm. As he did, Staines started to scream in mortal terror. McCann looked away; he wouldn't stop it now.

Bridget's eyes once more caught sight of Danny's image, smiling back at her through the years. She knew she couldn't stop Brian now, no one could, except maybe….

"What would Danny tell you to do?" she asked, shouting above Staines' own pitiful wailing. Brian's left arm moved down in a blur, muscles coiled and bunched, to drive the strychnine-filled syringe into the heart of the beast. The words reached him, apparently too late, as he continued driving his closed fist forward. As his hand came within a few inches of Staines' body, the hypodermic needle fell from his grasp, landing on the floor next to the foot of the chair. Brian mumbled something that neither Bridget nor McCann could hear as his fist ploughed into Staines' midsection, eight inches below his heart.

Brian faced Bridget again, unable for the moment to speak, the tears of a lifetime of pain streaming down his red, anguished face. He'd remembered--the most severe punishment Danny could think of, when he'd found Brian guilty in the death of his beloved Bandit. He took a step to one side, and Bridget and the detective could both see Staines, eyes bulging, gasping for breath, retching as he prepared to vomit yet again, such was the force of Brian's blow. But he was still very much alive.

"A box in the belly," Brian sobbed, tears streaming down his face. "That's what Danny would have chosen!"

An hour later, the squad car pulled away, Staines the back seat passenger. Brian, Bridget and McCann stood at the curb, watching it drive off into the darkness.

Inside the house, McCann had cut the plastic ties, freeing Staines' arms and legs, while Brian and Bridget stood to one side, watching and wondering what would happen next. For his part, Staines had regained some of his earlier bluster, once he'd gotten his breath back and realised he would live through the night.

"Aren't you going to arrest him?" he'd asked McCann.

"Arrest him? Why would I do that?" McCann had asked the incredulous man. "As far as I can see, you're still breathing, and by the way, do you have a permit for that gun? I doubt it. Ex-convicts normally have a lot of difficulty getting gun licences, and somehow, I don't think they'd make an exception in your case. You do know that carrying that thing is a serious violation of your parole conditions? Consider yourself cautioned and arrested," McCann said, not bothering with the formalities. "Parole violation, concealment of an unlicensed gun, assault with a deadly weapon, and weren't you supposed to meet your probation officer this afternoon? Mister, you're going back to Mountjoy for a long, long time."

"It's not my gun," Staines said weakly.

"Oh, really? Then I guess this man over here just happened to bring his revolver into your bed sit, where he shot himself. Clumsy, isn't he? Get up!"

"But what about those things?" Staines whined, pointing at the table.

"To the best of my knowledge, it's still legal in this State for a man to carry his power tools with him. Now shut up, you're giving me a headache, and for God's sake, put some clothes on. You could catch your death on a night like this!" Staines had forgotten that he was still stark naked, and he hurriedly threw his hands over his groin, covering himself as best he could. Grinning slightly, Brian pointed to one corner of the room where he'd discarded the clothes earlier that night.

The night air no longer felt chilly; rather it was cool and soothing around them. Brian turned and faced McCann for the last time. "What now?" he asked, as Geoffrey Staines was driven out of sight.

"No one else got hurt. You promised me that, and you kept your word" McCann answered honestly. "You also promised me when this — this war--was over, I wouldn't hear from you ever again. Not that I don't want to see you from time to time—under much different circumstances mind you--but now I'm asking you. Is it over?"

Brian looked from McCann to Bridget, then back to the detective. "Yes. It's over. Next time he gets out, I won't be waiting. You have my word."

The detective looked at the bloodied, shattered man, and thought for a moment of what he'd been put through since the night his child had been taken from him. He made his decision, and felt it was the right one. "Then, as far as I'm concerned, it's over, too," McCann said. "If you can live with that, so can I. Now you'd better get that arm seen to, and do it tonight. Do you want a lift to the hospital?"

"No, thanks, I've got to drop this van off first thing in the morning, or I'll be stuck paying another day's rental. I'll make my own way, ok?" He thought for a moment, and his face became a bit sadder. "Would you mind taking Bridget with you?"

"But I...no, I want to go with....Brian, we should talk," she said.

He didn't want to hurt her any more. Nothing could be put back the way it was, no matter how much he, and she, might want to try. Brian knew that a large part of him was buried with Danny, and could be neither exhumed nor resurrected. What he had left to give, he couldn't be sure was enough. Slowly, he stepped away from her side.

"Thank you," he said quietly to McCann, then to Bridget, "I'll call you."

It was the last lie he ever told her.

EPILOGUE

It was another eight years before Geoffrey Staines received word that he had, in the opinion of the State, paid his debt to society and would be released. Now in his 40's, Staines had been drug free for the last five of those years, and had convinced himself that he would remain so for the duration of his life. Morality had little if anything to do with that decision. Staines had contracted hepatitis from using a shared needle. His liver was severely damaged, and he had spent more than three weeks in the prison hospital, two days of that literally at death's door. The doctor had told him in direct, passionless tones that one more bout would, without any question, finish him off for good. Ecstasy didn't suit him, either. It only made him nauseous and gave him violent migraines. Cocaine was too expensive; cannabis too dull. Staines made the decision, and in his own mind was certain that he'd stick to it, that drugs was one mug's game he no longer wanted to play.

Job prospects were non-existent; he had been advised that the Fas schemes, so popular in the 80's, 90's and at the beginning of the new century, had been phased out due to lack of funding. Window cleaning was still a possibility, but he was hoping to find something that would keep him indoors during the long, wet, cold winter months. He'd noticed during the last few years that his bones and joints ached when the air was damp and chilly. He thought he'd even prefer working as a cleaner — maybe in a hotel or as part of a contract cleaning company — at least until the summer months came around.

"Maybe," he thought, with a little surge of pleasurable anticipation, "I'd be able to get a job as a janitor in a primary school. Lots of happy little kids running around. Now that would be nice!"

Staines wasn't that desperately excited about getting out of Mountjoy again. Neither did the thought disappoint him. He didn't think he'd be back; he'd made no links with the organised prison gangs who could send an inmate straight from his cell to an outside "job", sometimes literally on the day of release. As in his first "stretch" at the Joy, he'd kept his head down, and largely stayed out of trouble. "Nope, not coming back here," he muttered when told of his impending freedom. "Yeah, and that's what you said the last time you left here," replied the desperately annoying, squeaky little voice that occasionally invaded a space at the rear of Staines' skull.

He still had no friends on the outside, male or female, nowhere to go, nothing to do, no one to do it with. He would have the money from working in the prison, and his intent was to make it last considerably longer than when he was last released. He thought he'd like to buy a little car; ironically, given his age now, and the number of years that he'd been claim free, his insurance would cost him a fraction of what it had the last time he'd owned a motor.

So it was that, two days before he was to be released, Geoffrey Staines faced another new beginning, neither dark nor bright, but falling somewhere in between. At four o'clock in the afternoon, he received his post. He was surprised that anyone would be writing to him, but not shocked; he received the occasional unsolicited letter from prisoners' rights groups, new churches, even the odd bit of junk mail. The Justice Department also sent him his formal notification of release through the post, but he'd received that already. This envelope was slightly larger than that containing a standard letter, but it didn't have a greeting card inside. Staines read the message.

At 7 a.m. the next morning, Prison Guard Brendan Kane was walking past Staines' cell, and immediately saw that something was amiss. Firstly, Staines appeared to be slumped, half sitting, half crouching, his right leg out straight, but his left bent at an awkward angle underneath him, against the door of his cell. There was no sheet on his bed. He had torn off a length of that sheet and tied one end around the bars of his cell, the other around his neck. It would not have been possible to hang himself from the ceiling; there was nothing there to which he could have tied off his makeshift noose. But this also meant that his neck couldn't have been broken by a sudden, violent drop.

Geoffrey Staines was dead, but to take his life in the manner that he chose would have meant that he suffered horribly in the moments before he lost consciousness. The body's natural will to survive would have meant that Staines' had to resist, for some considerable time, the urge to simply reach up and remove the ligature from around his throat.

His will to die must have been incredibly, horribly powerful.

"I don't understand it," Kane said to Paul Carberry, one of his fellow officers, after Staines' body had been removed to the morgue. "He was getting out of here tomorrow, and he didn't strike me as being desperately worried about it. Quiet enough guy, but not depressed, if I'm any judge. What the hell was this about? Was he high on something?"

"Who knows?" Carberry replied, with obviously less concern than his colleague. He picked up the note that Staines had received the day before and read through it. "This looks innocent enough, but we'll probably have to try to find out where it came from," he said, and he read the message aloud. "Can't wait to see you when you come out. We'll have to get together at some stage, and relive those good ol' times. See you soon."

"Not signed?" asked Kane.

"Nope, that's all there is," Carberry answered. "Strange, though, that it's written on the back of a piece of sandpaper."

THE END

Acknowledgements

Given this was my first book, I needed so much help and information, it's difficult to know where to start saying "thank you," but it's also important to me that the people involved know how grateful I am for their support.

Michael and Linda Hall were immensely helpful with their information on police procedures—without revealing anything they shouldn't of course! I would also like to thank Paddy McCauley for the "chemically-related" tips, and Mark Felton, who gave me the benefit of his legal expertise and some insight as to the goings on in the legal world. To all of the above, I'm eternally in your debt.

Equally as important as those who supplied me with information are those who lent their never-dwindling support. These include, but are not limited to, my son, Denny, who acted as proof reader and constant source of encouragement, and Mr. Gene Shumate, whose opinion I value greatly, given the complete, utter (and sometimes blunt) honesty he invariably brings to the table.

My mother and father have both been an inspiration to me throughout my lifetime (oh, by the way, sorry about the odd swear word, Mom!)

Finally, my lifelong companion, wife, and best friend, Mary, has shown incredible patience from the inception of this project. She has never once wavered in her support. My sun rises and sets with this woman; she makes life worth living, and I want to thank her, not alone for her constant back-up, but just for being there. When I wake up in the morning, if she's there next to me, it's going to be a good day. Thanks, Mary.

—Kevin Klatt

September, 2004

ISBN 1-41204062-0